RELUCTANT
REDEMPTION

RELUCTANT REDEMPTION

REG QUIST

Reluctant Redemption
by Reg Quist

Paperback Edition

CKN Christian Publishing
An Imprint of Wolfpack Publishing

6032 Wheat Penny Avenue
Las Vegas, NV 89122

Paperback ISBN: 978-1-64119-984-1
Ebook ISBN: 978-1-64119-983-4
Library of Congress Control Number: 2019953870

FOREWORD

Post Traumatic Stress Disorder, or PTSD wasn't officially diagnosed and named until 1980. But as far back as the Roman and Greek era, and possibly into the ancient Babylonian era, manuscripts exist that point to conditions very similar to what the modern soldier, policeman or others facing traumatic situations experience.

The condition appears to be as old as human conflict. Clearly, it is not exclusively a twenty-first century ailment.

In more modern times, from the US Civil War, through two world wars and multiple conflicts since that time, PTSD has been known as soldiers' heart, shell shock, and battle fatigue, among other diagnoses made by unaware medical people.

Symptoms of PTSD vary widely throughout historical records. In ancient manuscripts there are recorded incidences of mysterious blindness, sometimes becoming permanent, and visitations from the ghosts of those killed in battle. Other reported symptoms include nightmares, flashbacks, depression, hyper-vigilance, negative thoughts, impulsive or self-destructive behaviour and difficulty sleeping, among others.

In World War One, with the years-long trench warfare, gas attacks, incessant rains and indescribable carnage, some soldiers were known to simply 'blank out', as if their minds could take no more trauma, and their souls could absorb no more hurt.

It is estimated that up to forty percent of recorded, non-fatal, battlefield casualties fell into the category that, today, would be named PTSD. At that time, very few, if any, received any helpful treatment.

It was not unknown for insensitive field commanders to name the victims of PTSD as cowards. The British military court-martialled and convicted approximately 3,000 soldiers, condemning them to death. Over 300 of these sentences were carried out.

There is still much to learn about PTSD, but the good news is that the situation is being taken seriously by militaries and governments worldwide. And the medical profession is making some small inroads into this devastating condition, although there is still a long way to go.

The severity of PTSD varies from patient to patient; from mild to life changing.

***

In Reluctant Redemption we follow the life of Zac, a Civil War survivor, as he works his way through his sleepless nights, flashbacks and bitter memories, in his struggle to find his way in a world not of his making.

CHAPTER ONE

The dejected, shell-shocked troops didn't notice the lengthening shadows of late afternoon, as the westering sun broke through the smashed and broken forest. That the guns had fallen silent and they were no longer being killed or maimed was enough for this one day.

Even though the gray clad troops had held the higher ground, the end of the conflict was at no time in doubt. The enemy's superior numbers and materiel proved to be an unbeatable combination.

In late afternoon, the Captain himself had ridden down to the enemy lines, holding a white flag draped from the barrel of an unloaded rifle. Battle weary troops from both sides stood in wonder, as the commander of the enemy forces stepped out to meet him. The two commanders closed on neutral ground. The guns fell silent.

The troops still in the field turned and trudged slowly back to their own lines. A few men stooped to help a fallen comrade.

On his return, with assurances of a ceasefire,

the captain ordered the few remaining cannons be turned away from the enemy, signifying the end of hostilities.

That the guns had finally fallen silent was a reprieve the boys feared wouldn't come before more hot lead and steel poured out of the heavens, claiming them one by one, until all were taken.

Signalling the end of this last, long, sad, foolish day of battle, the bugler stepped forward, readying himself for Assembly and then the Retreat ceremony. The captain had negotiated a dignified striking of the colors. This would be the last call. The very last call for a tired and beaten group of warriors, all that was left of a proud fighting force.

The torn and wind-whipped flag would be lowered from its crooked, pine tree pole, neatly folded, and then removed from sight.

Everyone knew what it meant and welcomed it with sadness and resignation in their hearts.

The weary, defeated, hollow-eyed soldiers only waited for the official word. Hunkered down in whatever safety they found, or created for themselves, they waited for the bugle's call.

Other armies of the Confederacy would be fighting on; a day; a few days; a week, before they arrived at their predestined journey's end. But this tattered army was finished.

Down to the last of their food, ammunition almost gone, hardly enough troops left to stand to assembly, few officers able to answer the call; it was over.

Still wary of the enemy, no one stood or exposed themselves. Most held loaded weapons, their eyes fixed on the line of guns across the narrow battlefield. The cannon barrels, those black hollows that rained down such destruction earlier in the day, were still aimed their way. The lines of blue clad soldiers were hidden away in their own safe shelters. Neither group trusted the other.

But it was over. Had been over for a long time, if anyone in command could have brought himself to admit that depressing fact.

But on this last day they had fought one more battle in this remote, far flung edge of the war. A waste. A horror of destruction and inhumanity; the callous wish of proud, thoughtless leaders. The evidence, the demonstration of the cost, lay strewn between the worn-out men in gray and the equally spent forces in blue.

A man who has not experienced the carnage, the waste, the horror of a closely fought battlefield, has no real possibility of understanding. Nor is there any way to grasp the impact of continuous slaughter on the soul and spirit of a man.

Zac Trimbell had experienced it all. And yet, could even he really understand? Does a man fighting for his life, in the midst of a fire or a flood or a battle, stop to consider the flames or the water or the enemy soldier? It is the nature of fire to burn; of a flood to rampage waters over everything in its path.

Fighting and killing is what a soldier, in wartime, does. A man mired in the depths of a battle has no time to assess the enemy. Nor does he have the ability, even if his curiosity moved him in that direction. He sees only what is in front or beside him. The larger picture is left to the generals who study maps and issue orders, usually from a safe distance.

It is much more likely that the soldier will un-thinkingly revert to the basics, the animal nature within him. And at the base of animal nature, un-derneath it all, is the need, the will, to survive. For if a man fails to survive, there is nothing else.

Zac was a survivor. For three years he had sur-vived. As friend and foe alike died in their dozens, their hundreds, around him, many by his own hands, he survived. During those three years he had witnessed, and caused, soul-destroying may-hem and destruction.

The first time he triggered his rifle and watched a man fall, he wept all the following sleepless night. To think that his once orderly life had come to this! But it was shocking how quickly he hardened. When it came to fight or die, he found that he wished to live.

Day by day, battle by battle, a piece of who he was, died along with the battle casualties. He was no longer shocked by death. His heart no longer recoiled at the sight of broken bodies and spilled blood. He had become a warrior. A warrior with a duty to his country. A warrior doing what he must do in order to see one more sunrise.

Zac had ever been a godly man, grown to adult-hood amidst the influence of godly parents. His beliefs rested easily on his shoulders and in his heart. He couldn't imagine another way of life or thinking.

But until then he had never been to war. Never sighted his rifle or squeezed a trigger on another human being. Had never felt the burning slash of hot lead as it tore flesh and meat from his own body. Had never looked a man in the eyes as he met the charging enemy with his bayonet and watched that man's countenance take on fear and resignation before finally falling at his feet, his mouth open in agony, his life's blood draining onto the welcoming ground.

He had yet to have a good horse shot from under him, fearing that the next ounce of lead would find his own flesh.

No, his beliefs, his faith, were not shallow, he was simply inexperienced. Had never been seriously tested in the ways of the world. But after three years of battle, the first few months in the infantry and then in the cavalry, he had seen and felt it all.

He couldn't have said exactly when his faith had begun to slip, if indeed it had slipped. Perhaps it was simply shadowed in a dark part of his heart. It might be more honest to say that he no longer thought much about it.

If God was somehow on the battlefield, he had seen little evidence of Him.

He was wise enough in the ways of God to know that not all things were laid bare. He knew that in the story of Elisha there were hosts of unseen angels, with their chariots of fire surrounding the enemy, but Elisha's servant couldn't see the angels until God opened his eyes.

In a time of deep despair Zac had prayed that if there were angels anywhere close, his eyes would be opened to see. If God answered that prayer His answer was 'no'.

But then, with brother fighting brother, who really, is the enemy? If there were protecting angels, where would they be standing? Had God chosen sides on this sad conflict?

After the first couple of battles, never once in the three years of conflict had Zac found the need or the desire to think about the reasons or the purpose of it all; to try to figure it out. It was easier to block it out of his mind, as much as possible, and simply do his duty. Of course, there were still the nightmares. But he knew of no way to block those.

When not preoccupied with actual battle he only waited for it all to end. End so that he could get back to his life. The life with his small plot of land in East Texas, where Maddy and his little girl waited.

In any case, Zac wasn't the naturally introspective kind. In battle he simply followed orders. And tried to endure. Regardless of the details of the ordered battle plan, the bigger picture for the soldier was to live. To do what had to be done in his own self interest, and the interest of his fellow soldiers and his country. If that meant killing more of the enemy than the enemy killed, so be it. It was all about survival. Winning and surviving. Let the officers huddled over their maps make the plans, sending those battle plans down to the infantry or, in Zac's case, the cavalry. Zac would follow those orders without worrying over details he could not change.

When the bugles blared out their terrible message and the men rose from their huddled safety, bayonets fixed, their eyes glassy with fear, their hearts filled with hope and determination, there was no time to think. There was only time to kill. Kill and survive, if that was possible.

But now it was over. The big guns were silent. An eerie stillness had fallen over the battlefield.

The dead and dying from the last hopeless battle still lay in the grass and bush between the lines.

The end had been expected. Everyone knew. The morning's battle had been nothing more than wasteful pride. Officers' pride paid for by young men, some mere boys, who should have been released to go home to their loved ones.

At the sounds of Assembly, the men, one by one, and then in small groups, left their points of safety. Most of their gray uniforms were merely tatters of what had once been a proud declaration. Many men were barefoot. Some had wounds wrapped with bloody and dirty rags. A few walked slowly, ever looking back, reluctant to take their eyes off those dreadful cannons that still stared up at them.

Some, barely able to walk, dragged their rifles beside them.

A smattering of soldiers had not answered the call, remaining hunkered down in their small hovels of safety. Some didn't hear the call, their ears permanently destroyed from working the big guns. Some didn't care anymore, weary of officers' orders. A few were weeping, their pain and hopelessness on open display. In most cases a buddy stepped back, encouraging the tardy one to rise and assemble.

CHAPTER TWO

Captain Charles Jenner, looking weary and combat fatigued, greeted the assembled men. The day's battle saddened and horrified him. With the future no longer in any doubt he had pled with his seniors to strike the flag, to call an end to hostilities, but to no avail.

He was awarded his battlefield commission only after the loss of most of the old guard officers. He didn't want it, didn't like it and would shed the title as he shed the last remnants of his uniform. Nevertheless, he had one final task.

Seeing the men stagger towards him, the captain motioned the bugler to stand down. These men had heard the first call. They were slowly assembling. Charles Jenner, for that was still how he thought of himself, just plain Charles, not captain, watched the men with great sadness. These were men he had fought beside for months. Men he shared pain and sorrow with, his own uniform as tattered, and his belly as empty, as the lowest private.

Nevertheless, he was still a captain. He would

act the part for one more day, or for as long as it took. He looked over the weary assembly, standing as straight and tall as his battle-damaged body would allow, setting an example.

"Men, it's over. The war is over. You fought well. Don't ever let anyone tell you otherwise. But conditions on the field were not to our advantage.

"I know you're not surprised. I also know how it hurts. It hurts me too. But it's over. For better or worse we're going home."

Captain Jenner didn't know if his action met all the protocol associated with surrendering. He couldn't remember ever having the act of surrendering laid out for him. He had never been to officer training classes, but he somehow doubted there was much emphasis placed on this situation. He would simply do the best he could and let the results speak for themselves.

Captain Jenner motioned for the bugler to blow Retreat. As the sounds rose over the silent battle grounds Charles Jenner turned to the flagpole with a smart salute. The gathered troops followed his example.

Although few noticed, the enemy ranks across the bloody ground rose from their shelters and stood in silence as their victory was acknowledged. These men were as anxious to get home as the men in gray were.

With the flag no longer in sight the Captain said, "I need the medics and stretcher bearers to see to the wounded and dead. If some of you wished to assist, I'm sure that would be appreciated. The enemy will be doing the same. I advise that you ignore them. Let's not do anything that would cost more lives.

"We have negotiated a dignified end to hostilities. Stack your weapons where they can be seen and do nothing that would raise suspicion.

"We will put together the best dinner possible this evening and get as much sleep as conditions allow. We will assemble at 0700 for roll call. You will then be dismissed. Thank you and God bless each one."

Zac listened as the Captain laid out his plan. Or perhaps it was the plan the senior officers laid out to him. Or, conceivably it was all wishful thinking.

Zac didn't believe a word of it. It was naive in the extreme. Perhaps it was because of his years in the cavalry that caused the doubt.

The cavalry troops were always a bit more independent, a bit more self-assured. They were often in the center of the action, taking the brunt of what the enemy had to offer. And they paid the price. Zac's troop was reduced to just twelve poorly equipped riders. Eleven now, after losing Jakes in the morning's battle.

Too small to be an effective force and lacking any replacements of men or officers, the troop had been attached to a worn-out infantry group.

Zac was reasonably sure the victorious Blue Coats would be making their way across the land, taking anyone in Gray as prisoners. He couldn't imagine the Southern boys being freed to head home, carrying their weapons and their hatred. Reflecting on this for perhaps thirty seconds he figured it was time to take care of Zac. Swinging aboard the big bay gelding he had ridden for the past two-and one-half years, he quietly, and without speaking to anyone, rode from the assembly.

His only stop was at the supply wagon. No one was around. It was a matter of less than one minute to drop several handfuls of cartridges for his Henry rifle into his saddle bags.

He draped two half-gallon canteens over his head, to hang one on each side. He glanced longingly at the wagons pulled up behind the cook's tent, knowing that was the only source of edibles, as scant as that supply was. The crowd of gathered troopers made an approach impossible.

Accepting the situation as it was, Zac swung back onto the gelding and walked the animal into the bush surrounding the camp. He was out of sight in seconds. No one watched him leave. No one cared.

Zac had no clear idea where he was. Over several weeks the chain of battles had swung from the east to a north-east direction before being driven several miles to the west and then further south. He knew he was in western Tennessee, close by the Arkansas border, but how close was purely a guess. In any case, he had only a bare understanding of the larger lay of the land. He wasn't sure he had ever seen a full map showing how the states locked into one another. Nevertheless, he hoped that by riding carefully, travelling by night as stealth required, he could make his way across Arkansas, angling south and west, and eventually making it back to his home in East Texas.

It would take some time, but if he accomplished that goal, he vowed to never again leave Carob, Texas, the little town his family called 'home'. And to never again leave Madelene and baby Minnie. Of course, Minnie would no longer be a baby. She was six years old now. Zac had been gone for three years. The little girl wouldn't even remember her Pa.

He hoped Madelene would remember him. He hadn't had a letter from his wife for many months. And he had no idea if his own letters had ever been delivered.

Zac had only the barest notion of how broken his mind and soul were. He knew he had changed; was no longer the quiet, confident young husband and father, with dreams of a family and a successful farm. The change; the damage, happened slowly, accumulating bit by bit as each battle was fought, as each loss of a fellow soldier was witnessed or acknowledged.

The cruelties of close battle would have been unthinkable to the Isaac Trimbell that saddled up three years earlier. How his mind absorbed all he'd seen, and caused, was something he'd never seriously considered. It was easier to push it all back into his forgetfulness. It didn't matter anyway. The past was the past. It was only the next battle that mattered. And he was always prepared for that.

Zac rode carefully, his Henry repeating rifle held across his lap, the muzzle pointing to his left, his fingers never far from the trigger. The rifle had been his constant companion since his cavalry troop liberated a few of the repeaters from a defeated Union position. They'd gathered up all the rifles, distributing one to each man and then loaded themselves down with boxes of cartridges, before heading back to their own lines.

Breaking out of the bush, Zac warily approached a fifty-acre plowed field. The land carried old corn stocks smothered in a rank growth of weeds. There was no sign of farm work being attempted, no plowing or seeding, although the sunshine and warm winds of April said that spring was upon the land. Turning his head constantly to watch for hazards dressed in blue, Zac lifted the gelding into a trot and headed for the brush on the opposite side of the field, scaring up a bunch of squawking crows along the way.

He had come all of five miles since leaving camp but that wasn't enough to offer any kind of safety. There could be patrols almost anywhere.

As he neared the brush line three horses stepped out. Zac pulled up, facing three ragged and unshaven men. Slowly the riders walked their animals his way. The men held their weapons in the same manner as Zac was holding his, a comfortable and effective way when riding.

One rider swung his rifle over the horse's neck, resting it on his right leg. Zac noted the action and marked the man as his biggest threat.

That rider, a man with corporal stripes on his blue jacket, the only sign of a uniform on any of the men, pulled his horse to a stop and dropped his hand to bring the others to a halt, an easy shouting distance from Zac.

"Where ya head'n fer there, Reb?"

Zac knew trouble when he saw it. These weren't regular troops under the discipline of recognised officers and orders. These were freelancers, rene-gades, perhaps deserters, out for whatever spoils of war they could gather to themselves, now that the end of hostilities was in sight. The one blue jacket was enough to convince Zac of where the threesomes sympathies fell. It was time to be careful. Careful and vigilant.

"Going home boys. The war's over. You won. Ain't nothing more to keep me here. Got a wife and child might be need'n me."

The three soldiers glanced sideways at each other. The make-believe corporal spit a wad past his left knee, and grinned.

"Don't know as how yer gett'n off all that easy, boy. Might have someth'n to say about that my own self."

The three rode a bit closer and stopped again.

"I'll be ask'n ya to step off'n that there animal, boy. Lay yer weapon on the ground. Careful ya don't go ta gett'n no dirt down the barr'l. Ain't got no clean'n kit. Might want ta use that there rifle my own self. Good look'n piece. Taken yer horse too if'n ya don't mind. Or even if'n ya do mind."

The corporal thought that was worth a laugh. The others joined in.

Zac knew as much about his horse as a man can know of an animal. Two and a half years in battle together left man and animal both scarred from bullet and saber, and fully knowledgeable of each other. He knew the horse had nerves of steel. When the guns went off and the black smoke filled the air, the gelding stood like a marble statue until his master told him to move. Then the big bay would fearlessly step forward.

Zac also knew the animal would respond to the lightest touch of the spurs. He wasn't one to abuse his rides. The gelding had never felt anything but the lightest touches.

Only the most observant watcher would've noticed Zac working the toe of his left boot against the brown hide, with just the slightest movement. At the same time, he tickled the animal's ribs with the spur on his right foot. The gelding shook and pranced a bit before pivoting to the right, in a clockwise motion. Zac lifted the reins and spoke for the benefit of the soldiers facing him. "Whoa there now. Steady down boy."

While he spoke, he continued tickling the animal with his left toe. Just a bit more to the right. A bit more. There. "Stand," he said quietly. The animal became a statue, a steady shooting platform.

Knowing there was no way out of this confrontation, Zac did what he had been doing for three years. Still held firmly across his thighs, the Henry belched fire. The corporal had time for one last startled look before falling to the ground. All three horses facing Zac were suddenly prancing and sidestepping. Shooting without lifting the carbine, Zac required four shots to bring down the other two men. One of them had tried to raise his rifle to aiming position. Zac felt no pity at all as the slug from the Henry tore into his ragged, red checked shirt.

"Gotta learn your weapon, boy. Gotta shoot like the bullet was coming out of your pointing finger. Should'a known that. Too late to learn now."

Zac quickly rode forward, bailed out of the saddle, and ground hitched the gelding. He had no way of knowing if these three were part of a larger bunch or if there were just the three of them, out to get what they could find. He didn't plan on hanging around to find out.

It took only seconds to slip the saddles and bridles off the three horses, turning them loose. He then flipped the corporal onto his back. He grabbed up the handgun the man wore in an open holster, pushing it behind his own belt, adding it to the one he already had holstered over his left hip. He found the cross draw easier and faster while sitting the saddle. He was about to pull the dead corporal's pockets inside out when he noticed a strange bulge across the man's belly.

Ripping and pulling, he opened the jacket and then the bloody shirt. Wrapped tightly around the dead man's waist was a light, leather belt with four pockets. Zac lifted the flap on one pocket. Bills. US currency. A whole sheaf of it. A quick examination confirmed that the other pockets were similarly loaded.

Zac sat back on his heels and studied the situation.

"Well, now. I'm guessing I'm look'n at a thief. No way a renegade like y'all came by this legally. Looks mighty like army money. Maybe a small payroll. I'm bett'n you've been dream'n of having a high ol' time, you and your buddies, when you get to some big city. But now you're dead. You got no further use for the proceeds of your thievery. I'm alive and in need. So now I'm a thief stealing from a thief."

Without thinking further, Zac felt for the tie string and soon had the belt free of the dead man. A quick look through the pant pockets of each man and feeling for any more bulges on the other two,

Zac had the most of what he could use. He left the old, worn weapons lying in the dirt and corn stalks.

Only the man in the corporal's jacket had saddle bags. The big US burned into the flap confirmed that they were stolen too. Not wasting time examining the bags, Zac untied them from the saddle and flipped them over the neck of his own horse. Remounting, he drove his gelding into the bush and headed west. The shots would be heard for a mile or more. He needed to be gone; to be somewhere else.

CHAPTER THREE

Five days of hiding out in daylight hours, while travelling at night, took Zac deep into unknown territory. He guessed his distance travelled was about seventy-five miles. He met no one along the way, mostly because, at the slightest noise or the sight of a farmer's lighted window, he took whatever cautions were available to him. He lit no fires, left few tracks and made no noise.

He was hungry and lost. He saw no towns and few villages, avoiding the ones he did see. There was no way for him to know what sympathies lay in the minds and hearts of the townsmen, or the farmers along the way. He dared not push his good fortune by asking for a meal, even if he could pay. But he knew he was going to have to take a chance soon. He couldn't go on with his scant rations already used up. To steal something from a smoke house or a chicken coop would expose him to the charge of theft if he was caught.

Nearing the end of his endurance, he squatted beside the gelding at the edge of a spring-worked field, studying a small trading post backed against a hillside of brush, about one half mile away. It was too early in the morning for the place to be open. But he knew that, risk or no risk, at the first sign of life he was going to ride down.

The small trading post made its home on the side of a two-track trail laid out north to south. A narrow dirt road intersected the two-track on an east to west axis. No other buildings were close by, although the bush might conceal any number of structures.

He had already folded a couple of small Federal notes into a shirt pocket. The rest was still tucked into the money belt. He purposely allowed his shirt to sag outward in the hopes of hiding the bulge.

Zac kept nothing from his brush with the renegades that was obviously Federal, except the money. Each renegade had carried a belt-knife but none were as good as the one Zac already had. The dead corporal had nothing worth keeping in the saddle bags, so they were dropped in a bit of bush along the way. Now he needed to shed his worn and stinking gray uniform.

At the first sign of chimney smoke, Zac swung into the saddle. In a matter of minutes, he dropped to the ground and tied the gelding to the hitch rail in front of the small store. He looked all around. Seeing nobody, he pushed the door open with the barrel of the Henry and entered the darkened, smoky room. A brass bell clanked as the door opened. A half-awake voice hollered out, "Early yet. Stand by whilst I get this coffee on."

Zac went directly to a table displaying rough canvas pants and checked woolen shirts. Wasting no time, he picked out what he needed and dropped them on the counter. He then went to a shelf displaying wide brimmed hats. A hat, a jacket and a pair of long johns completed his clothing purchases. He would cut the long legs off the underwear when opportunity allowed.

By the time the trader stepped into the store Zac had a small stack of hardtack, a block of cheese, a few cans of sardines, three cans of peaches and a few other edibles laid out.

The trader started saying "Good morn..." but cut his talk off at the sight of Zac standing there in his gray uniform with the Henry pointed his way.

"Stand easy friend. I mean no harm. Just being careful. I need to make my purchase and shuck the uniform. You tote this up so's I can pay. I can shed the uniform and be dressed back up in just a couple of minutes. I'll be gone and you'll never see me again. It would help if you were to forget I was ever here. You can burn the uniform if you have the mind to."

The clerk stepped forward and moved behind the counter.

"No need of the weapon. I don't carry one, and those I have for sale are tucked away, high up, hard to reach. Anyway, the news is that the war's over. Around these parts, anyway. Might still be kill'n each other further east. I wouldn't know about that. Far as that goes, I never took no firm position. Either way. Time it ended."

He fingered each piece of clothing. Sliding a dog-eared account book towards the pile, he started tallying.

While Zac waited for the final tally, he unbuttoned his uniform jacket and dropped it on the floor. He was starting to slide the pants down when the clerk cleared his throat and ran his fingers through his unwashed and uncombed hair.

"Bit more than it all cost before the war. Hard to get supplies."

He named a price, almost sounding like he was asking a question.

Zac gave him a hard study before reaching into his shirt pocket for a couple of the bank notes.

"I expect you can charge about what you want. You're a greedy old man but you know I need the clothes so take this and count me out the change."

Stepping behind a display of men's pants, Zac started to peel off the shirt, hoping to keep the money pouch hidden from view.

The clerk made the change and held a closed hand over the coins.

"For another two-bit piece you can step into the back and have an all over wash. Ain't got no tub but there's a barrel of water and a wash basin. Couple of hardly used towels. Leave the uniform on the floor. I'll get rid of it for you."

Zac hated to spend more time. but he desperately needed a bath. Even if it was a standing-up bath, the opportunity was too good to pass up. Kicking his soiled and worn pants aside he stepped out in only his shirt and long johns. He gathered the new clothing into his arms.

"Keep another coin then and give me the rest. Sack up this grub and have it ready for me."

Ten minutes later, standing as naked as the day he was born, Zac finished his wash and was wiping his hair with the cleanest part of the dirty towel, when he heard voices from the store. He couldn't make out every word, but he pieced together, "In the back. Bath. Cash money."

Zac picked up the carbine he had leaned against the wall, stepped behind the barrel of water and waited. His belt gun hung from the peg the towels had been on, close by and easy to lay a hand to.

Two men pushed their way past the canvas flap that separated the two rooms. If they were thieves, and Zac guessed that was exactly what they were, their first mistake was entering the room with their belt guns drawn but hanging uselessly at the ends of their arms.

Allowing the canvas to fall back into the doorway, the men turned to look at Zac. Their eyes widened at the sight of the Henry rifle trained on the first man.

"Morn'n fellas. Come in here where I can see you. Actually, you'd look better without those belt guns. Just drop them in this here barrel of water. I'm in a bit of a hurry so best you do it now."

The man in the lead, a tough, belligerent type, tried a bluff. "I ain't gonna drop nothin' in that water. There's two of us here and another in the store. Best you pass me that carbine and do as we say. You just might come out of this alive."

Believing the odds were in his favor, and they were, if you just counted noses, he started to lift the Colt, holding his other hand out as if to take the Henry from Zac.

Zac waited as the man took one more step towards him, watching his every move. When the two were within a few feet, he suddenly levered the stock of the Henry sideways, using his right arm as the driving force, his left arm steadying the barrel and allowing the weapon to pivot. With no mercy, he whacked the fella above his right ear, with the rounded side of the hardwood stock. The sound of bone breaking was clear.

As the first thief fell to the floor Zac turned the weapon again, thrusting it with full force into the throat of the second man. That action brought forth an awful choking, gagging sound.

The thief fell to the floor, holding his two hands firmly around his throat. His eyes were rolled back into his head in agony. Blood and torn flesh clung to his grasping fingers.

Zac reached for the new long johns. He dressed as quickly as possible, watching the thieves the whole time, and listening for threatening movements in the store. He wasn't sure either fallen man was breathing. He didn't care. But just to be cautious, he unloaded the handguns that dropped from the men's hands and flipped them into the water barrel.

"Would've been a might better for you two if you'd a just done as I told you. Or if you'd a stood in bed this morning."

Leaving his filthy uniform crumpled on the floor, Zac re-entered the store, his Henry pointing the way. The clerk stood behind the counter, fear radiating from his troubled face and his trembling hands. He licked his lips and glanced at the doorway, as if looking for his two friends. He said nothing.

Zac walked over to a display of light rope. He cut off a twenty-foot length and came back to the storekeeper.

"Turn around. Hold your hands behind you."

The store man started to object.

"Now see here, fella. I don't know those other two. Don't know where they came from. You just gather up your purchases and be on your way. Far as I'm concerned, I never seen you."

Zac responded, "Don't end your life with a lie on your lips. I don't know how you signaled them two but signal them you surely did. Now turn around."

Zac stepped behind the counter. Taking the terrified man by one shoulder he turned him around, jamming him hard against the back shelves. Reaching for one wrist he soon had a loop fastened tightly. The second arm followed, with the same result. Zac pulled the rope tight and dropped a half-hitch around the storekeeper's neck. He turned the man around again and dragged him from behind the counter. With each reluctant step the hitch pulled a bit tighter until the trussed-up man had no choice but to follow.

Zac pulled on the new jacket, snugged the hat on firmly and picked up the sack of trail supplies. Tugging the rope again, he led the way from the store, stepped into the saddle and put the bay gelding to a walk. He didn't bother looking at his prisoner. The stumbling, half-choked storekeeper trotted along behind.

Zac hadn't felt pity for three years. He wasn't about to start again over a man who intended to rob him or maybe stand by while his friends killed him.

The strange caravan walked about one mile, arriving finally at a short but steep hill leading down to a small, fast-flowing river. The two-track trail led directly into the water and up the bank on the other side. Zac made the assumption that the trail showed the way to a shallow ford. He chose to step his horse upstream, towards deeper water.

Zac pushed his animal into the river, the bay sliding down the short bank on his haunches. The store man fell, rolling into the water, tangling himself in the rope. Zac waited while his prisoner found his footing again, and then proceeded to cross the river. The rise of water came to the gelding's belly.

The lassoed man fell again, going completely under this time. Zac simply dropped the rope and rode on, never looking back. With two short lunges the horse was up the other bank and back on dry land.

Zac figured the fella would either drown or have a chance to learn a lesson.

CHAPTER FOUR

After three more weeks of careful riding, now recognising the country around him, and somewhat relaxed, with the uniform shed and gone, but still cautious, Zac was getting close to the small town he called home before the war. His excitement and longing for home and family were tamped down firmly until he figured out the lay of the land. This was not the time to be making a careless move.

He had joined the war effort three years before as a naive, trusting, inexperienced young man. He was arriving back as a hardened veteran, his memory stuffed to overflowing with horrible mind-pictures, weary of the fight but still suspicious of most things and people he saw. Ready to do what had to be done. And do it before the other guy had the chance.

Now that the fighting was over and the direct threat to Zac's life was past, he was able to let down a small portion of his guard. But in the letting down, the relaxing, his emotions were allowed freer range than he had tolerated in battle. Feelings barely recognised or understood came to the surface. He found a deep sadness overwhelming him, sadness that delved into his very soul. Sadness that threatened to blot out all his other thoughts and feelings.

Along with the sadness came feelings of hopelessness. His inner mind asked, 'why bother'? 'Nothing matters'. 'The foolishness of war proved that'.

Steeling himself with grim determination, he closed his mind to these silent thoughts, as best he could.

He remembered his father often warning him, as a boy just coming into his formative years, "Be careful you don't talk yourself into something."

Thinking of his father added a moment of something approaching joy to his day. It was quickly gone.

He couldn't control the sadness, but by force of will he could shut his mind down. He even shook his head in determination and said, "No", a couple of times to still the unwelcome thoughts.

With a blank mind he rode forward. West by south. West by south was home and Maddy. Another short day's ride should take him to Carob, Texas. Since leaving the last battle site he had often been unsure of his location but now he knew. Just keep riding.

He kept telling himself, "West by south. All will be well at the end of this short trip."

CHAPTER FIVE

Before and during the war, strange alliances had developed all over Texas. Determined men of every stripe had been set loose on the land. Some took hard positions, forcing whole towns and counties to bend to their wishes or face the consequences. In some cases, the most radical, on either side, never went to battle themselves, choosing instead to remain safely at home, forcing their way on others.

With so many of the young men in uniform choosing the side of the conflict that satisfied their personal beliefs and choices, a zealot with no one to stop him and with just a few followers could hold sway over a town or an entire county.

What had transpired in the friendly village of Carob, Texas, Zac had no idea. He might be awarded a hero's welcome or he might be hauled before some zealot's drumhead trial, charged with treason. He was prepared to shoot his way through town if that proved necessary.

The modest cabin housing his wife and daughter lay five miles south. His parents had the fifty acres next to his own. That little cabin with the loving wife and child waiting was his goal. Nothing was about to stop him now.

He rode into the little village without drawing any attention. The heavy beard, the slim hardness showing under his shirt and the gauntness of his face, held little resemblance to the man the town folks knew as Isaac Trimbell. That his face and body had taken on considerable age, he was unaware of. He hadn't seen a mirror in months.

No one on the boardwalk could see his hat-shaded eye; the battle-weary eyes that held a cold guardedness, like an animal avoiding danger he could smell but not locate.

Zac knew the man who left for war three years before would not stand out in a crowd. It never occurred to him to describe himself, but if he did, he would simply think, 'pretty ordinary'.

At three inches under six feet his height was about standard for the day. His shoulders were broadened by a lifetime of physical labor. His arms were iron hard. But that would describe most men he knew. His face was too long for him to be considered handsome. His hair was black and straight. His beard was equally black, and heavy; a shave lasting only hours before new growth painted a shadow across his cheeks and chin. Unlike most men, he didn't favor a mustache.

At a casual glace he would look like any one of the men who rode through and around town each day.

As a show of his peaceful intentions, he dropped the Henry into the scabbard.

Zac made a single stop on his way through town.

Before he greeted his wife again, he needed a shave. Tying the bay directly in front of the small barbershop, where he could keep his suspicious eyes on him, Zac stepped inside. He didn't recognise the barber, which he felt was just as well.

A half hour later, with his hair cut, but still longer than most men's, and freshly shaved, he rode out of town. His excitement was growing as each minute passed.

One half mile north of Zac's homestead lay the farm of Jubal Watson. The main house was partially hidden behind a grove of shade trees that Jubal preserved during the land clearing. Zac had a mind to stop for a quick 'hello', but the thought of home overrode that initial urge.

Riding closer, he was able to see a man hoeing a garden patch. With the gardener's back turned to him and the big floppy hat shading everything above the shirt collar, Zac couldn't be sure who it was.

Hearing the clop-clop of hooves in the deep dust of the trail, the gardener turned towards the road and looked up. Zac immediately saw the black face and hands of Lemrich, the former slave. Jubal Watson had brought Lemrich and his wife to Texas with him years before.

Disagreeing with slave ownership and in horror of his father's treatment of these two faithful black servants, he had purchased them, freeing them when he entered Texas. But even being free, the former slaves had to earn their living somewhere, so they stayed on the Watson farm, working for small wages, living in a shed behind the house.

"Morn'n, Lem."

The gardener was a long time studying the rider, but he finally whipped off his hat and asked, "Mister Isaac? That you? Dear God, Mister Isaac. We all's give you up fer dead."

Lem dropped his hoe and approached the fence. Still holding his hat across his chest, he said, "Word from town is that nothn's been heard from you in a year or more. Thought sure you was shot 'n dead."

"The mail was pretty unreliable, Lem. I haven't heard from home in many a month. Maddy, nor my folks, either one. I'm hoping they're still here and doing alright."

Lem looked the picture of sorrow.

"Then you don't know, suh?"

Zac was instantly startled. He sat up straighter in the saddle and said, "Know what, Lem? What's happened."

"I's sorry to tell you this, Mister Isaac. It was the raiders. Good for noth'n raiders. Not soldiers, although they called theirselves such. Bout, well, 'bout one year ago they come terr'n through the countryside, steal'n an burn'n and kill'n. Killed poor Mister Watson first off. His Missus too. Stole everyth'n. Horses. Cattle. Anyth'n they could take away. Burned the house.

"Phoebe an me, we was work'n the field out back of the bush. W'al hid ourselves. Fer sure we'd a bin dead too if'n we warn't hid."

"Killed others to the west of here. Then they went to yer place. Yer father, he come a-runn'n 'n fought 'em to the death. Kilt a couple of 'em. But got kilt hisself too. Kilt yer Ma. Burned their house.

"Oh God, I's so sorry, Mister Isaac! Kilt yer wife and yer little girl. Burned the house. Took everyth'n, Mister Isaac. They's noth'n left down there. No mor'n a burned-out house 'n bad memories. I's so sorry, Mister Isaac. Awful thing."

Zac sat his horse in stunned silence. Everything he'd dreamed of. All that had kept him going during those terrible years. His future. His and Maddy's and the baby's. His purpose in striving for life during battle. All gone. It was no more. Had been no more for the past year and he hadn't known.

He took a deep breath, turned from Lem and nudged the bay gelding into motion. Without saying a word, he left the former slave standing with his hat still held in an almost reverent position. There were no words to say.

CHAPTER SIX

Zac sat his saddle, studying the blackened and weathered timbers; all that was left of their little cabin. Grass was growing vigorously between the scattered boards. Something kept him from stepping down. He had no desire to walk on this once special, now almost hallowed ground, where his wife and child died. Where his dreams died. Where his hopes vanished in last year's smoky blaze.

He remained in his saddle, holding his hat at arm's length, alongside his right leg. Tears were streaming freely. Ugly thoughts of revenge and despair came to his mind. With great force of will he shut them out.

He studied the sky and the white clouds drifting slowly by, as if he was looking for God. He would like to ask God why this had happened. And where He was when his precious little family needed protection.

Zac had turned from many battle sites without even a look back, or ever thinking about it again.

He knew he wouldn't be doing that here. These images were now a permanent part of his mind and heart.

Holding the gelding still, Zac studied every corner, every garden fence post, every shade tree, every flower plot he had dug for Maddy, burying the imagery indelibly into his troubled mind. The little fence he built to keep baby Minnie from wandering was still there, although it was now badly weathered, and two posts were fallen over, or perhaps pushed over by wandering cattle.

Zac felt dizzy. Unconsciously he grabbed for the saddle horn on the officer's saddle he had claimed after most of the senior men had fallen. The regular troopers' saddles had no horn. All this ran through his mind with no conscious effort on his part.

It was too much. He felt himself slipping, both emotionally and physically. He gripped the saddle with fierce strength and repositioned his boots in the stirrups to correct his physical slide.

But what was he going to do about his emotional slide? That slide that held him somewhere between furious anger and hopeless despair; between the wish to tear across the country killing every renegade he could find, and his despondence that said, 'you might just as well quit. Simply sit down and quit'.

Needing to do something, anything at all that would feel like activity, he nudged the bay forward to ride around the shed and the well house, both still standing. It had taken a long summer of labor to hand dig the well but, in the end, the young family had a steady source of clear, cold water.

Behind the shed sat his high-sided work wagon.

A little larger than a buckboard, yet not so large as the typical Studebaker covered wagons that carried so many emigrants to the western country. It had served him well, and could again, if need presented itself.

He reluctantly stepped out of the saddle to see what was left in the shed. Pulling the door open, scraping it through the overgrown grass, he peered into the dim interior. There hung the harness he had so often laid on the backs of the team of grays. A bit dried out but still usable. For some unexplained reason, he was pleased to see it had survived.

Around the little shed, leaning against the walls, and in each corner, were tools bought with hard-earned money. Shovels, a pick, one hay scythe, a couple of garden rakes, a milk bucket. Maddy would have used the bucket every morning and evening unless she turned the calf into the cow pen. A bridle from his saddle horse hung on its peg. The saddle was gone.

He stepped into the sunlight again and closed the door.

Zac repeated his motions at his parents' home, on their nearby plot. The result was much the same. Obviously, the raiders had no use for tools that might require physical work.

With the plan that was quietly forming in the back of Zac's mind, a plan he had no conscious thought of before this time, he would have no use for the tools either. He might take a few with him, but only for times of need on the trail. What trail, he didn't know. He only knew he couldn't stay here. The plan was germinating almost of its own free will, with no effort from himself. He would let it grow to maturity the same way.

Suddenly, ashamed he hadn't thought of it before, he wondered if there were graves, and where they might be. The answer came silently.

The churchyard. Of course. Where else?

He turned the gelding back onto the town road. Riding north, he again passed Lem, still working in the garden. The former slave stilled his hoeing and watched him ride past. Zac neither looked his way nor spoke. He had other things on what was left of his mind.

At the edge of the little village stood a white painted, clapboard-sided church. On the end of the church building furthest from the road was a small addition, the home of the pastor and his wife.

***

Rev. Moody Tomlinson asked for little from life. With their children grown and scattered, Moody and his wife were perfectly content in the tiny village of Carob, and with the small gathering he ministered to. No soft handed desk sitter, Moody was constantly finding something to do in town that would benefit from his labor. Beyond the preaching and teaching he wrapped his love around, he was often seen building a fence, helping to break and train a horse, walking behind a plow, driving a team for a neighbor who needed help, and a dozen other things his neighbors would find helpful.

Zac found him at home, working up the soil for his own garden. "Afternoon, Rev."

Rev. Tomlinson jumped a bit at the greeting and turned to see who it was. His actions nearly paralleled Lem's, when Zac had ridden past the old Watson place.

The pastor left the short-handled spade stuck in the ground and whipped off his hat. "My Great Good God, is that you, Isaac?"

"It's me alright, or what's left of me, Rev."

Moody Tomlinson pushed open the fence gate and in three long strides was standing beside the bay gelding. He grabbed Zac's hand. Wordlessly, he studied his old friend. Tears of sorrow and compassion flowed. Nothing was said for a long thirty seconds.

As happy as he was to see this good man, Zac had only one thing in mind.

"What can you tell me about my family, Moody? Are their graves around somewhere?"

"Step down. I'll show you. My God, Zac. We were sure you were dead. No news for so many months. It's a sorrowful thing you come home to, but I'm beyond happy to see you."

Zac stepped down and tied the gelding to the wire fence surrounding the garden. He had no desire to discuss matters with the pastor. They had been friends for years, but this wasn't the time. Perhaps the time would never come.

Silently he turned and followed the pastor to the sunny side of the old church building. There, enclosed within a picket fence painted the same white as the church building, lay the generational graves of the people who had called the little settlement of Carob, Texas, home.

The pastor pushed the gate open and the two men wordlessly walked in. Without making a sound, Moody stopped before a short row of four graves. A roughly hewn and carved stone lay at the top of each one. Zac studied the names and the dates. Four. All on the same day. It was almost too much.

Standing side by side, the two men thought their silent thoughts. After a minute, Moody put his arm on Zac's shoulder and prayed a short prayer, thanking God for bringing Zac safely home and reminding Him that His Word said to rejoice with those who rejoice and to mourn with those who mourn.

With that, Moody left Zac alone. He stepped out of the small cemetery and took a seat on a bench, nestled in the shade of a towering live oak. As his friend mourned, the good pastor silently prayed for the soldier's soul, and his peace of mind and heart.

Zac was not long at the graves. Many, many times on the battlefield he had watched friends fall. Grieving was a luxury saved for quiet moments and there were too few of those during the past three years. There, the sense of loss was swallowed up in the probabilities of war. He had learned to cope, becoming a bit harder of heart each time he was confronted with hurt and loss.

But this was family, his hoped-for future. He knew he would mourn the rest of his life. Mourn at some level of his mind and heart, even if he couldn't quite describe it.

Still, he was alive. He had to move on, build a new life. And Carob, Texas was not the place to do it. He knew that as surely as if he had seen it written in the sky, or on a chiselled stone carried down from a mountain. There was nothing to be gained by delay.

Zac had questions to ask that he didn't wish to

hear the answers to. The rumors of what the many raider gangs had done across the land were deeply troubling. Women, especially, had suffered horribly. He walked to the bench and stood in the shade. His pastor friend studied him, seemingly understanding what was to come.

Zac was holding his hat in his hands, his lips forming questions.

The wise Pastor stood, looked directly into Zac's eyes and spoke quietly but firmly before Zac had the opportunity to voice his questions.

"Isaac, you've suffered a terrible loss. Please know that the town folk did what they could. Lemrich Watson did more than most. He was there first. Must have run the whole way from the Watson place when he saw the smoke. He tried to fight the fire, but it was over so quickly he could do nothing. But he did manage to pull the bodies free of the flames before the townsmen showed up. He took on some burnt flesh and hair in the doing of it.

"Those four graves are the resting places of people we all loved, Isaac. And now you have questions. Let it go. Know that you were much loved by those you lost. And we know how much you loved them. They are at peace. They are in God's care. Let the rest go."

Zac made no response.

Into the silence of the churchyard the good pastor said, "I know you'll not be staying here, Zac. I understand why. Wherever you go, go with God. I will continue praying for you. For peace and for happiness in your future."

The two friends strolled slowly to where the gelding was tethered.

Zac untied the animal and swung into the saddle. When he turned towards the dirt trail, Moody Tomlinson gently took hold of the bridle. The horse stopped and Zac politely waited for whatever words his friend had for him.

Moody let go of the bridle and stepped a bit closer to Zac.

"I can't let you go without asking you, Zac. It's my job, after all, and you're my good friend.

"No one can even imagine what you've been through in the war. And what you've come home to is horrible beyond description. Nevertheless, my friend, tell me the truth. "Is it still well with your soul?"

Zac couldn't answer, nor could he look at the pastor. The feelings were too fresh, too tender. And he had so many unanswered questions. With a single nudge of one spur the gelding stepped forward. Zac glanced back once, as he rounded the corner towards his land and home. The pastor was still standing where he had been before, soaking in the sad sight of his departing friend and, no doubt, praying for good travels and a better future.

CHAPTER SEVEN

Zac hadn't cared deeply about another human, man nor woman, other than his family, for a long time. On the battlefield he had a level of caring for his mates, but the losses were so often and so hurtful that even with his fellow soldiers, his caring couldn't be called love. Not in the real sense of that word, it couldn't.

Beyond his own family, he wasn't sure he had the capacity to care, to love. And now he had even lost the anchor his family had provided. But somehow Lem and Phoebe touched a part of his heart that he had kept firmly locked during the war.

He had known them for years, of course. Watson was a good farmer and a kind man so Lem and Phoebe were well cared for and needed nothing from Zac. Perhaps until now, if he had the right of it.

With his fractured mind and soul, he had to sort out his doubts about everything he did. But he thought he saw the future of Texas clearly. And the future he saw was grim, and not far away.

He rode back to the Watson farm. A plan was taking shape in his mind as he rode. Lem was no longer in the garden. Zac rode to the small shack Lem and Phoebe were calling home, and dismounted when Lem came to the door.

Phoebe stood in the open door and listened as the men talked.

Lem, somewhere around forty years old, black, but not dark black, with graying curly hair and a perpetual smile when life was close to normal, had always shown a keen intelligence. As a former slave, freed years before the war, with no education, unable to read or write, he lacked opportunity in the world he was freed into. But the intelligence still showed in his thoughts and actions. He was strong to work and asked for little. These were the attributes that caused Jubal Watson to decide to bring him to Texas as a freed man.

Phoebe was a bit younger than Lem, but not by much. That put her, perhaps a decade older than Zac. Tall and angular, hard work and heredity keeping her slim, Phoebe would be considered a beautiful woman in any society.

Before coming to Texas, she had never been offered any education either. Mrs. Watson began almost immediately upon their arrival in Texas to teach her the necessities of life, beginning with her letters and numbers.

Zac got right to the point.

"What are your plans, Lem? You don't own this land. Now that the war is over, I expect someone will buy it, or claim it, and you'll find yourselves without a home. What will you do then?"

Lem clearly had no answer for Zac's question.

Zac waited through a moment of silence before moving on to ask another question.

"I'll be needing a wagon team. Where might I find someone with a team for sale?"

Phoebe stepped from the doorway to stand beside her husband. She was the most of an inch taller than him. Phoebe was all angular grace, standing straight, holding her head up, ready to look the world in the eye.

Lem was a bit stooped from time, abuse as a slave, and hard work. His sleeveless shirt exposed his powerful physique.

Where Zac was tall and lean, with long, stringy arm muscles, Lem was rounded, his bulging muscles a natural complement to a strong man.

Lem and Phoebe studied each other. A silent signal seemed to pass between them. Lem said nothing. He studied Isaac for another moment. He then turned and walked towards the nearby grove of trees. Zac hesitated, then followed.

The two men walked a hundred yards into the bush. Lem still didn't speak. He simply stood aside so Zac could see the small corral. Inside, eating grass hand-cut from the surrounding area was a pair of big, gray mules.

The two men studied each other; the unspoken message clear. In the aftermath of war, ownership was an uncertain thing. With so many land-owners dead or missing, many things were done that would have been unacceptable in other times.

The mules were a part of the Watson farm. They didn't truly belong to Lem and Phoebe. But the Watsons were dead, and the mules were there.

When enough time had passed for Zac to think

it through, Lem quietly said, "We was work'n the mules in the back field, behind all this bush, when the raiders come. We hid ourselves in the bushes, us and the mules. Far as anyone knows, these mules be either dead or gone."

Zac decided that if Lem didn't have a plan, perhaps he should provide one. Even a partially formed one was better than no plan at all.

"Lem, it won't be many days before this country is overrun by bluecoats. We have to get out of here. We have to do it now. We're going west. You and Phoebe and me. All the way to the goldfields in the Rocky Mountains, maybe. Or maybe we'll find some available farmland along the way.

"You go tell Phoebe to pack up everything she needs for a long trip. Bedding. Warm clothing. Food. Cooking things. Bring a waterproof sheet to cover everything, if you have one. I have only the clothes on my back and my small bedroll so there'll be room enough for your stuff, and a bed along side it all for Phoebe.

"You walk those mules down to my place with the first darkness tonight. Try not to be seen. With Watson dead and gone, you have as much right to the animals as anyone. I'll go ahead and get the wagon ready. Grease the wheels and tighten everything up. I have harness. Hurry now. Get your stuff sorted out.

"With first dark, we'll harness up and come back here for Phoebe. We need to be gone from here before anyone sees these mules."

Lem looked at Zac as if a rescuer had just ridden into the yard. Then he turned and trotted off to talk to Phoebe.

Zac caught up his horse and rode quickly to the old place.

CHAPTER EIGHT

At the first sign of darkness the strange caravan took the long way around the village and headed north-west, winding their way down country lanes, and seldom-used trails.

Zac had no idea what had transpired between Lem and Phoebe. But if Phoebe's energetic loading of the wagon was any indication, that good woman had jumped on the idea with enthusiasm. Or perhaps it was resignation. But the reason didn't matter. With no lasting home and no way to make a living, they had to get out of Texas. That or end up as sharecroppers for the remainder of their lives.

There was no one to say goodbye to. The three survivors, each attempting to get beyond their past lives, stepped into a future as dark as the night they travelled in.

Zac rode the gelding while Lem handled the lines for the team of mules. Phoebe rolled into her blankets and slept in the back of the bumpy, rattling wagon.

Zac hadn't slept for most of the past two days. He

was now afraid to sleep, afraid of the new nightmares that would be added to the nightmares the war left deeply imbedded in his mind.

He couldn't stand the thought of seeing his lovely Maddy and his little Minnie walking through his dreams. Or his parents either, come to that.

Pushing himself relentlessly, until fatigue drove him to his blankets, was the only solution he could think of that might still the memories. The memories of a foolish war. The memories of his murdered wife and daughter. The memories of four rough carved stones in the church yard. The thoughts of what they had suffered before they died.

He couldn't have put a name to what was going on in his mind, but he knew it scared him. Sometimes it angered him. Sometimes it filled him with melancholy.

Pointing the wagon north and west, driving by moonlight, occasionally paralleling the trail that led him home just hours before, left Zac's mind empty of thought.

He had no idea what lay ahead and no clear idea of where Colorado was, or the fabled goldfields. Or if that should even be their destination. Perhaps they would find another promised land somewhere along the way. They would simply keep moving, hoping to find their way by one means or another. There was no purpose served in thinking about something he knew so little about.

But, of course, there is truly no such thing as an empty mind. Something will always rise up to fill it, often something unwelcome.

In Zac's case, even when he was awake and riding, unbidden by conscious thought, his mind filled with horror and hurt and despair.

He tried to push aside the roar of cannon that had so often been a part of his existence, and the rain of body parts that fell around him, and sometimes on him, in the aftermath of the deluge of lead and steel. But when he thrust that aside, the screams of the dying pushed their way forward.

As clearly as if he was seeing them in bright sunlight right before his eyes, he saw empty saddles on wounded horses, saddles where his friends and mates had ridden just minutes or hours earlier. But in truth these men were in their graves, weeks, months, years before. Their names slowly scrolled through his mind. He blinked his eyes and tried to think of something other than war. But with one vision supplanting another, there was a steady kaleidoscope of horror for his troubled mind to sort out.

When he somehow pushed that aside he saw his wife smiling at him, holding out the new-born baby for him to hold. He shook his head to dislodge the memory, only to have it replaced with a new vision.

He saw the baby as she was running across the farmyard on wobbly legs, screaming in delight as her mother chased her in a happy game. In his mind's eye he smiled and watched. But his smile faded as, to his horror, the baby and her mother ran into the burning cabin.

More screams, more rifle shots. And then a band of laughing men driving the cattle and horses before them as they callously left their trail of destruction behind them.

Aloud Zac cried out, "NOooo."

He reached out to help Maddy and the baby. But they were gone.

Zac realized he had screamed out loud and was

thankful for the noisy wagon. He hoped Lem and Phoebe hadn't heard him.

"I'm going crazy. My mind is broken. I can't control my thoughts anymore. I don't even know what I'm doing myself, and now I've gone and talked these good people into following my lead. God help us all."

The wagon rumbled on until the first sign of a cloud shrouded sunrise. Zac cantered ahead to take a look at a promising copse of trees just off the trail. He found a small clearing and a tiny seep of water, outlined by the green of spring grass growing along its edge. He stepped down from the saddle and tied the gelding. He then walked stiffly to the edge of the trees and waved Lem in.

Phoebe, who had joined her husband on the wagon seat for the past hour jumped down like a young girl, as soon as the wagon stopped, amazing Zac. He shook his head, feeling the pain in his joints, and knowing he might never again feel well enough to jump anywhere, ever again.

Zac built a small breakfast fire while Lem dealt with the mules, first taking them to water at a small bulrush slough that came and went, depending on the recent rains, and then staking them on good grass. He would take them to water again before lying down to sleep. Phoebe made coffee from the barrel of clean water strapped to the side of the wagon.

With Phoebe having slept most of the night, she sat, awake and watching, as the two men went to their own blankets. Zac slept better than he had in some time. Perhaps sleeping every two days, holding his eyes open until exhaustion forced him down, was the solution to his nightmare problems.

Phoebe prepared a modest meal after the men awoke. Seeing little reason to travel at night now that they were away from Carob, and anyone who might enquire about the mules, they decided to travel only until sundown. They would travel in daylight hours from then on.

A few days later they entered a small village busy with foot and horse traffic. There were other travellers on the trails, all heading generally north or west, perhaps taking advantage of the opportunity to get away from the destruction of war and put old plans into place in some new land.

So many had lost everything, including loved ones, that a new start, even from almost nothing, was better than trying to sort out the rubble of the old.

For some, those plans would include joining the westward march, all the way to California or Oregon. Others would stop somewhere along the way.

Zac was careful to keep the money belt well hidden under his layers of clothing. Without even letting Lem or Phoebe see what he was doing, he dropped back when the village came in sight. Hoping the dust thrown up by the wagon wheels would cover his actions, he dug out enough bills to cover their needed supplies.

They pulled up at the general store and went in, with Zac, as usual, toting his Henry .44. There was no threat in his movements. The proprietor greeted them warmly enough, but two women customers turned from picking over a table of work clothing and gasped at the sight of the black couple. They were too shocked to speak.

Finally, one of the ladies huffed herself up like a Banty rooster.

"Comry?" She studied the store owner. "Is this what it's come down to now? Are we decent folks expected to mix with their likes when we're doing our shopping?"

She said it with a glance at Lem and Phoebe.

Zac was about to speak when the store owner said, "Missus Reynolds. I appreciate your business, just as I appreciate everyone's business. When folks are in need of supplies and have the wherewithal to pay, they're welcome. I doubt as how that policy will have any long-term detrimental impact on your life."

The two women were stunned into silence.

Turning to the three new arrivals Comry asked, "What can I get for you folks?"

Zac, ignoring the outspoken woman, who was stomping out of the store with her friend, said, "Didn't go to cause you any problems, friend. We just need some trail supplies."

Comry chuckled, "No problem. Those two just don't have enough experience to know how the world works. Good enough ladies though. I'm friends with both their husbands. Still, you might want to get what you need and move on. I'm afraid you're going to run into difficulties from time to time. A few around here don't take kindly to mixing the races. There's a lot of healing needed in this country. A lot of new things to get used to. Take time, it will."

Phoebe had shopped many times back in Carob, but always with Mrs. Watson at her side. Still, she knew what she wanted and immediately began piling items on the counter. A few pieces of clothing were followed by a small mountain of packaged and canned foodstuffs. Two fresh sides of bacon topped off the lot, along with a large can of ground coffee and two small sacks of beans. Zac had assured her that he had the necessary funds.

Zac wandered over to the rack of weapons. A couple of new pieces were held apart from an assortment of used stock. After looking over the choices and enquiring about the costs of the used ones, he picked out a .56-.50 Spencer carbine for Lem and a Smith &Wesson #2 Army .32 handgun for Phoebe.

He added three boxes of ammunition for each weapon.

Zac looked at Comry, and said, "Add it up. We pile anything more here I'll have to sweep out your store to earn enough to pay for it all."

About the last thing Zac wanted anyone to know was that the travelling trio were solvent beyond what most folks had ever seen. He hoped that acting like he was down to his last dollar would be convincing enough.

As an afterthought Zac walked over to the clothing table. He picked out a beaded leather reticule, with a strong leather carrying loop. Lying it on top of the pile of goods he nodded at the storekeeper.

Comry found a used sugar sack to pile some of the canned goods in. The remainder was hauled out in an armful each for the three shoppers. Lem checked the mules while Phoebe stowed the goods, tucking the tarpaulin as tightly as she could around the edges, to keep out at least some of the dust.

The Spencer was carefully placed under the wagon seat, on a folded feed sack. Lem tucked the

.32 ca pistol into his big jacket pocket.

Zac was reaching for the gelding's reins when a loud, mocking voice said, "Well, looky here. We got us a couple of blackies and a Nigra lover, judging by looks. And that there's a might fine look'n woman. These here your blackies, boy?" He was looking at Zac.

Zac stepped back onto the board walk. What he saw was two rough dressed men, grinning and acting tough. The talker spoke to his friend in a voice loud enough to attract attention up and down the boardwalk.

"What ya think here, Gus? Think we ought'a take and see how fast that blackie can run? Maybe have other ideas about the woman. That's, of course, after we deal with this here Nigra lover."

The storekeeper, who had stepped onto the boardwalk, spoke up. "They're just leaving, Archer. Let them be."

The man named Archer laughed. "Why sure, we'll let them be, store man. Just as soon as we decide what we's gonna to do to them before we turn them loose."

Zac took a slow step forward. Archer hooted loudly, "Looky here, Gus. Fella's got a mind to try to stop us. You want the pleasure of lay'n him down, or should I do it?"

Zac took two more steps, bringing the Henry up from his side. At the sight of the rifle Archer quit hooting and looked over at Gus as if questioning their next move. He hadn't seen the Henry the way Zac was holding it.

Archer was given no chance to think it all through. As casually as you might twist the neck off a chicken for Sunday dinner, Zac drove the Henry forward, with a swinging drive; a brutal drive, into the big man's overgrown belly. It was a wicked blow, driving the barrel well into the fat and muscle, tearing flesh. Zac didn't care if he killed the man or not. Archer's eyes went wide, his mouth opened in terrible pain and he started slumping to the sidewalk, turning a bit to the side as he crumpled.

The sideways turn was perfect for Zac's second blow. Pulling the Henry from the man's ruined stomach he swung it sideways, catching Archer's lips and teeth with the side of the barrel. Blood, broken teeth and torn flesh flew through the air. Archer dropped without another sound.

Gus, a slovenly man, his shirt half out of his trousers, was scrambling to pull a revolver from his holster, but it was caught on his sagging shirt. Zac kept the Henry moving, slashing it down on Gus's wrist. The revolver fell to the sidewalk as Gus screamed and grabbed his shattered arm. Zac swung the butt of the rifle, taking Gus above his ear. He dropped and stayed down.

Zac turned to the startled Lem. "Get 'em moving."

He spoke to the storekeeper as he was mounting the gelding.

"We're friendly folks. Don't go to cause any harm. Won't be threatened or put-upon though. You spread the word, if anyone should take a notion to follow us, they'd best say goodbye to their loved ones before they step out. I won't abide any nonsense."

The storekeeper watched Zac ride away, catching up to the wagon. He glanced down at the two men sprawled out on the boardwalk.

"I'll be sure to spread your warning."

CHAPTER NINE

An hour north of the village, Lem pulled the wagon to a stop.

Zac rode up. "It's too early to stop, Lem. And still too close to that village."

"That's all true Mister Isaac, but I need to take and load these weapons. I wouldn't want someone to come up on us and we'uns not be ready."

Zac studied the black man for a moment wondering what to say. Finally, he asked, "Do you know how to use a rifle, Lem?"

"Yessir, I surely do. Mister Watson, he showed me some. Long time ago. Showed Phoebe too. Only thing is, she's not had much practice."

Lem was readying the weapons as he spoke. Digging into his pocket for the pistol, he continued talking.

"Mister Watson, he wanted us to know things. Phoebe and me. Taught us rifle and pistol shoot'n. Some about the care of horses and mules, though I had a good bit to do with the beasts back on the plantation. Tried to teach me letters and numbers. I wasn't too good at learn'n, but I can make out, given time.

"Missus Watson, she taught Phoebe. Phoebe picked up real good on the letters and numbers. And the proper way 'a talk'n.

"Missus Watson say she didn't want no more 'a that slave talk. Taught Phoebe to speak proper and all. I learned a bit along de way but Phoebe, she talk like she been to school an all that.

"Yassir, I know how to load and shoot these guns. Mister Watson, though he say I don't want to shoot nuth'n but varmints and maybe sometimes a deer fer the kitchen. He say if'n I shoot a white man I's gonna get hung. I don't expect the war changed any 'a that."

Zac said, "Phoebe, you dig that leather reticule out and put your pistol in it. You carry the bag everywhere you go. Those two back at the store aren't the only ones holding a hard attitude. Don't you be shooting anyone that doesn't warrant shooting, but when the need is upon you don't hesitate. And you don't have to pull the gun from the bag. You can shoot right through the leather if the time is tight.

"You have to be prepared to take care of yourselves. By and by, we'll find somewhere out of the way to get in some practice shooting."

Four days later, the little caravan crossed the Red. The river was a bit higher than they were comfortable with, but they followed a well used trail, hoping someone had located a ford. The river came to the hubs of the wagon wheels but no higher, although the current was enough to cause the wagon to sway.

After crossing the river, they pulled the team

to a halt and stepped down themselves. Phoebe walked the kinks out of her legs while Lem took the animals to water.

Zac looked around. "I do believe we have left Texas."

Studying the green, slightly hilly country around them, Lem asked, "What would this place be called then?"

"I don't know much more than you do. Might be the corner of Arkansas or it might be Indian Territory. We'll just have to have our eyes open for trouble and keep following this trail."

Phoebe, hands on her hips, studied the land before them. "Not much of a trail. I wonder where it goes."

Zac had no idea himself where the trail led.

"We'll just have to wait and see."

The procession made its slow way north and west, still following the faint outlines in the sod. All the trail told them was that others had been this way, probably many times, to leave wagon tracks like these in the grass.

For Lem and Phoebe, slave or free, farming had been their lives. They knew no other. Lem was admiring the land around him, sparsely treed and unused with just a few head of cattle staring at them from time to time.

When they stopped for lunch, Lem said, "Be farms all through here one day."

Zac, standing with his plate in his left hand, his coffee cup balanced on the iron rim of a wagon wheel, looked all around as if seeing the land for the first time.

"Yes, but it's not for us. I'm not interested in

farming and if I left you here to work up a place for yourselves, you wouldn't be safe. Someone would come along who never accepted the new way. There's no telling what might happen then. Anyway, it takes a pocketful of money to get a farm up and going."

Zac was quiet for a while, studying on another matter that he felt needed to be discussed. Finally, although he was uncomfortable with his thoughts, he pushed ahead anyway.

Squatting on his heels to bring his eyes level with Phoebe's, his cup cradled between his two hands he said, "Phoebe, there's something you may or may not be aware of. We need to talk a bit about it."

Again, he hesitated before proceeding.

"It's just this. Black or white, you are an uncommonly beautiful woman. You're going to draw attention no matter where we go. Back in Carob everyone knew you. You and Lem both. Everyone knew you were a married woman and a lady.

"Then, you were always with Missus Watson, under her protection.

"Out here it's different. No one will know you or anything about you. Your beauty could attract attention that you wouldn't welcome. That could lead to all kinds of grief.

"You stay close to Lem and don't do anything to make anyone doubt that you're a married lady. I'll stay as close by as possible too. Even the roughest sort of men will usually respect a married lady but still, you watch and be careful. And keep that reticle hanging on your arm."

Neither Lem nor Phoebe chose to push the conversation any further.

As the days wove their way into another week, the emotional exhaustion started catching up to Zac. He often felt like he just didn't care anymore. It took every ounce of resolve he could find to keep putting one foot ahead of the other, when he'd much rather take to his bed. He remembered the same feelings coming all too often towards the end of the war, wondering every time he saddled up if it would be the last time. And not really caring one way or another.

It was probably his father's teaching, and the never-ending needs of the farm that had ingrained in him the habit of moving forward, of keeping going, regardless of his feelings. And now he had the added burden of living up to the trust Lem and Phoebe had placed in him.

It was true that the idea to travel was his. But now they were underway, so where the idea came from no longer mattered. There was certainly no going back.

He couldn't allow himself to stop. The little caravan had to keep going, regardless of feelings.

He was still having his nightmares, waking up sometimes in a cold sweat. If he cried out in his sleep, neither Lem nor Phoebe mentioned it. He knew it was possible they were just being polite.

In addition to Zac's exhaustion was his overwhelming sadness. He had been telling himself for three years that the dying and killing he was a part of was just the way of war. And anyway, there was no one there that he knew or felt close to. There was no one he would miss in future years. He told himself that time after time. But he didn't really believe it. And the evidence was all against him.

To fight old battles and see men who had been dead for years, being blown up again by the artillery shells night after night had cost him countless hours of sleep and wearied him to the bone. As much as he told himself he didn't actually know those men in any personal way, that they weren't really close friends, in his sleep he named them off, one by one.

Then there was the loss of his family. Put together, the burden was greater than he could have explained. It was almost too much.

Although the temptation to simply stop, to quit, was strong, he feared that if he gave in, his mind might go over some edge that he could not pull it back from.

His mind hurt. His brain was tired beyond description. He had trouble making decisions. Several times he let Lem take the lead while he sat his saddle unresponsively. With a slackened rein, the horse followed the wagon, plodding on without direction from its rider.

He seemed to be forever fighting tears that he couldn't explain.

When his eyes finally opened to each sunrise, it took all his will to simply push back his blankets. He worried that if he had set out alone, with no one to travel with and care for, he might have stayed in his bedroll and never gotten up again.

Zac was always a strong-willed man. A self starter, needing no one to push him along. No others could hope to be successful with a pioneer farm. He didn't know what it might be like to lean on anyone or anything. He had never felt the need. But now that strong-willed nature was put to a severe test.

Still, it was that will and determination that kept the little caravan pushing forward. But for how long? Some days Zac felt himself slipping. Slipping in his mind. Idly he wondered if he was the only one who came home from the war with these feelings.

And then there was the awful tendency towards violence, towards lashing out at enemies and perceived enemies. The old Zac would have found a more peaceful way to deal with the two crude men back in the little village. Or at least made the attempt. The new Zac was perfectly willing to kill them. Or wound them almost beyond recovery.

But they were on the road. Heading for the fabled goldfields. There was no going back. Push ahead. That was the only choice. So, he rolled out in the morning and tried to hold himself together during the day.

Lem and Phoebe seemed to accept him just as they found him, day by day. Still, sometimes he caught them studying him as if they had unspoken concerns.

After being on the trail for nearly two weeks Phoebe gathered up all her courage and spoke to Zac after the evening meal.

"Mister Isaac. You gave me good advice a while back. Would you let me tell you what I see in you?"

Zac showed a half smile. "You've earned the right to speak anytime you see the need, Phoebe."

She was a long time working up more courage. Finally, she glanced towards her husband. He returned a quick nod and she started.

"I see awful hurt in you, Mister Isaac. I expect the war was real bad. I don't know what you did or what was did to you, but it hurt you, I'm thinking. Then with your family and all, the loss was almost too much.

"You might think that Lem and I don't know about that kind of loss, but we do. It's different. But it's still a grievous loss."

When Phoebe hesitated, Zac gently said, "Tell me about it, Phoebe."

Remembering was obviously causing her great pain, but finally she started.

"Lemrich and me, we birthed two sweet little babies. A boy and then a beautiful little girl. Master usually liked it when the darkies birthed a free slave. But then Master, he told the overseer to bring me to the house. Lemrich was to stay in the fields but he wanted me to be a house slave. Lemrich and me, we would be separated. I wouldn't be allowed to see my husband no more.

"I cried and pleaded with the overseer, but it was no good.

"Master, he said no house slave could have children to bother them. My little boy was seven years old and his little sister was four. Old Master Watson, he called the slave trader and sold my children away from me and Lemrich. Those children were too young for work so why did he do such a cruel thing?

"I screamed and fought the slave trader, but the overseer dragged me away and beat me. Lemrich, he tried to protect me but that was the wrong thing for him to do. Overseer, he hung Lemrich by his hands from a tree and beat him awful.

"The night after my beating I was cleaning Lemrich's wounds when I lost my unborn baby. Master didn't know I was carrying another child. Overseer, he had hit me somth'n awful in the stomach. Killed my new baby. Made it so's I could never have another child. When he heard about that the next day, he beat me again.

"Mister Jubal Watson, he was very angry with his father. They had a terrible fight. The slaves could hear them fighting up in the big house. Next day, Mister Jubal, he bought Lemrich and me from his father.

"After another big fight, he left the plantation and brought us to Texas. He set us free, but it was too late for my babies. My three beautiful little babies are gone.

"Mister Jubal, he tried to find out what happened to our two children, but he found nothing. We don't know if they be dead or alive.

"You see, Mister Isaac, you are not the only one who has lost someone from your life. But the Lord, He still loves you, even though He doesn't tell you why things happen.

"I see you hurting, Mister Isaac, and wish there was something Lemrich or I could do to help. But all I can do is pray for you and do our part on this trip.

"You aren't ever going to forget what's happened to you but with God's help, perhaps you can rise above it. It will take some time, just as it did with Lemrich and me, but you have to believe there's good times ahead."

Afraid that she might have taken too many liberties, Phoebe dropped her head and cast her eyes at the ground. She had been legally free for several years. But free and equal were still not quite the same thing.

The campsite was silent as each sufferer agonized over their own losses, considering the past and looking to the future.

CHAPTER TEN

The travellers saw only a smattering of people as they moved along. Once a small band of Indians stopped them. Knowing nothing at all about Indians, Zac had no idea what band or group these riders were a part of or what they might be called, or if they represented a risk.

Zac and Lem held their weapons in plain sight. Phoebe kept her hand close to the reticule, the drawstrings loose. One Indian rode forward and spoke for the group.

"This Indian land. Where you ride?"

He spoke to Zac, but his eyes never strayed from Lem and Phoebe.

Zac answered, "We ride west, to the mountains. We will take nothing from your land. We will stop only to rest the animals. We will bother no one."

The Indian continued holding his eyes to the black couple while Zac spoke. Zac wondered if these men had ever seen a black woman before. Or a black man, either.

After a long study on Zac's words, the men re-grouped and rode away.

Zac tried to relax but, as in the war, he remained diligent, watching every move of a branch, listening for any sound. Expecting an attack at any moment.

Their chosen path led them to several river crossings, only one of which was a challenge. Gritting her teeth and holding fast to the side of the wagon, Phoebe swung her eyes from the roiling water to her husband and then back to the water.

The mules balked but Lem got them settled back down and pulling. Although the flow was faster than most plains rivers, it wasn't particularly deep.

Zac's big gelding had seen many rivers during the war. This one presented no special challenge. Plunging forward, it moved directly to the far bank. Zac was wet to the knees, but the horse didn't have to swim.

After the crossing, Lem pulled the team to a halt. The three travellers immediately started pulling the bedding and purchased stores of food and supplies out of the wet wagon box.

The bedding would dry, and little was lost from the food supply. A small sack of sugar was wet and would dry hard. They would chip out what they needed for their coffee and try to ignore the taste of the river water.

Lem dug out a small feed of oats for the mules.

After making a meal for themselves and resting for an hour while the animals grazed, they moved on. The bedding was spread over the top of the wagon box, allowing the sun to do its drying work.

Three days later they arrived at Fort Gibson and got their first look at the Arkansas River.

Zac accompanied Phoebe to the sutler's store, staying with her until he was assured that she was safe enough. She shopped carefully but generously, purchasing what they needed to make their travels as comfortable as possible. She ignored the stares of the other shoppers.

They camped for one night only, wanting to get along as quickly as possible. Zac asked the sutler for travel advice. The talkative man was more than eager to sketch a rough map on a piece of brown wrapping paper. The general directions received would get them to Fort Dodge, if they followed the river and then headed west when the river took a big bend to the north.

"You'll meet folks enough along the way. There's lots of people on the move. And there's trails to follow. Might be wise to join up with other travellers for safety."

Leaving Fort Gibson, they followed the river except when it made one of its hundreds of twists and turns. Seeing no threat to their safety from other travellers or from Indians, they chose to travel alone.

But several days after leaving Fort Gibson, Phoebe turned from her wagon seat to look at their back trail. Zac often did that, but he had been riding in a haze of depression and bad memories for the past two days, neither speaking nor noticing what was around them. Phoebe worried about him but had no idea how to help. The best she could do was keep up her end of the responsibilities and perhaps pick up this one safety precaution that Zac was ignoring.

She took just a quick glance behind the wagon and shouted out a warning, pointing at the black sky. Her shout brought Zac out of his reverie and caused her husband to jump to his feet, turning to see what had startled her. They all knew what a tornado looked like.

The black swirling wind and dust storm appeared to be bearing directly down on them, growing in size as it danced across the landscape, now touching the ground and then, rising hundreds of feet into the air, only to fall again.

Phoebe could see small trees and other debris twisting in the whirling funnel. The threat was still miles away but with a tornado there were never enough miles separating the storm from exposed travellers.

Zac was shocked into reality. He hollered at Lem, "Get those mules moving. Head for that hill over there. Try to get behind that grove of trees."

With that, he galloped the gelding towards the hill, hoping to find some bit of shelter large enough for the wagon and animals. The screaming, outer wind was on them now, picking up dirt and more debris as it thundered across the land. The funnel was perhaps a mile away, twisting and turning, changing direction slightly, but still coming on.

Turning into a break on the off side of the hill, Zac rode into the bush at full gallop, cottonwood branches smacking his head and shoulders. He hung on to his hat and pulled the animal to a sliding stop at the base of the hill, as he leapt from the saddle. There was a bit of an undercut in the hillside, only partly blocked by trees. He thought it might be large enough to provide some shelter to the animals and wagon. They might be safe if the hill would be enough to turn the twister just a bit to the south.

He tied the gelding firmly to a large cottonwood, where it would not block the entrance for the team. He then ran to the edge of the bush and waved Lem towards the opening.

Still standing, working the reins with all his strength, frantically trying to control the terrified animals, Lem managed to point the mules into the opening, nearly running Zac down in the process. The low hanging branches forced Lem to a sitting position, with his folded arm protecting his head. Still, branches pounded him, tearing his clothing and leaving bruises.

Phoebe rolled over the seat, dropping horizontally into the wagon box to escape a beating from the waving branches.

Lem needed no instructions. He spotted the overhang at the back of the bush immediately. Pulling the mules down to a controlled trot he directed them behind the last row of trees and into the slight shelter of the hillside.

Leaving Phoebe to manage for herself, he vaulted off the wagon, grabbed up the tether ropes from the floor under the seat and moved to secure the mules.

Zac untied the gelding, moving it tight against the hillside in a space behind the wagon. He grabbed a tether rope and a halter from the wagon box. The animals were soon tied as securely as the situation allowed.

The screaming wind made it impossible to talk and be heard. With the wind came a deluge of rain. Using hand signals Zac indicated that they should get under the wagon, grabbing something strong to hold on to.

Lem and Phoebe wriggled into the tight space between the wagon and the hillside. Phoebe lay down and squirmed under the wagon's shelter. She then slid out far enough to wrap her arms around one of the poplars. Lem fiercely gripped a close-by tree, wrapping his right arm around the base. He then wrapped Phoebe as tightly to himself as he could, with his strong left arm.

Zac was lying on the ground at the rear of the wagon with his own desperate grip on a tree.

The shelter was soon a whirl of dust, dry grass and tree branches. Too late to do anything about it, Zac hoped the hillside wouldn't come down on top of them. The frightened animals stamped and thrust themselves against their tether ropes. The wagon rocked with the movement of the mules but unless the tethers broke, or the trees they were tied to were ripped out of he ground, there was no danger of the wagon breaking loose.

The three travelers had all witnessed violent storms before, but always from a safe distance. This was a close-up experience. Zac found himself praying that the worst of the funnel would veer away.

The threatening winds blew on and on, as time seemed to pass slowly, the fear of imminent death a living thing in the copse of trees. In reality the storm passed quickly. The downpour of rain and the trailing winds, however continued.

As the worst of the howling, screaming winds abated, Zac crawled out and stood up.

"Stay where you are," he hollered at the other two sheltering people. "Let me take a look around."

He walked from the bush far enough to look in all directions. Only the hillside blocked his view.

Although they were still being drenched by the rain, he could see sunny skies breaking through scattered clouds to the east and north, many miles away. It appeared the storm had veered to the south and west. It was over. He was sure of it.

Zac made his way back to the wagon through the mess of broken trees and the hundreds of branches cluttering the way.

"It's safe. The storm's gone off to the south."

He was dragging their torn tarpaulin and an unopened can of coffee with him. They all knew the swirling wind had helped itself to anything that wasn't firmly tied down. They would gather up what they could and wait for the next opportunity to replenish their stock of supplies.

Zac threw the tarpaulin and coffee into the back of the wagon and went to his gelding. The animal was still prancing a bit, fighting the tether rope, its eyes glazed with terror. A gentle touch on his neck and a soft word from Zac seemed to have a quieting effect.

Lem went to the mules who were showing signs of settling down.

Phoebe had fallen on something hard as she rolled into the wagon box, hurting her hip bone. Now she limped to the back of the wagon to see what could be salvaged. The rain still poured down, soaking what bedding and provisions hadn't been taken by the wind.

Some bedding and a few other items were hanging from branches in the poplar grove. Most of them were too high up to ever be retrieved.

She stuffed the tarpaulin around the remaining supplies in the wagon box as well as she could, knowing nothing more could be done until the rain moved on.

Lem untied the mules, released them from the wagon, and walked them out of the bush so they could graze. Zac did the same with the gelding.

The two men stood looking into the distance.

Zac said, "I'm thinking we'll stay hunkered down right here until the rain stops. I never remember hearing of a tornado turning back on itself, but I'd as soon not take the chance. I'll go see if I can get a fire started."

Lem simply nodded. He was still in a bit of shock himself.

"I'll get to clear'n out these branches. Don't know how we's goin' to get that wagon out of there without we back it all the way. Hard enough fer the mules without we have all this broken wood block'n us in."

When Zac took a good look at Phoebe he said, "Why don't you go to Lem. Maybe the two of you can find a drier place to rest for awhile. Maybe go for a walk or something."

The frightened and shattered woman nodded her head and started making her way out of the bush.

At Fort Dodge they rested for three days. The storm had ruined much of their food supply and the wind took most of their bedding. The sutler's store stocked what they needed to re-provision, and they were soon ready to take the last leg of their long trip.

When they and the animals were rested, they joined a freight outfit on the westward trail. The freighters were taking the Cimarron Cut-off, but when the time came to part, they pointed out the way to Bent's Old Fort. The fort was no longer in use but was still a guide point for the now weary travellers.

After leaving Bent's Fort they saw large herds of buffalo and a few scattered cattle. A couple of wandering white men stopped for a visit but no Indians were sighted.

Again, following directions from the men they met along the way, they, at long last, pulled into Denver, Colorado.

Looking at the booming frontier mining town, each of the weary travellers was silent with their own thoughts. Regardless of the details of those thoughts, they amounted to one question: 'is this where we can make a new start?'

CHAPTER ELEVEN

Dominik Kowalski was hungry. This was not a new experience. He had often been hungry since arriving with nearly empty pockets, at the Colorado goldfields. He had been hungry the day before too. And the day before that. He was having trouble remembering a time when he wasn't hungry.

At least the little trickle of water that found its way along the hillside he had built his poor shelter on kept him well supplied with that other essential of life. On the trip west he had known times when he would have wrestled a bear if the animal was keeping him from water. But with that matter put aside, all he had to worry about was starvation. He admitted to himself that starvation amounted to a considerable concern, but what he didn't know, was what to do about it.

The little bit of money he brought with him was soon used up. He had needed more tools; a short-handled pick, a heavier hammer, a selection of rock chisels, a shovel, a water bucket, a bed roll. With these purchases made, his pockets had been nearly emptied.

He really needed a wheelbarrow, but the cost was beyond his meager resources.

After one more trip to town for supplies he was broke. And now those supplies were gone. And the wild game on the nearby mountainsides had been pretty much hunted out by the many gold seekers who prowled the hills.

Over the weeks, he had snared a few rabbits and, just that morning, a racoon. The rabbits were small, but they served the purpose for a single meal.

He skinned out and set aside the racoon hide, to join the rabbit skins. He knew how to tan and soften them, but time didn't allow. The best he could do in the time he had was to stake the hides out for the ants to clean off. That would save him the trouble of scraping them at some date in the future. For now, he needed to get back to his mining venture.

But first the racoon. He had to eat.

After skinning and gutting the thing, he trimmed off the feet and head, readying it for the metal spit that sat in the two forked branches suspended over his fire pit. He was surprised at the amount of fat on the underside of the hide, as well as the fat oozing out of the meat, even before it was cooked. He knew little about racoons, but he thought this might be an old animal. Old, and fat with age. He threaded the metal spit through the skinned-out animal, readying it for the fire. Nothing about what he was doing filled him with any positive anticipation.

He managed to knock a deer over with a well thrown rock about one month before. It wasn't a large animal, but it offered enough meat to stave off starvation for another short while. Unfortunately, there was nothing left of that kill and no other had come his way.

In any case, he didn't own a rifle and hitting a deer with a rock was a chancy thing, so anything larger than a rabbit was not likely to grace his larder.

So, good or not so much, he was cooking the racoon.

As the racoon carcass heated up, big droplets of fat found their way to the surface, dropping and sizzling in the flames. The odor of the evaporating fat reminded Dominik of burning garbage barrels he had encountered on his many travels.

He was familiar with racoons in his native Poland. He had never heard of anyone eating one. But had anyone ever been as hungry as he was?

Working long brutal hours, chipping and hammering and shoveling, he had made a start. His hands were a series of blisters and calluses. His fingers and wrist were sore and often bleeding from where he had missed hitting the steel with his hammer. His ears echoed with the ring of steel and the last rock chip that landed in his eye was still there, defying any amount of washing, squinting or rubbing.

But he had a tunnel. It was only a few feet deep and not high enough to stand up in, but it was a tunnel. And he had exposed a very small seam of color that he believed was worth following. But he could do no more work without food.

Squatting on his haunches, watching the fire as if he had to guard against someone stealing his kill, his mind wandered back over the months and years since he last saw his native land, and the farm he was raised on. Would he ever sit around the big kitchen table with his parents again? Were his three sisters and two brothers healthy and raising families? He missed them. But he didn't miss them enough to return across the sea.

He missed Bianka too, the lovely neighbor girl from two farms over. Of course, she would be married with a couple of kids running around by this time. She was probably fat from the eating of sausages and cabbage soup, and weary with work and birthing, and not nearly so attractive as the young girl that resided so firmly in his memory. He consoled himself with these thoughts, balancing his loss against his imagination.

Returning from his time at the university in Warsaw, he had announced to his parents that he intended to go to America. They responded with head shakes and silence, unable to imagine such a thing.

His brother asked, "So, what will you do in America that you can't do right here on this good farm?"

Dominik knew these questions would be coming. He hoped his answers would be adequate.

"I studied to be a geologist, Roman. To find minerals for mining. There are no minerals to mine on this farm. Anyway, many people have searched out Poland for minerals. For many years they have searched, and there are several good mines as a result of those explorations. My work is not needed here. In a new land across the sea there is much room. And not so many people.

"There are rivers that might offer good clay for bricks. There are great mountains. High mountains. Mountains where almost anything might be found. I must go and do some of the finding."

The family discussions were long and, sometimes, loud. There was little money in the metal box Dominik's father kept hidden away. Certainly not enough to carry someone across a sea none of them had ever seen and could scarcely imagine.

"How will you go?" asked Dominik's father. "The cost of your university has not left much for other ventures. And your brothers will have needs too."

He didn't mention the daughters. Their husbands would take that burden from his hands.

There was a pause as the family members let this truth sink in, before the father continued.

"But if you are determined to go, I would sell one calf. Not more than one. Perhaps that would bring enough money for some food along the way. But how will you travel? I think it will cost much to travel all that distance."

Dominik himself didn't know the answer to the question. His view or knowledge of the world was limited to looking at maps he found at the university. He knew these maps disguised the real distances involved, for how can you look at a hand's breadth and imagine it to be a thousand miles?

And then there was the talk of the other students, all as ignorant as he himself, disguising their ignorance with foolish comments and loud laughter as they took their tea at lunch time.

Dominik's only response to his father was, "I am strong to walk. If a cart should happen by, I might be invited to ride. Then I will see what comes next."

There followed many weeks of walking, from his home close to Krakow, sometimes riding a farmer's cart, and always carrying his sack of miner's tools.

Along with the tools, the sack contained a few pieces of clothing, and sometimes a loaf of hard, black bread, made from good Polish rye flour and saturated with molasses, when one could be found to purchase with a small coin.

Only very cautiously could he spend the money set aside from the sale of the calf.

But the walking, wagon rides and the black bread eventually took him to the port city of Hamburg, Germany. He still had enough money to feed himself for a short while, but he could only look longingly at the big sailing ships readying for their departures to many romantic, far away lands.

The steam powered side-wheelers held him in rapt attention.

Knowing he needed to find work, he looked around at the busy dock crews, searching for someone in charge. Narrowing his choices to two shouting, arm-waving men, he slowly approached one of them. Again, he was confronted with the language problem that became apparent as soon as he crossed the border and was to travel with him over many miles and many months and years.

He had managed the purchase of his bread with finger pointing and a smile, but this shouting, harried man intimidated him almost into silence. Finally, desperately, he made his approach.

"I am seeking work." He shouted over the turmoil and clatter of the riverside.

The foreman barely glanced at him. Shouting back at Dominik, the man pointed towards a small building placed on the back side of the dock. "Da drüben." (Over there.)

Dominik knew nothing of the guttural German language. The harsh words and the bark of the big man startled him. Needing work and hoping he might find a job if he followed the pointing finger to the little shack, Dominik overcame his fear. Trudging among the hundreds of laborers and the mountains of supplies yet to be loaded on the ships, he made his way to the building.

On this warm day the single door stood open. He took that as an invitation to approach the man inside. Setting his sack of tools and clothing on the doorstep, and scrunching his soft, cloth cap in his hands, he stepped in. Not sure what to do next, he waited to be noticed.

Sitting on a high stool, hunched over a sloping table hung from the back wall, was a huge man, bulky with fat, but still looking fearfully strong. The man had his back to the door but, somehow, he knew Dominik stood waiting and wondering. Perhaps Dominik's arrival in the doorway had blocked the sun, alerting the man to the visitor at his door, or perhaps the frightening man had eyes in the back of his head.

The job seeker had little time to think of those possibilities before a strangely high-pitched voice barked out, "So Polack, tell me. You are hungry. You are lost. You wish to board a ship. You wish to go to America. You have no money. You wish for a job. What else?"

Dominik was hearing these questions in his own native tongue. That alone filled him with hope.

"You speak my language. I am happy to hear that. But how can this be? Am I not in Germany?"

The German still hadn't turned around, his eyes

studying forms laid out before him and his hands busy with a pencil, filling in spaces on the papers.

"Right off the farm are you Polack? Off the farm and ignorant of the world. Many Germans speak your strange tongue and a small number of Polacks manage a few words of the Master language. The few of you who are smart enough. Well, do you want a job or not?"

"Everything you say is true except I am not just from the farm. I have two years in the university. I am a geologist. I would go to America to seek minerals for mining. Yes, I need a job to earn my fare."

The big man's answer was a guttural grunt of some indecipherable meaning. Clearly, he was not impressed with the educational claims of his Polish visitor.

He slid off his high stool, pushed past Dominik and bellowed at a man working close by. Shouting something else Dominik couldn't understand, the man pointed at the job seeker and went back to his high stool and his work.

Dominik hadn't asked what the pay would be, but he had a job.

Staking out his own sleeping space in an unused freight shed, sharing the rough wooden floor with a hundred, or more, snoring, stinking labourers; men from many lands; Dominik joined the large group of workers who, by day, shouldered their heavy loads onto the waiting ships.

He toted heavy bales of freight onto sailing ships for two weeks. Then, with the promise of a working passage on a ship bound for New York, Dominik joined a crew loading the hundreds of tons of coal required to heat the boilers on a steam powered side wheeler.

Once on board and floating freely on the high seas, he settled into the routine. Along with many other workers, Dominik spent his days shoveling and moving the heavy, dusty coal, piling it where the firemen could most easily heave it into the burning maw of the huge cast iron boilers.

By the end of the first week he wondered if his hands were permanently curled into the shape of the wheelbarrow handles.

The living conditions below decks were almost impossible to imagine. The voyage was rough. Sea sickness was common. His few pieces of clothing were worn to shreds.

But, finally, the day he longed for arrived.

Even from below decks the crew could hear a multitude of steam whistles from other ships blaring a welcome, drawing Dominik from the filthy engine room. He stepped onto the deck, well away from the paying passengers, coal dust from top to bottom. His body was fatigued from work. His muscles were as hard as the hickory shovel handles his hands had gripped hour after weary hour, day after exhausting day.

All the coal dust in the world couldn't hide Dominik's smile or the hopeful glint in his blue eyes. His handsome face, disguised by beard and black dust, would again become visible once he got off this accursed ship and found a bucket of water to wash in. Or a hundred buckets, if that was what it took.

Behind him were the hundreds of miles of open Atlantic, the romance of side wheeler travel buried in the depths of that cold ocean.

Before him lay New York. He was in America. And wrapped safely in a tied rag, stuffed to the bottom of his pocket was a handful of coins, his wages from the loading of ships.

He spent one winter laboring on the New York docks, and three years in the stockyards of Chicago, leery of venturing further west, due to the turmoil of the Civil War. He saved every possible penny from his poor wages, but his small hoard grew at a pitiably slow rate.

Along the way he learned to speak passable English.

As the war was winding down and travel was becoming a bit less hazardous, he joined a group of freighters traveling west, towards his coveted mountains, again earning his way, this time caring for the mules. He arrived in Denver and then, after carefully asking questions, moved on to Idaho Springs, thankful at last to be truly on the goldfields.

Stopping in Idaho Springs only long enough to buy some cooked sausage and a loaf of hard, dark brown bread, and some much-needed rock tools, he set out walking and climbing. It seemed he had been walking forever, since leaving home.

This time the walking was different. This time he would stop only when he found his pot of gold.

He chuckled to himself, wondering how hard he would have to work to fill that imagined pot with the shiny mineral.

The high cost of food and supplies pushed the intrepid gold seeker into frenzied activity. Hoping for some little success, some small showing of gold that he could sell or trade for supplies before his funds ran out, drove him forward. He prowled the hills trying to remember everything he was taught at the university.

CHAPTER TWELVE

Standing back, Dominik took an overall view of the hillside he had spent the morning climbing. He studied the lay of the land; the upthrusts, the shattering of the rocks, the type of rock, always looking for signs of mineralization. The sun glinted off some quartz deposits, but they were too high up on the hillside for a hands-on examination. He could only stare. And wish he could fly.

He found his first sign of mineral where a back-eddy moulded a small pool in a little creek that tumbled down the rocky steps formed by the shattered rock. He didn't have a pan for sorting out the sand and minerals but with slow, careful moves he managed to separate a small amount of sand scooped from the bottom of the creek. Repeating this motion for most of a day produced three small flakes of gold and one tiny nugget. It wasn't much but it was at least something.

Moving from the creek to the adjacent rock wall, he scraped away a bit of moss, carefully studying the face of the granite, looking for tell-tale signs.

Where brush had grown close to the vertical rock wall, he pulled the offending greenery away, tearing a nasty gash in his hand from a brutal thorn, but also exposing a small quartz vein.

With the rock hammer he had carried all the way from Poland, he chipped and tapped. He pried out chunks of quartz. He carefully studied each chunk, and the rock he had pried it from. There were no signs of gold, but he kept looking.

He worked his way step by step up the hillside above the spot where he had found the evidence of mineralization in the creek. Where the rock became too steep for climbing, he moved to one side or the other, continuing upward, hoping to re-locate the quartz trail. He examined outcrops for signs of brecciation and quartz-carbonate veins which might reveal a source for the flakes of gold. Steady progress through the low brush was rewarded with a large exposure of brecciated and oxidized outcrop. At each promising sign he peeled back more moss.

With renewed energy he continued breaking rock with his hammer, finding a zone of fresh copper, lead and zinc sulphide mineralization. It was a strong structure. This was exciting and beyond his expectation, considering it was his first venture into the mountains.

He could hear hammers striking iron, not too far away. Someone else was breaking rock on a close-by hillside. The sounds encouraged him. 'If others have found mineral so close, why not here'?

The English words for what he was seeing in the rocks were not in his limited vocabulary. He thought it all out in Polish. He laughed to himself as he thought, 'I don't think the rocks care what language I talk'.

Finally, he stood back, studying the ground, the rock face and the surrounding topography. The zone of mineralization was most evident right where he had peeled back the big growth of moss.

He had climbed past the steep rock at the base of the cliff, had circled halfway around the small hillside, following the quartz trail, and now stood where the slope had given way to an almost flat area. He was about fifty feet below the crest of the hill.

He didn't know the English word for plateau, but he could easily visualize the level portion as a starting point for his digging.

Although there was no established trail to town, he could see the marks left by passing horses or mules, where other men had wandered these hills.

Turning to look back down the hillside, he tried to imagine accessing the position with a team and wagon. The downward slope behind him could be made into a passable trail without too much work. He believed it could be done simply by hacking and removing some brush and rolling some boulders out of the way.

Even in his enthusiasm he held to a practical side. If he found something worth digging, he would need wagon access to carry ore away for processing. To construct a trail through rock country was beyond his experience or financial imagination. But a wagon can roll over natural rock if the need was evident and trail not too steep. He thought it could be done.

Reverting to English and scanning the hillside

once again, he said, "Ya, I tink so dis is da place. I dig here."

That had been a month ago. In that time, he hadn't been to town and he hadn't seen another soul, coming or going on the rough trail. The sounds of close-by hammering had ceased, as if the prospector had given up.

He was still convinced of his judgement; believing the quartz would lead him to pay rock. But without more supplies he couldn't stay. He was going to have to find a job in town to earn food money.

A teamster on the trip west had told him how some prospectors were able to find someone to provide money for food and other small necessities in exchange for a portion of the find. It was called 'Staking'.

Perhaps there was someone who would do that for him. But where to start? Who to talk to? He had no idea.

Hiding his tools under a pile of broken rock at the back of the small tunnel and rolling up his bed, he was ready to walk to the village. First, though, he had to disguise the very small showing of color in the tunnel. That little bit of color was not enough to sell, but it might be enough to cause a rush of other prospectors to his hillside. He didn't want that.

Mixing mud from the little stream with crushed granite, he plastered over the opening he had pulled the quartz from. It wouldn't fool an experienced miner, but it was the best he could do.

He piled some rocks in front of the tunnel, hoping that would indicate the claim was not abandoned.

He gave up on the racoon after one bitter bite. The taste was beyond description. He couldn't chew through the tough meat and the odor was about to make him nauseated.

Flinging the carcass down the hillside, away from his camp, he thought, 'if I had a dog, I could feed the racoon to the dog and then eat the dog'.

CHAPTER THIRTEEN

As Lem guided the mules through the crowds of riders, wagons and foot traffic, Phoebe cast her eyes from side to side of the busy Denver streets, taking in one shop after another. She had never seen anything like the bustle of activity everywhere she looked. It was nothing at all like Carob, Texas.

Zac followed along on his weary gelding. He was hoping to find somewhere to bed down for a couple of days, and a café that would serve his black friends. After weeks of travel they all needed rest, both the animals and the people.

Nearing the end of the business street, he spotted a lady dressed in a beautiful light blue dress, her head and eyes mostly covered by the tipped down brim of a white sun hat. She was carrying a large wrapped package. Only her hands and the lower portion of her face were visible from where Zac sat on his gelding, but he could see that she was black.

Zac moved ahead of the wagon, motioning Lem to follow along slowly. He then trotted the hundred yards to where the lady in the blue dress was walking. Tipping his hat, he spoke to her.

"Excuse me, Ma'am, may I speak with you a moment please?"

Two white women glanced his way but the lady in the blue dress held her head straight forward, not acknowledging him. He trotted a few yards ahead and dismounted. Pulling his hat off and holding it at his side, he spoke directly to the woman.

"Please, Ma'am, if you would take a moment."

She could no longer doubt that Zac was speaking to her. Several people on the walkway stopped to stare. She glanced at Zac and sped up her steps, moving to the inside of the walkway, as if to hurry past the intruder.

Zac spoke again. "Please, Ma'am. Just one moment. I'm thinking you can help me and my friends."

She stopped and wordlessly turned her head Zac's way.

"Thank you, Ma'am. My friends and I just arrived in town. You can see them on that wagon back there."

The lady turned enough to catch a glimpse of Lem and Phoebe and then turned back to Zac.

"Ma'am, I assure you, Phoebe is a lady in every sense of the word, and Lem is a gentleman. They have accompanied me from Texas. They were freed several years before the war. They're good people and good friends of mine. But we don't know this city or where they might be welcomed for a bed or for dining. I'm hoping you can offer some suggestions. They're a Christian couple, Ma'am. They're tired and in need of rest. Can you offer any suggestions?"

When the woman hesitated, Zac motioned for Lem to move the wagon closer. When he again pulled the mules to a stop, Zac said, "Ma'am, this is Lem and Phoebe. Can you give us some guidance so we don't do anything that would make us unwelcome in Denver?"

The woman still hadn't spoken. She took a long study of Zac and then an even longer study of Lem and Phoebe.

Finally, she spoke.

"Follow me. I'll take you to a boarding house."

As the wagon started slowly moving, keeping pace with the lady, Zac rode alongside and passed a gold piece to Lem and another to Phoebe.

"You'll need some money. Pay what's asked for the boarding and use the rest for clothing. Make sure the place you stop at is safe and decent and the food good. We'll stay a couple of days at least. Get some rest. Perhaps the wagon can be left at the boarding house, but we'll have to find a livery for the mules. I'd like if you could do that, Lem. I have to find someone who can talk me through the mining laws, and such. I'll come find you when I'm done."

The small cavalcade moved at the pace the lady in blue set with her walking. She led them three city blocks and then turned down a dirt lane that wound through some trees, following a shallow creek. Coming out of the trees, they saw ahead of them what might have been a small village, with a couple of vegetable farms tucked up close. The houses were not large, but most were well kept. At the end of a side road stood a church. Several people were outside their homes, working in their gardens or strolling to what looked to Zac like a small store. Everyone he saw was black.

Their guide motioned for Lem to stop and wait. Opening the front gate on a picket fence surrounding the largest house in sight, she stepped onto the covered veranda and knocked on the door. A single knock and then she turned the knob and pushed the door open.

"Rebecca, are you to home?"

"Morn'n, Abby." The shouted response came from somewhere deep inside the house.

A few moments later a large black woman arrived in the doorway, wiping her hands on a cloth.

"Just mixing up some dough. Mak'n bread. Will you set and have some lemonade?"

"Another time, Rebecca. Brought you some house guests if you have room to take them in."

The woman named Rebecca stopped wiping her hands, hung the cloth on the doorknob, and started walking towards the wagon. Lem pulled his hat off and brushed his fingers through his stiff, curly hair. Phoebe squirmed a bit on the wagon seat, feeling like she was under examination from someone who held her fate in her hands.

Zac rested his hands on the saddle horn, his back straight, as any cavalry soldier is apt to do.

Rebecca studied the pair on the wagon as she walked their way. At an easy speaking distance, she stopped, continuing her study. She looked back at Abby.

"Where did you find these folks?"

Abby nodded at Zac. "Man on the horse stopped me on the street. Asked if I could guide these folks to a welcoming place."

Rebecca was still studying the wagon passengers. "I'm thinking you two must have names."

Lem smiled and nodded his head. "That's a good guess. I'm known as Lem. This here is my wife, Phoebe. Our friend on the gelding is Isaac, called Zac by most folks. And I'm hearing your name called as Rebecca.

"We've come a long way from East Texas, Rebecca. Zac has his own things to do in town but Phoebe and I, we're in need of a place to stop. Been camping out through the many weeks, but a bed and kitchen cooked food would sure be welcome. And a bath if that can be managed. Kind of this lady to guide us here. We're hoping you can take us in for a few days."

"Don't take in single men but with you two married I imagine we can work it out. You are married fit and proper ain't you?"

"All fit 'n proper Rebecca. In sight of man and God. Married as slaves. Married again, under God after we's set free, six – seven years back."

Rebecca continued studying the pair, but her real question was Zac.

She finally got up the courage to speak her question.

"How do you fit into this Mister Zac? Were these your people before they were freed?"

Lem jumped in to answer the question.

"Oh no. you figured that wrong Rebecca. Mister Zac 'n his wife, they were neighbors before the war. Phoebe and I, we worked a farm close by. Mister Zac came home from the war 'n found everyone killed and buried. The raiders done it. Killed our Mister Watson. Killed Mister Zac's wife 'n child.

Burned everything. Stole the cattle 'n horses. Mister Zac, he helped Phoebe 'n me get away from all that sadness and come out here for a new life. We sure look'n forward. Anything is better than all the hurt'n back in Carob, Texas."

Rebecca was slow making up her mind, but she finally said, "Three dollars a week for each of you. You can put the mules in the corral out back. You care for them yourself."

Lem had no experience in any transaction like that. He glanced at Zac for guidance. Zac simply gave a small nod.

"That be fine, Rebecca. I'll take the mules 'n wagon out back right now."

Rebecca stepped up to the wagon holding out her hand to help Phoebe. "You look exhausted, Phoebe. Step down here. We'll find you a bath and then some lunch. A couple days of rest and you'll be fine."

Abby had turned and started walking away when Lem agreed to the cost. Zac rode over to her, pulling his hat off again.

"Miss Abby, I can't thank you enough. I'm sure Lem and Phoebe will be well taken care of here. Phoebe needs to shop for some city clothing. Lem too I suppose. But that can be another day. Perhaps you would have some suggestions on that. She has the money to buy what she needs."

Several people had again stopped their gardening to watch suspiciously as Zac approached Abby.

Abby kept on walking. "I'll drop by tomorrow."

With that simple statement she turned down a side lane towards her own home.

CHAPTER FOURTEEN

Zac pulled his duffle from the rear of the wagon, slung it over his shoulder and re-mounted the gelding. He rode back to the downtown area, looking for a hotel. He found one that had a dining room attached that looked satisfactory. He tied his horse to the rail in front, brushed some of the trail dust off his pants and shirt front and walked in. The daily cost was a bit more than he expected, but he paid it and registered. He took his duffle and his weapons up to the room and stowed them in the tiny closet. He then locked the door and went looking for a livery stable and a barber shop.

There was no shortage of livery facilities, but the barbershop required a bit more walking. He was finally shaved and had his long hair trimmed just a bit. He liked it long, hanging black and straight over his collar. The hotel had bathing facilities, so he turned down the barber's offer of a tub and hot water.

After a long soak back in the hotel tub Zac eyed the bed, thinking a short nap might be just the thing, after the long weeks of dawn to dusk riding. But he had been fighting past terrors within himself all morning. The urges, the feelings, came and left on their own timeframe.

Many of his nights were little more than hourslong nightmares, studded with the roar and boom of cannons and the screams of dying comrades. Lately, the feelings had been creeping into his daytime thoughts. He knew he needed more to lock his mind onto and point it into a safe direction. There is little to hold a man's thinking on a straight path when he's sitting a horse, walking at wagon speed.

He often found himself planning ahead, thinking of the new life he and the friends riding the wagon could build for themselves. Those thoughts were filled with pleasure, or perhaps it was simply fantasy, although he knew nothing would be easy.

But then, as if out of nowhere, he might feel a tear forming. Or he might have a shudder run through his chest as if his lungs were reminding him that he'd forgotten to breathe.

Then the voices of Maddy and Minnie came to his ears and mind. Or the faces of his parents. All shot down and buried.

Sometimes, the worst visions were of men he himself had killed. It was almost as if their ghosts were pointing accusing fingers at him, filling him with guilt and causing him to shudder in revulsion at the insanity of war.

No, he couldn't take a nap. If he did, he just might sink into a reverie and not return. He had to keep busy. Busyness was his emotional salvation, at this time.

He had always known great determination. His

father spent his life demonstrating it and Zac found the concept an easy fit.

Zac steeled himself, getting control of his thoughts. He wrapped the much-depleted money belt around his waste, tucked in his shirt and left the room. He purposely chose to leave his gun belt in the closet.

Zac didn't know enough about mining to develop a plan. He simply started out, seeing where his footsteps would take him. His first stop was a miners' supply store. There were no customers in the store, which suited him fine. He had no desire to share his ignorance with others.

Gaining the attention of one of the clerks he said, "I'm just in town after a long ride from East Texas. I don't know the first thing about prospecting or mining, but I'm prepared to learn. Where do you suggest I start?"

The clerk chuckled and said, "Well, right off I can see that you're different than most. A step ahead you might say. At least you're prepared to admit your lack of knowledge. Most just come in here in a frenzy, desperate to reach the gold country and start spending money on things they think they'll need.

"I'm no miner myself. I wouldn't know a gold mine from an outhouse hole. What I do know is tools and equipment. That's what we have on offer, and nothing else. I can't tell you one single thing about minerals or what to look for. What I can tell you about is tools. Come on over here. I'll show you the standard hard rock items. You might want to take a look at tents and field-kitchen equipment too."

Zac looked at shovels, picks of all sizes and weights, drill steel, short handled and long handled hammers, called single jacks and double jacks by the miners, lamps, wheelbarrows, tents and a range of other equipment. The clerk then led him to the tents and field equipment.

The store clerk completed the tour by saying, "We have a branch outlet at Idaho Springs. Everything available in Denver is also available up there. I'll be pleased to help you here when you're ready to go. Or you can travel light and purchase the same pieces up country."

Zac took another long, slow look around the store, amazed at the variety of equipment and the choices that would have to be made. He thanked the clerk and turned to leave.

The clerk stopped him by saying, "I should mention. You're going to want powder to blow the rock. Take you till you're old as Methuselah to open a hole, without powder.

"You seem like a man that can take advice. Now listen, even if you forget everything I've just told you, don't you forget this. When the time comes, you hire yourself a powder man. You try to do it yourself your tunnel could become your grave. It's happened manys the time."

Zac nodded and looked at the clerk. "That's good advice. I'll remember. And thanks again."

Zac went from the supply store to an assay office and then to the land office. In both places he picked up valuable information. The assayer gave him a few brochures showing mineral bearing rock formations.

By the end of the second day he felt he was ready

to venture into the mountains. He didn't try to hide his ignorance, especially from himself, but his several enquiries led him to believe that he was not much worse off than the majority of amateur prospectors.

Zac spent the next two days grooming his horse and generally lazing around the town. He was cautious to sense his feelings, and control them, not wanting to give way to the sadness that sometimes threatened to overwhelm him.

On the third afternoon since arriving in Denver, Zac saddled up and rode to the boarding house. Lem and Phoebe were sitting on the veranda with Rebecca. They were each holding a glass of what looked like lemonade. Zac tied his horse to the brass ring mounted on a post outside the picket fence.

Rebecca called out, "Come sit, Mister Zac. I'll get you a glass."

Zac opened the gate and approached the house. His eyes were on Lem and Phoebe as he said, "Thanks, Rebecca. A cold drink on this warm day would be welcome."

He nodded his head towards Lem.

"Well, you two are looking rested and raring to go. Looking fine too. The new clothing suits you both."

Zac wasn't sure he had found even a single reason to smile since he looked at his burned-out house and the graves of his family. He smiled now. His black friends truly did look good and it was best he acknowledge it.

"If I wasn't going mining, I'd be tempted to find some better clothing for myself. But I expect I'll be getting dirty enough in the next while to ruin anything but these old canvas pants."

Lem perked up. "I 'spect we're ready just about any time you say Mister Zac. Never done so much of noth'n in all my born days. Mules is look'n over the corral rail too, wonder'n what's goi'n on."

Zac took a seat on the floor of the veranda, leaning against the railing post, one foot resting on the top step.

"Rebecca. It looks like you took good care of my friends. I need to thank you for that. But I'm thinking we need to be on the road in the morning."

Rebeca hesitated before responding but finally said, "We were just talking about church in the morn'n. Have you forgotten what day this is Mister Zac? Saturday today. Church day tomorrow. Can't hardly leave for the goldfields, what with all the sinn'n goi'n on up there, without you take the Lord with you. Church, ten in the morn'n. You welcome to join up with us."

Zac took a big sip of lemonade. "Haven't known what day it is for weeks now."

He smacked his lips after taking another sip. He looked off into the distance and appeared to be silently contemplating something.

"I'm sure there'll still be gold to find if we get there a day later."

There didn't seem to be much to talk about so Zac drank his cool lemonade and made his departure.

He had a single drink before supper in the dining room and then made himself comfortable in the hotel foyer. He claimed one of the overstuffed wing-back chairs for himself and started thumbing through newspapers left there by other hotel guests. He wanted to tire himself out before going to bed.

Zac read for an hour and then went for a long walk. Finally, he climbed the stairs and turned the key in the door. He lay down, praying that his memories would take a night off.

At ten on Sunday morning, after a serious argument with himself, Zac tied his horse outside the little church.

The singing had already started as he slipped into the back row, feeling totally out of place. Everyone in the hall was standing, clapping, weaving to the music. A few had their hands lifted high, their eyes closed, their voices raised in a melody of worship.

Zac heard no piano. But the acapella voices filled the small hall with as pleasing a sound as he had ever heard in his limited church experience in the little town of Carob, East Texas.

He couldn't spot Lem or Phoebe or Rebecca in the joyously singing crowd.

As far as he could tell he was the only white man in the room. Several people glanced his way. He tried not to let the passing attention bother him.

Most folks were well dressed, showing their best. Even the weary looking, hard used men, probably mine labourers, poured themselves into woolen suits, some of them old and threadbare, but gratefully worn on this Lord's day morning.

He became self-conscious as he looked down at his clean, but trail-worn work clothing.

He had never been a singer and he didn't know

the hymn the folks were enjoying so loudly. He was content to remain quiet and let the others sing their praises.

Gradually, as folks quit staring at him, he started to feel more comfortable, remembering old times in the little clapboard church back home, with Rev. Moody Tomlinson leading.

Zac hadn't been in a church for three years or more. He was almost frightened at the possibility of opening up old memories; memories that were perhaps best forgotten.

As the service went on, with the black preacher's rumbling voice echoing off the walls and ceiling, Zac's uncontrolled mind soared over the miles, back to that little church in Carob. As if looking down from above, he seemed to see himself sitting with Maddy at his side and with Minnie resting on her father's lap.

A loud sniffle followed by a deep breath, caused several people to turn and look at their white visitor. Knowing he was going to have trouble this day, trouble that he would have difficulty controlling, he stood and quietly slipped out the door. He rode back to the livery barn and stabled the gelding.

He found lunch in a little hole-in-the-wall shop. The food was excellent; heavily spiced, just the way he liked it, and the coffee was hot.

Again, he walked the streets of Denver, mile after mile, hoping to become tired enough to get through one more afternoon and one more night.

CHAPTER FIFTEEN

Zac enquired about directions to Idaho Springs as he was saddling up.

The livery man, lonely in spite of all the coming and going in the big barn, grabbed up the opportunity to talk.

"Well, son. Far as that thar goes, there's just the one trail up inta them thar hills. The trick is to find your way outa this here big metropolis. Folks been known to go 'round and 'round and arrive right back here, putt'n thar animals up fer another night. Lost. I don't mind, long as they got the coin ta cover the tab."

He stopped talking long enough to cackle at his own joke.

"Now, if'n yer in a rush ta get thar you jest faller this here road out front. It'll take ya north a ways till ya sees the Gold Country Hotel. Not really much of a hotel, if'n ya was ta ask me, but it makes a good 'nuff landmark. Ya take a turn to the left thar and jest keep on a-going. Trail winds around some. Pretty soon yer climbing. Trail rises 'bout a thousand foot, might could be a bit more, in the thirty miles ya cover. Ya jest keep a plodd'n along, you'll git thar bye 'n' bye."

When Zac arrived, Lem had the wagon rigged out and the mules tied off at the hitch rail in front of the boarding house. Phoebe was on the veranda saying her goodbyes. They were on the road in a matter of minutes.

The winding trail was uphill most of the way. A good saddle horse could cover the distance in a single day, but the trio of travelers kept the mules down to a steady walk. After one night of camping they arrived in the gold town the evening of the second day. They looked for a camping spot rather than a hotel, thinking it was not worth the problems that could develop over Lem and Phoebe.

The following day, the three hopeful prospectors secured the animals and the wagon at a livery and walked the small town, trying to get a feel for the gold country. They entered the land office to confirm what Zac had been told in Denver.

After being hurriedly dealt with by a harried clerk, who explained the process of claim staking, Zac asked his last question, "So, who can file on a claim?"

"Any American citizen." the man answered. "Or any newcomer who's applying for his citizenship. There's really no effective way to police the matter. People are pouring all over these hills by the hundreds. In some places it's by the thousands. Most of them don't have any papers to prove who they are. We generally register the claims and if anyone ever complains we'll let the court sort it out."

The clerk glanced at the black couple several

times as he spoke, but he kept his thoughts to himself.

He reached under the counter for a pamphlet.

"This outlines the process of staking a claim and how to register it. You will need to follow the directions carefully. You also have to make sure your claim does not overlap another claim. Look around for corner posts or rock cairns that someone else has put up.

Without enquiring any further Zac thanked the man and ushered Lem and Phoebe out the door before any question could be thrown their way.

He had seen no other blacks on the streets or in any of the businesses. He figured that any blacks living there would be up hours earlier, working one of the hundreds of active claims.

As noon approached, Zac chose a small café, hoping for the best. He held the door while Lem and Phoebe stepped inside. The dozen customers all looked up and stared, but no one spoke. The waitress simply pointed to a corner table, seemingly not bothered by the color of her customer's skins. They took their seats and waited. The busy waitress came to their table a few minutes later.

"The menu never changes, folks. Roast beef, potatoes, carrots, or whatever vegetable I can find. Soup and bread if you'd prefer. Coffee and apple pie. Fifty cents. And don't bother complaining about the price. This is my establishment and I ain't listening to no complaints."

Zac grinned at her. "You'll hear no complaints from this table, miss. The beef sounds just fine to me."

Lem and Phoebe agreed that the beef would suit them as well.

There were no other women customers in the small café. Zac was impressed by Phoebe's dignity and self assurance as she ignored the many stares of the working men that filled the other tables.

Nearing the end of their meal a dishevelled man wearing badly abused clothing and a filthy cloth cap staggered in the door. The lady owner threw him a suspicious look.

The man pulled his cap off, crunching it in his hands. "Miss, please, I have to have food. What I can do for to earn food? I good chop wood. I, how you call, brush floor? I geologist. Know rocks. I have goot find. Much mineral I tinking. But I no got money. Please kind lady, I got to have food."

The café owner was trying to serve all the tables by herself. She had no time for beggars.

"I'm sorry for you mister, but the hills are run over with people like you. Fresh off the boats and hoping for a handout. If I feed you, I'll soon have you Dutchmen lined up outside waiting for a free meal. Go ask someone else."

The pathetic man looked as if he just might collapse to the floor. Hunched over with hunger and fatigue, wringing his hat until Zac thought he might twist it in two, he pleaded.

"Please kind lady. I not Dutchman. I Polish. I tell no one else to come here."

Phoebe had her back to the man but Zac and Lem were both listening to every word. Zac had picked up on the word geologist. He looked over at Lem. Lem nodded.

The waitress had gone back into the kitchen.

The forlorn man looked as if he might start crying. Zac lifted his hand in the man's direction. The hand was seen in a flash. Zac waved him over, pointing to the unused chair between Lem and himself. The beggar stumbled a bit getting around another table, but he was soon standing beside Lem, looking at Zac.

Zac said, "Sit down."

The waitress had come back into the room with her arms laden with steaming hot plates of beef and potatoes. When she had delivered the orders, Zac called her over.

"Bring this man some beef and potatoes please. I will cover the cost."

The sceptical woman said, "That's all well and good. But so far I haven't seen the color of your money either."

Zac dug in his pocket. The strained grin he pointed the owner's way could have meant almost anything. He dropped a ten-dollar coin on the table.

"Bring this man a generous plate and some more coffee all around, please."

In no time at all, the waitress laid a heaping plate before Dominik. Zac thought the starving man was close to tears at the sight of the steaming food.

Before beginning his meal, Dominik closed his eyes and bowed his head, only slightly. He spoke silently, his lips forming unheard words. He completed his thanks by crossing himself, right to left, as those of the orthodox faith were in the habit of doing.

He picked up his fork and looked at Zac. "T'ank you. T'ank you." He looked again at Lem and Phoebe. "T'ank you."

He sliced off a bite of beef, lifted it to his mouth and laid down his fork and knife. With closed eyes he tilted his head back just a bit and slowly chewed the modest banquet. Tears formed in both his eyes.

Lem and Phoebe watched in wonder. Instead of frantically gobbling the life-saving feast, Dominik ate slowly, savoring each delightful bite. Zac understood. He had frequently missed meals during his time in uniform. He knew the pleasure of relishing something long anticipated.

With a piece of apple pie and three cups of coffee put away, Dominik leaned back in his chair in great satisfaction and gratitude.

"I Dominik. How are you called?"

Zac introduced himself and then looked across the table.

"These are my friends, Lem and Phoebe."

Dominik offered his hand to each one, again saying 't'ank you'. He started to say, "I am geol…", but Zac cut him off with a raised hand.

"Let's find somewhere quiet to talk."

With that he rose from his chair and moved towards the door. The waitress was waiting for him. She held out a handful of coins.

"Your change, Sir."

Zac quietly said, "I'm certainly not wealthy, but I've been hungry more times than I wish to remember. You keep that change. Feed a man or two as opportunity allows."

CHAPTER SIXTEEN

On a bench built against the shady side of the livery barn, Lem and Phoebe sat down. Zac and Dominik pulled a couple of weather-worn wooden chairs up close, forming a small circle.

Zac spoke to Dominik.

"Sir, in the café you said you were a geologist. That you know rocks and minerals, and that you have a claim. You also said you were without funds. Do I have that all correct?"

Dominik pulled his cloth cap off again. It seemed to be a reactionary move, showing up whenever a problem peeked around the corner.

"What you say I tink is truth. I not so goot with the English. I don't know what is this claim. What I found is gold, and I tink so maybe some other tings. Maybe copper."

He pressed his hand against his chest, indicating himself.

"Dominik, he go university. Poland. Am geologist. I come to America look for mine. Maybe gold. Maybe copper. Maybe sometink different. I look in hills where is other mines."

He waved his arm towards the hill behind Idaho Springs.

"I find. Goot mine I tink. I dig. Much rock to broke. I find. Gold. Just little bit, I find."

He held his thumb and one finger close together to indicate the smallness of the find.

"But no food. No money. I come dis place, ask for food. Maybe so find partner. We build mine, two mans. Partner and Dominik."

Zac listened to all of this and wondered at the foolishness of this young, naive immigrant geologist.

"Dominik, you have to be careful who you trust. The men in that café were all miners looking to get rich. You have to keep your find secret. Have you filed a claim on your mine?"

"What is this claim? I don't know about claim. I just look. I find."

Zac turned to Lem and Phoebe.

"What do you two say? Should we go see if we can work with this man?"

Lem glanced at Phoebe. She was already forming her answer.

"I enjoyed going to the stores in Denver. I've never done anything like that where I wasn't spending someone else's money. I'd like to do it with my own money.

"I liked being able to buy nice clothes. I know it was your money Mister Zac, but I still enjoyed the buying. I think I would like to buy many things. I think I would like to have a gold mine. I think we should see what this man has found."

Zac chuckled, looking at Phoebe.

"It hasn't taken you long to learn to enjoy the freedom to look after yourself, Phoebe. I think you are correct though. Let's go see this mine."

Lem silently rose and stepped towards the livery.

Zac said, "Dominik, we will come with you. If we like what we see, we will work with you. I am not rich, but I should have enough to get what we need. for a while, at least. We will go now."

Dominik said, "Is long walk. Is too long for lady?"

Zac patted Dominik on the knee.

"Don't you worry about this lady. She will walk as far as any of us. But today I think we will ride. You wait here just a bit. We'll be right back."

Lem and Zac soon had the team ready and the gelding saddled. With the wagon hitched and driven from the shed, Lem pulled it to a stop beside Phoebe and Dominik. He jumped down to help his wife, although she really needed no assistance. He retook his seat and spoke to Dominik.

"Climb aboard, sir."

With Dominik pointing the way, the group of novice prospectors were soon nearing the claim. There was no real trail.

Dominik had been walking when he located the quartz outcrop, paying little attention to the possibility of wheeled access. Only after he located a place to dig, did he give the access some thought. He studied the hillside on his walk to town, deciding that a good team could get the job done. For most of the distance, a natural, rocky swale provided a passable route to the diggings.

Lem's big mules would be the first to test it out. The animals had to work a bit, but they managed to pull the wagon over the rough terrain, climbing higher with every step.

Nearing the top, Dominik pointed out a rocky hillside surrounded by aspen and pine forests.

Rounding the last fold in the granite hillside, nearing the small tunnel, Dominik was about to tell them they had arrived. But the words froze in his mouth. Two men were holding fast at the entry to the small digging.

One was sitting casually on a flat rock, at the mouth of the newly dug tunnel. He was rolling a small block of quartz from one hand to the other. Dominik saw immediately that it was the rock he had found the trace of gold in. His attempt at hiding the quartz seam had obviously been inadequate.

The second intruder had his shoulder propped against one corner of the tunnel. He had an insolent grin on his face, and a cigarette hanging from the corner of his mouth. He held a carbine in the crook of his elbow, halfway into firing position.

"Move along, folks. This is our claim. No visitors wanted."

Dominik leaped off the wagon seat, falling to one knee in the process. He scrambled to his feet and ran around the rear of the wagon ready to charge the two men. Zac leaned from the saddle and grabbed his shoulder, taking a grip on his shirt, holding him back. Dominik twisted to get free, but Zac held an iron grip.

"Hold on, Dominik. Let me handle this."

Turning his face to the two men, Zac asked, "Just what makes you men figure this is your claim?"

The man standing, leaning against the rock wall, patted his carbine stock.

"This here is Mister Winchester. He speaks for

me, fella. Unless you wish to hear his bark, you best just move along."

Zac hadn't been fully relaxed since his first battle, over three years earlier. Even with the war's ending he had never given up his vigilance, nor the habit of carrying the Henry across his thighs. He didn't make a show of the Henry, preferring that it not be noticed. He had also learned during battle that delay almost never brought the desired results.

With no words of warning, fire and grayish-black smoke and a half ounce of lead belched from the muzzle of the Henry. Shattered rock sailed from the wall the man was leaning against. Four rapid shots had rock chips flying in all directions.

The fella sitting on the flat rock dove to the ground, wiggling behind the rock, as best he could.

The standing man dropped his carbine, grabbing his face. Blood ran through his fingers from where the chips had torn his cheek open. Rock dust had flown into his eyes, temporarily blinding him. He staggered a few unseeing steps and tripped over a rock. He lay on the ground, one hand over his eyes and cheek, with the other arm wrapped across the top of his head, as if that might stop the next bullet.

Dominik dove under the wagon. He had no experience at all with weapons. Lem held his rifle at the ready. Phoebe had her pistol lifted from the reticule, pointed towards the intruders.

When the shots quit echoing around the hills, Zac spoke.

"Boys, in case you think I missed those shots, let me assure you that if I wanted you dead there would have been no doubt of it. That was just a warning. Now pick yourselves up and clear out. I ever see you again there'll be no more warning."

The two men stumbled from the mine site, leaving the Winchester and the small sample of gold on the ground where they had been dropped. The intruder with dust forced into his eyes was being led by his friend. Their saddled horses were tethered a few yards up the creek. They were soon sitting their saddles, edging down the trail left by the wagon wheels, and out of sight.

One man was leading the second horse with the blinded claim jumper gripping the horn.

CHAPTER SEVENTEEN

It took a long time for Dominik to decide to crawl from under the wagon. He looked with fear and awe at his potential partners, twisting his cloth cap in his big hands.

Lem and Phoebe took the shooting casually, but privately Lem was thankful Zac chose not to kill the two men.

Lem tied the team off after leading them to the little creek for water. Zac was still mounted on the gelding. He rode around the hillside, alert for more potential problems.

Lem and Phoebe walked together to the small tunnel. Dominik had started the work well above the surrounding ground level, placing a small series of rocks at the entrance to act as steps. Lem and Phoebe stood on the steps, leaning into the mine opening. The tunnel wasn't high enough to stand up in. The light in the workings was poor, the walls hidden in shadow, lending more mystery to the tunnel.

The darkness of the small tunnel didn't matter

much to Lem and Phoebe. The entire matter was a mystery to them.

Dominik joined them, standing at ground level. He picked up the dropped piece of quartz, bearing the show of gold.

Phoebe was becoming braver and more outspoken as she and Lem lived and traveled with Zac. She touched the rock walls, wondering at all the chisel marks.

Turning to Dominik she asked, "Did you dig all this rock out by hand?"

Dominik smiled and nodded his head. "Wit hammer and, how you say, chisel?"

Phoebe looked from Dominik back to the rocks. She spoke to Zac, who had just walked up, standing beside Dominik.

"Well, if nothing else is true, I'd say this much is; the man is not afraid of work."

Zac rolled the gold laden quartz over and over in his hand. He looked into the shaded mine shaft and then turned to study Dominik, who was still twisting his cap into knots. Lem and Phoebe stood silently, having no idea where the conversation should go from there.

Zac finally asked, "Where did you find this?"

"I show."

Dominik pushed past Lem, stepping up the stacked rocks and into the short tunnel. Zac joined him. Once inside, their eyes gradually became adjusted to the dimness.

With his improved vision Zac could see a clear outline of the tunnel wall, with all its thousands of chisel marks.

Dominik pointed out the vein of quartz. The

whitish trail held a very slight upward angle, towards the low roof. Dominik used one finger to brush away the remaining mud from the slot he had tried to disguise. He now understood that he should have pocketed the six-inch-long chunk of quartz instead of trying to hide it.

Dominik took the quartz piece from Zac, placing it back where it came from.

"See. Here is white rock. Called quartz, I'm tinking. Gold in rock."

He pushed some rocks around on the floor and dug out his hidden chipping hammer. Passing it to Zac, he pointed at a spot close to the tunnel mouth. Lem and Phoebe bent close to watch.

"You break white rock here. You see."

Zac took the hammer, aimed the pointed end at the quartz and started tapping. The white rock was harder than he expected, but with another, harder tap a crack developed in the narrow end. He repeated the process a few inches away. Satisfied with the cracks, he tapped and pushed until the chisel end of the hammer was part way into the opening. A solid pry, using the leverage of the hammer handle, loosened the rock. With a bit more work, one end of the quartz came loose, but the opposite end was still partially wedged in the space it came from.

The excitable geologist couldn't wait to see what the rock was hiding. He pushed Zac's hands aside and grabbed the loose end of the quartz with strong, brutalized fingers. He levered it free from the surrounding granite and turned it over. Even in the poor light they all saw the glint of gold.

Zac was struck silent. Lem simply sucked a big breath between his teeth. But Phoebe laughed out loud. Dominik shook the rock in front of his three visitors, grinning from ear to ear.

"Is gold. I am tinking will be much gold, dis place."

He traced his fingers along the quartz seam that disappeared into the native rock at the end of the tunnel.

"You see? Goot mine, I'm tinking. But much rock to move."

Dominik lay the quartz on a flat portion of rock at the mouth of the tunnel. The three newcomers all bent in to get a closer view.

Ignoring the pain in his knees as he knelt on the shattered rock of the tunnel floor, Dominik picked up the larger hammer and started gently tapping the chunk of quartz, breaking it into pieces. Sheltering the pieces that were breaking off with his other hand, so they wouldn't get lost, he continued carefully hammering. Soon there was a mound of broken quartz with gold lying among the pieces. Some larger chunks of Quartz still had gold clinging to them or embedded within.

Dominik spread the shattered quartz into a shallow circle, then leaned back on his haunches. He spoke to Phoebe.

"You can pick out gold."

He was smiling like a man who had just seen the promised land.

Slowly, Phoebe began to sort out the gold, picking it up and placing it into the palm of her other hand, as she looked in wonder at the treasure lying before her. She found no words to add to the moment.

Zac crawled out of the low tunnel, stretching the

kink out of his back as he stood. He looked for some kind of message from Lem and Phoebe. Lem was silent, his brows lifted, his eyes enlarged, although he looked as serious as Zac had ever seen him.

Phoebe's face was lit up with a giant smile. He guessed those looks were all the answer he was going to get to his unasked question.

Dominik had taken a seat at the entrance to the tunnel with his legs dangling over the edge. He was picking small pieces of gold from a handful of shattered quartz. Zac gave him another long study before making his final decision.

"Dominik, I think we will work with you. I will buy what we need for digging and for a camp. Lem and I will help with the digging. I'm hoping Phoebe will keep us all fed. We will want half."

Dominik was a few moments processing the English into Polish before he thought it all through. Finally, he scratched a large circle in the dust on the tunnel floor. He drew a line through the center of the circle.

Pointing at himself and then at the top half of the circle, he said, "Dominik?".

Zac nodded and then took his finger and drew a line dividing the lower half of the circle into two portions.

He pointed to one portion and then to Lem and Phoebe.

"One quarter to Lem and Phoebe."

He pointed at the other lower portion and then to himself.

"One quarter for Zac."

Pointing out the top half of the circle again he said, "Half for Dominik."

Dominik studied the dust for another moment before turning to his three new partners with a big smile.

"Is goot, I'm tinking. We work hard. We find more gold, maybso otter tings. We sell. Make money."

He then jumped to his feet, throwing his arms around Zac, giving him a big hug. Zac backed away, never having been hugged by a man before. Dominik repeated the process with Lem, who had no idea how to respond, and then turned carefully to the beautiful Phoebe, suddenly unsure of himself.

Neither Lem nor Phoebe could ever have imagined being hugged by a white man. Phoebe broke the ice by laughing and then hugging the startled Dominik.

Zac brought them all back to reality.

"The first thing we have to do is get this claim staked. As it is, if someone else came along and staked it, the mine would belong to them."

The western lands were still new and relatively unorganized. Laws governing settlement, whether for ranching or mining, were not yet clear or cast into law.

The information Zac had gathered from the assayer's office was that they could claim the land around their prospect hole and stake it, claiming the right to the minerals, if not actual ownership of the site.

The partners decided to stake just the single claim, registering it in all their names, by their agreed-to shares of ownership.

The staked claim would take in the entire hillside as well as a large portion of the downslope on the other side.

The leadership seemed to fall to Zac. He would pass it off to the geologist once they got a bit more established. But to get started he laid out something for each to do.

"Lem, I would like if you would take the axe and that small saw and cut some posts. Make them four feet long and four or five inches through. We will need a dozen or so to mark out the hillsides between the corners.

"Square one end for about a foot. Make it smooth enough to write on. We will need to record our information there.

"Phoebe, we are going to be camping here. You see if you can scout up a reasonably level camp site and get a fire started. We'll all enjoy a cup of coffee. We'll buy a big tent when we get to town. Try to find a place close by where we can stay for the summer. We'll all come later and clear the rocks away."

"And hurry, everyone. We need to get this done before sundown."

Turning to Dominik he said, "You need to show me what land we should claim. I'm thinking this whole hillside should be staked, with the tunnel near the bottom, claiming everything that looks promising. Do you agree with that?"

Seeing the bewildered look on Dominik's face, Zac scratched the outline of a claim in the dust, with the tunnel centered near the bottom. It would be a sizable piece of land, most of which Dominik had not yet explored.

The geologist had trouble with the concept of the land claim and the tunnel location, but more scratching in the dust solved the problem.

Zac almost laughed out loud when he saw the realization of what a claim meant, lighting up Dominik's face.

"Ya, ya. Is goot. We claim. Find much mineral."

Lem was soon back with an armful of pine posts. After a second trip to bring the balance of what they needed, he used the smaller hatchet to flatten the four sides for writing. Phoebe had a fire going and the coffee pot filled from the little stream.

It took almost until twilight to locate and post all the corners. With Dominik standing at the first corner, below the tunnel, he sighted down one arm, while waving Zac this way and then that with his other arm, until he was forming a straight line. As the claims snaked over small hills and through a couple of swales, Dominik had to move to the first established post and give directions from there. He held his two arms straight out from his sides while Phoebe sighted over and past him, giving directions to Zac.

Zac paced off the distance being claimed. The paces were only rough attempts at measurements. Being of an orderly mind, it was Zac's intention to hold the claim to a rectangle with ninety-degree corners if possible.

The steep, rolling terrain and the bush struggling for life in the few areas where a bit of soil might be found, meant Zac had to compensate for his uneven gait as he added up the steps taken.

With the hillside being solid rock, with just a fractured surface here and there, where windblown soil had accumulated, supporting the growth of a few trees and some small brush, it was impossible to sink the posts into the earth.

The accepted method of staking was to stand the post upright and stack a large mound of rock around its base, holding it in place. Much of the broken rock had to be gathered from a distance, creating a wearying chore.

It was a time consuming and tedious task but when they were finished, they all felt they had done a good enough job, considering they were not surveyors or engineers.

As they all sat around the fire with their coffee cups, satisfied in the day's work, Zac said, "The next thing we have to do this evening is somehow mark those posts with our names. I don't have anything to write with. Perhaps we could carve our names into the wood.

Dominik, getting more excited as the day progressed, jumped up and went to his satchel. He was soon back with a thick, heavy pencil in his hand.

"Look. Is Ołówek. How you say? Pencil? Goot for mark in rain. We use, I tink."

Zac took the special marker and soon the posts were labelled. He then explained to Phoebe that they had to describe their claims.

"It's called a 'meets and bounds' survey. We have to locate all of this on the big maps down at the land office and we have to have a major landmark to start from. How would it be if we walk the perimeter again? I'll call out the details while you write it all down."

Phoebe went to get a cheap booklet of writing

paper that she brought with them and a much lighter pencil than the one Dominik had.

Zac then said, "Lem, I think it would be a good idea if you were to take the Winchester that fella donated to us and teach Dominik something about shooting."

Lem grinned and said, "Do you think that's a good idea, Mister Zac? Our geologist friend is pretty excitable."

CHAPTER EIGHTEEN

After taking turns standing guard during the night, they were ready to visit the land office. But now they were presented with a dilemma. If they all left together the claim jumpers could come in force and settle in, even re-writing the information on the claim posts.

To reclaim the registered property would mean they would have to hire a lawyer and go to court, and no one had any appetite for that. They also had no appetite for an all-out gun battle to roust claim jumpers from their property.

They settled on having Zac, Phoebe and Dominik go to town, leaving Lem to hunker down in the mine shaft. It was a tight fit for the big man, too low to stand up in and too shallow to hide all of Lem's bulky torso.

"We'll get back here as quickly as possible, Lem," promised Zac. "You stay back inside the tunnel and keep your eyes open. If anyone comes around, we'll hope that just the threat of you being here will be enough to drive them off. I'm not too sure how the community would take to a black man shooting a white man, so I'd advise that you be discreet and cautious."

After one half hour of misery, folded into the rough floored tunnel, Lem slid out and stepped to the ground. He would listen for approaching visitors and hope he was up to any challenge that presented itself.

At the claims office, the registrar looked long and hard at both Dominik and Phoebe but then proceeded to register the claims, using a large rocky knoll and a huge Ponderosa Pine growing out of a fissure in a side rock, apparently defying gravity, as the landmarks.

Dominik and Phoebe waited in a small café while Zac rushed back to the claim, taking his place as guard, while Lem rode the gelding to the land office. By mid morning it was all done and legal, and the mismatched group was ready to begin mining.

CHAPTER NINETEEN

That same afternoon Zac drove the wagon back down the hill, to the mine supply store. Working with Dominik, he had compiled a list of tools the group was going to need. Phoebe joined in to work out the camp supplies.

The buying went quickly. With the store clerk assisting, Zac soon had the purchases loaded and the wagon ready for the trail. Before leaving the store, Zac asked, "Where can I find a powder man?"

With the directions to the man's home, Zac mounted the wagon. A stop at the general store to fill Phoebe's list of camp supplies wouldn't take too long. He would then see if he could locate the powder man.

That turned out to be simpler than he thought it would be. Believing he might be wasting his time, hoping to find anyone at home during working hours, Zac was surprised when the powder man himself answered the door.

Zac introduced himself before saying, "I'm told that you might be available to do some powder work."

"That I am, young man, depend'n on conditions. I grew this old by sett'n some standards and never mov'n off'n them. Powder is a great friend when she's used well and proper, but she's a terrible enemy to the careless. Won't work in a dangerous shaft. Won't cut corners. You tell me what you got. I'll tell you if'n I'm interested."

Zac explained their situation. The powder man said, "Name's Black Wiley, son. Mostly answer to Wiley. You promise to bring me back down the hill, I'll come with you now. See what's to be done."

Less than an hour later Black Wiley was squatted on his heels in the short tunnel. Dominik and Lem had spent their time prying out most of the quartz while Zac was away. Dominik held out a piece for Wiley to examine.

He turned it over in his hands like everyone else seemed to do, before saying, "Boys, I'm think'n you just might, could have yourselves a mine."

He eased himself to the tunnel opening and stepped down to the ground. "Cain't squat like that no more. Too many cold winters, I'm think'n. Rheumatism's got the best of my old joints. Don't know why I stay in this cold country. Should be in California or maybe Arizona. Probably too old to make the move now.

"Now see here. Here's what ya got ta do. Ya got ta take this roof out. Make her higher. Yer not going ta get much work done all squinted over and work'n on yer knees. And there's a pretty good chance there's mineral up in that there roof rock too. Might's well git 'er out. Rock's solid. Shouldn't be no problem of cav'n."

He waved his hand at the solid rock roof.

"Hard work, drill'n holes vertical like yer probably think'n yer goi'n ta need ta do ta take "er down. But ya don't need ta do 'er that way. What's better is fer ya ta take and drill in from the outside, horizontal, like. Build yerself up some kind of a platform here and work off'n that. We'll blow 'er that way as deep as yer iron goes and then ya kin drill horizontal ag'in and we'll blow the rest. After that's done, ya kin work stand'n up, like a man should otta be able ta do."

They all huddled closer as Wiley explained the process and their part in it. He explained how deep the holes had to be drilled and in what pattern.

With all the talk finished Zac asked, "What's all that going to cost? Our funds are starting to bite a bit on the raw end, what with all the mining stuff and all."

Wiley laughed and said, "Well, son, whatever the cost, 'tis worth the penny. But it'll not be too terrible. Let's blow this roof, see what ya finds, and then ya kin count up the cost ag'in the prospects."

Zac didn't like open ended deals, but he saw no choice. Wiley was a strange kind of man compared to most a fella might meet, but then, perhaps a body needed to be a bit strange to spend his life working with powder. In any case, Zac could find no reason to mistrust the man.

"I'm sure we'd all like to work with you, Wiley, as long as you understand the situation. If we ever pull enough saleable metal out of this hole to cover the costs it will be full steam ahead. For now, we'll do what's necessary. I'll come find you when we have the holes drilled and ready. We'll be a couple of days or more. I expect we're going to be the most of a day building that scaffold out here before we can start."

Wiley had more to say.

"If'n it were my claim, I'd find me a surveyor to lay 'er out right 'n proper. Ya got a good claim here, I'm think'n. But yer short'n yerselves on yer measurements, follow'n the lay of the land like yer doin."

Zac could almost feel his pockets and money belt shrinking as they talked.

"So, do you know a surveyor?"

"Sure as shoot'n I do. Good man too. I'll send him along ta see ya."

Zac hunched his shoulders, as if the costs were physically hurting him. But he resigned himself to the situation, since he was anxious to get working.

"Well, Wiley, I'll take you back down the hill. You've laid out a mess of work for us. Best we get at it."

CHAPTER TWENTY

While Zac was gone, the remaining three partners cleared away the offending rocks and laid out the new tent. Again, they were dealing with solid rock. There was nowhere to drive tent pegs. They did the best they could do, piling rock on a few inches of folded canvas along the bottom edge. Zac had agreed to bring back a few mill-cut boards for shelving. Until that happened, Phoebe sorted the camp supplies into manageable piles.

Dominik and Lem went to the bush to cut pine poles. By the time Zac returned there was a wobbly scaffold standing at the face of the shaft.

Dominik had laid out the drilling tools, ready to get to work.

Zac laughed and said, "That scaffold's a good start, men, but I'm thinking we had better brace this rig up a bit before we lose a man to a broken leg, or worse."

Another couple of hours adding cross pieces tied firmly in place with rope, and they were ready to drill. By that time the clouds were turning to crimson around their edges, a good sign that evening was upon them. The drilling could wait until morning.

Blowing the roof cost less than Zac had feared. It also exposed another quartz seam. But before they could work on the quartz or deepen the tunnel, they had several tons of rock to move. Dominik went through the rock waste looking for sign of minerals, removing any quartz he found, or anything else that caught his fancy, before Lem and Zac loaded it into their new wheelbarrow.

They used the waste to build the ground up to the level of the tunnel floor. They would extend it outward in a fan shape as the tailings were shoveled out.

Taking a break from the tedious work, the men went to the tent for coffee. They still had no chairs. They each joked about having found the softest rock to sit on. Phoebe had commandeered a packing box with a folded blanket on top for her personal use.

Struggling to express himself in English, not knowing how to say, 'in the future', Dominik needed a bit of help from Zac, but he finally made himself understood.

"In the future, I'm tinking maybe so you and Dominik, or maybe so udder big company, come take rock away."

He waved at the rapidly-growing waste pile.

"I'm tinking much good mineral. Maybe so silver. Maybe so copper. Maybe so udder minerals. Hide goot inside rock. Where is gold, many tings to be found."

Zac shuddered at the thought of loading all that

rock up again, no matter what minerals might be found.

"Well, let's leave that for the future. If we find more gold, I'll be satisfied for now."

They stacked the pile of mineral bearing ore to one side of the tunnel mouth and started again to drill, following Wiley's directions.

Zac had told Dominik, "Lem and I will drill. You take a slow walk over the claim. Take your time. You might find more places where we should be digging. Take Phoebe with you. And take that Winchester. Don't shoot anyone. But with the bears and cougars in these hills it's best to be prepared."

The survey crew arrived about a week after Wiley blew the tunnel roof. An accurate survey greatly expanded the area of the claims. They all pitched in, hauling rock and moving the claim posts to the new locations. The surveyor would adjust the maps at the land office.

There was now nothing holding back a full-on venture. At least as much as the work of three men could be considered full-on. It wouldn't compare with the big companies, but even they had at one time been small, and after all, who could see the future?

Standing by himself, on one of his many private walks, Zac looked at the almost flat money belt and shrugged.

"Well, it wasn't truly mine to begin with since I lifted it off a thief. So, if this mine proves to be a dud, I've lost nothing."

He didn't really feel quite that philosophical about it, but he wouldn't want to concern the others. So, he kept his thoughts to himself.

By the time Wiley blew the next stage of the drilling, and the rubble was mucked out, Dominik had pulled enough ore aside to justify a trip to the stamp mill. They loaded up their wagon and Zac drove it to the mill. The wagon was far too lightly built for the purpose, but if the venture proved successful, there were many contract haulers available.

They kept hammering and drilling while they waited for their turn at the mill. It took nearly a week but when their ore was finally milled and strained out, the results amazed everyone except Dominik. The first small load had proven to be comfortably profitable. Dominik simply nodded, as if he had known all the time.

Not needing the money at that time, they saved the small brick of solid gold, hoping it was just the first of many to come.

Dominik fondled the brick with a loving caress.

"I'm tinking, goot mine. Much mineral. Dominik happy wit mine."

Lem, who didn't often have much to say, offered an opinion.

"I'm thinking we's all pretty happy with the mine, Dominik."

Later that evening, sitting around the supper table drinking coffee, Lem said, "Dis here mine, she need a name."

Everyone else stared at him as if they had never heard such a thing before. But the truth was that mines all through the area were named.

Finally, Zac asked, "Did you have something in mind, Lem?"

Lem nodded and set his coffee cup down.

"This here mine be the last piece of the freedom

Mister Watson started us on, all those years ago. Because of Mister Watson, Phoebe and me, we no longer be slaves.

"Because we born slaves, we got no learning. We have no way to make money for ourselves except for farm work. Farm work all we know. That be no way for money freedom. We be like slaves to the landowner the rest of our lives.

"Now this mine showing us money freedom. I'm thinking we call this the Freedom Mine."

So, the Freedom Mine was officially born that evening.

On the next trip to town, Zak bought a small can of paint. From then on, painted on a slab of wood and propped into a crack of rock above the mine entrance, was the proud announcement. 'The Freedom Mine'.

CHAPTER TWENTY-ONE

Dominik found two more promising outcroppings on their claims. With the returns from the first milling it was tempting to hire a crew and open another tunnel. But Zac's natural caution, along with the almost flat money belt, held them back.

Zac had been going through another spell of serious melancholy. Several times he had disappeared for hours, telling no one where he was going or where he had been, when he returned.

What started it this time was the truth that he was, in all reality, alone. Alone in life. Alone in hopes and dreams.

Of course, he had known that since returning to Carob and finding his family dead and buried. But somehow that realization took on new depth.

The partners were becoming good friends, and they were important to him, adding dimension to his life, but that was a long way from having a home with a loving wife and a child.

Adding to his melancholy was his mind periodically tripping back to Rev. Moody's question: "Is it still well with your soul?"

Zac had no real answer and, in truth, was afraid to allow his mind to sort it out.

He wasn't quite sure why he was working so hard or what he would do with the money if the group fell onto riches.

When life started to appear pointless, he could feel the energy drain from him like sand draining from a suspended burlap sack with a hole in the corner. In his troubled mind he wondered if, when the last grain of sand fell to the ground, would he himself be as empty as the sack. The whole thing frightened him more than the battlefield had.

It sometimes took an hour, sometimes several hours. But eventually, the feelings that came un-invited, left the same way. Then, feeling guilty for having abandoned the partners, he would return to the mine, pick up the hammer or the steel, and work harder than ever.

But he was silent the whole time, seemingly lost in his own thoughts.

Although the partners had moved their sleeping locations to spots of their own choosing, giving each other space, everyone had heard Zac re-fighting old battles in the dark of night. It was as if the darkness in his mind and soul was at least as dark as the blackest night.

Zac often rolled from his blankets, taking up his Henry and wandering the claim for large portions of the night hours.

The partners could see the gradual change in him. He was losing weight even as his already strong body toughened up even more. He was si-lent most of the time.

The others didn't know it, but it took all Zac's internal fortitude to hold back from becoming morose. Even in his worst moments he knew that discouraging the partners would help nothing.

Privately he prayed again and again for the Lord to quieten the memories and to restore his health, both physical and mental.

Remembering the story of their lost children, Zac knew Lem and Phoebe had a bit of insight into his condition.

He was unaware of Dominik's history. They never talked about it.

Zac had no way of knowing, but the geologist had seen much that troubled him, back in his home country. Sometimes the cruelty of those that ruled the land, along with the widespread poverty, left him greatly disheartened. He was thankful to be away from it all. He chose to keep his thoughts on the matter to himself in this new land.

Even with all of that, the partners were unaware of the very depth of pain Zac suffered. He wanted to keep it that way.

When he bent over in abject pain from the knots in his stomach, he tried to make out that he was only out of breath. He learned a number of small tricks that he hoped were fooling the partners.

In truth he was probably fooling Dominik and perhaps Lem to some extent. But Phoebe wasn't fooled at all. She watched over the younger man like a mother, having no idea at all what might help the situation.

CHAPTER TWENTY-TWO

When the mill determined the results of the second load of ore, the news was meant to be private to the owners of the mine. But there is always someone who can't keep the secret. Someone who forgets that they were sworn to secrecy when they were hired. Someone who talks too much.

One of the mill workers sauntered into a miner's saloon to wash the dust from his throat. It was to be one quick drink before heading home to supper and his family. But being a man of uncertain self-control, the first drink led to another one, and then another. It wasn't long before his talk became careless.

Sitting unnoticed at the next table was Hammer Slake, a henchman for the self-appointed town controller, Big Mike Mullins. Big Mike was in reality, little more than a thug. He earned his name from standing well over six feet and tipping the scales past the two hundred mark; big, to be sure. His strength came from years of handling hammer and steel. Women had been known to call him handsome.

He was at ease in the company of saloon owners and small-time miners, and the lesser politicians, who he managed to charm and influence with glib talk and easy money.

That the real movers and shakers; the big mine owners, the businessmen and the respectable politicians, didn't even know who he was, bothered him not at all. He had his faithful following and he was raking in money. That's all he cared about.

As far as most knew, his wealth came from the saloon he owned, along with the establishment's gaming tables. In truth, his real wealth came from the mines he either possessed through violence or controlled through threats.

Mike had heavy-handedly bulled his way into the ownership of several small mining operations. Two frightened miners sold, taking what Big Mike offered. Another owner disappeared, never to be seen again. Three or four miners paid him a price off the top of each load milled, just to hold him at bay. No one but Mike himself actually knew how many mines he was involved in.

He figured another year or two at the gold diggings and he could bid the cold mountains goodbye. It would be San Francisco and easy living for him.

When Hammer knocked on Big Mike's office door, he was ushered in by a lovely young woman who was constantly at Big Mike's side.

Big Mike's greeting was, "What've you got?"

Hammer stepped to the desk and started to whisper his message.

Mike laughed at the man's attempt at confidentiality.

"Speak up. You don't need to hold back because

of Gertie there. She knows the score."

He raised his voice and grinned, "Don't you, Gertie, my love?"

"I guess so. If you say so."

"Well, I say so."

Looking back at Hammer he said, "Now, I'll ask again, what've you got?"

Hammer looked around at Gertie and then back at Big Mike.

"Heard something. Worker at the mill talked out of school. Seems there's a new working up the side hill, to the west of here. Freedom Mine, they're calling it. Kind of tucked behind some rocky knolls and bush. Couple other men tapping on rocks up there but no one else has opened a tunnel. Easy to miss it.

"First load to the mill, couple a weeks ago, showed exceptional color. Second, yesterday, was even better. I'm thinking you need to take a look before the operation gets much bigger."

Big Mike nodded his head, thinking. Finally, he looked back up at Hammer.

"Thanks. That's good information. I'll take it from here. Don't talk to anyone else."

Motioning towards the door he said, "Gert, can you find something to show Hammer our appreciation?"

The obedient woman picked a small gold piece out of her pocket and held it out to the pleased Hammer. She then opened the door, indicating that the meeting was over.

Holding a few gold coins in her pocket and passing them out at Mike's direction, was a small trinket of trust from Mike.

Big Mike sat quietly, considering the news. He was wondering why his friend at the assay office hadn't come to him. Big Mike expected that when he dropped a coin or two into someone's palm each month, that person would get news of this sort to him promptly. Yes, he would have to have a talk with the man.

Looking up from his desk he said, "Gert, see if you can locate Rowdy Hanson for me. Tell him I have a little job for him."

The sullen, but obedient woman silently left the room, gently closing the door behind herself.

Big Mike, an impatient man, was frustrated when Gert was long in returning, but he set those feelings aside when Rowdy rapped his knuckles on the door before walking in. Gert was not with him.

The tall, slim, tough-looking man, with the knife scar down one edge of his jaw, as if someone had attempted to cut his throat but missed by three inches, stood halfway between the desk and the door. He said nothing at all. He simply stood silently, waiting for Mike's message.

Big Mike, a tough enough man himself, survivor of numerous saloon brawls and miner's confrontations, secretly feared the man who stood before him. The coins that found their way from Mike's pocket to Rowdy's each month were a good investment, in Mike's calculation. Anything at all that kept Rowdy on his side was a good investment.

"I have a little job for you. Won't take long. Shouldn't be too difficult. There's a new opening up the hill to the west. I'm told they're calling it Freedom Mine. Might've put a sign up that you can find. I don't have any information on who owns it or how many men are digging.

"I'd like you to invite the owner to come here for a visit. Tell him I have a generous offer that will lift him from the need to swing a hammer for quite awhile. You might impress on him that the offer is only open for a couple of days. After that we will see about other options.

"Oh, and you might want to take a look around. See what we'd be facing if we were to want to root those folks out of there."

Rowdy had still not said a word. He waited until he was certain Mike had no other instruction. He then silently turned and left the room. There seemed to be a chill in the air when the door closed behind the silent man.

Mike had watched Rowdy since the moment he walked in the door. He wasn't sure the man had blinked even once the entire time. Everything about Rowdy scared and cautioned him.

Big Mike sat silently, excited at the prospect of picking up a new claim that showed good returns. He'd have to be careful though. If his name showed up on too many claims, the land office might start to wonder. It might be better to work out another silent partner program. He had several of those going already. They all came with their own complications, but they kept his name out of the public eye.

Still, his several ventures had been profitable up to this point. Why stop now?

Mike pulled out his pocket watch. It was lunch time. Where was that woman? They always went for lunch together. He knew she didn't really care for him. He wasn't that naïve. Hers was a bought and paid for presence, or more accurately, it was a forced presence. As he thought about it, he realized that everyone around him was bought and paid for. He wasn't sure he had ever had a true friend.

He was a bully as a kid, the son of the town bully and a shrew of a mother. The other kids in school shied away from him whenever possible.

Aw, well, why think of all that again. He had worked it over in his mind time and again, all to no advantage. He would finish what he started here in gold country and then clear out. Let them think what they wanted.

But Gert. Where was that woman?

He finally decided to go to lunch himself. Rowdy should be back by mid-afternoon and then he could make the necessary plans.

CHAPTER TWENTY-THREE

Black Wiley had blown another three feet from the tunnel face the afternoon before. The powder man's visits brought both excitement and dread to the miners. The excitement, of course, was because of the prospect of new and larger quartz veins with the accompanying gold. The dread was because of the tons of rock that had to be shovelled into the wheelbarrow, pushed out of the tunnel and dumped, expanding the fan of tailings that was taking on considerable dimensions. Zac and Lem were taking turns with the wheelbarrow while Dominik knelt on the rough tunnel floor, carefully examining each piece of rock.

From the day he first pulled the bush away from the rock face and spotted the quartz, Dominik's excitement and faith in the mine had grown. When he found a rock that he felt might hold hidden treasures he signaled for the shoveling to stop while he found the hammer and broke the prospective rock into smaller pieces.

Cleaning the rubble and tailings from the rough

tunnel floor was a slow, tedious task, made slower by Dominik's thoroughness. If anything was said about wasted time Dominik had a ready answer.

"Time not wasted. We not mining to build rock pile outside. We mining to find goot mineral. Take time to see what is maybe in rock. You wait. I look. I show you what is goot look like. You look too. Might be you find goot rock yourself."

The hard work, the rough living conditions and the tedious nature of the mining operation seemed to have no impact on Lem's normally placid nature.

Phoebe appeared content most of the time, if not truly happy.

Dominik worked like a man possessed, his excitable nature knowing no low points.

But for Zac, it had all compounded his emotional ups and downs. His determination kept him leaning into the task at hand, but some days he had nothing left inside him but determination. Everything else was closeted in a dark cloud of depression and pointlessness.

When his melancholy started to lean towards moroseness, and the temptation to quit was threatening to overwhelm him, it was only that inbred determination and work habit that kept him going. There might be a bit of left-over pride mixed in as well. To quit when the others were working and living under the same conditions didn't sit well at all.

Although, as a young man, Zac hadn't been one to show anger or a short temper, after arriving home from the war and then standing over the graves of Maddy and Minnie as well as his parents, that had changed. He was learning to push his anger deep inside, but as with the determination to keep working, he wondered if he might reach the limit of his endurance. He was aware of the possibility and it frightened him.

There was nothing about the Freedom Mine that angered Zac. That wasn't his problem. But his thoughts on the sheer stupidity of war on top of the fact that the murderers of his family were living free, without facing consequences for their actions, came near to pushing him to that limit he constantly feared.

He liked and respected his partners, and they were making money. He didn't want to upset that combination or blow it all up with careless words or actions. But some days...

Lem had just dumped the wheelbarrow and had turned to re-enter the mine. Zac was kneeling with Dominik, trying to learn more about rocks from his geologist partner. Phoebe was at the tent, singing as she prepared lunch. She had picked up the singing habit just a week or so before. Perhaps she hadn't found anything to sing about before then.

Since they drove off the original claim jumpers, they had seen no further visitors. The fear for the partners was that if news of their find should become public, the surrounding hills would be crawling with prospectors. But for now, they were enjoying the solitude.

The hail from a mounted man startled them all.

"Hello the mine. Need to talk with ya'll. Come out where I can see ya."

A few days before, Zac had drilled two holes high up on the side wall of the tunnel, just inside the entrance. He shaped and fitted short pieces of poplar branches, driving them into the holes as pegs. The Henry was resting on the pegs, wrapped tightly with a small piece of canvas to keep the worst of the dust out. He wanted it close to hand just in case. In case of what, he wasn't quite sure, but having the weapon close by was a comfort to him.

At the sound of the strange voice he lifted the Henry down, unwrapped it, and held it alongside his leg where it would not be easily seen.

The three men emerged from the dusty mine shaft, standing side by side at the tunnel mouth, squinting in the bright sunlight, curious but untrusting.

Phoebe edged close to the entrance of the tent. Zac noticed the reticule was hanging from her left wrist, her right hand caressing the top of the leather pouch.

Zac spoke for the group.

"What can I do for you?"

He made no attempt to sound friendly. The demand that they show themselves hadn't been friendly either. He took that as a sign of the nature of the call.

"Come to tell ya Big Mike Mullens wants to see ya. You're to come down to his saloon. Miner's Lodge. South end of town. Right away.

"Mike's not a patient man. Be best if'n you was to point that there wagon downhill just as soon as you can get them mules harnessed up. Don't be late."

Zac guessed the talker would seem like a dangerous threat of a man to some folks. Zac was impressed not at all. Nor was he in the least frightened.

"Never heard of this Big Mike. Wouldn't come

down the hill even if I had. We've got work to do and no time for galivant'n around. Best you ride back and tell him to forget about it."

The rider pushed his hat back a bit. The small smile on his face had no joy or humor in it.

"This here ain't what you might call a request. When Big Mike calls, people come. I won't tell ya again. Mike said to tell you this is a short-term offer to talk. He intends to name ya a price fer ta buy out the mine. You don't come and talk, we'll use another method beside just talking. Ya won't enjoy that. Best ya ride on down."

"You go back and tell your boss the mine isn't for sale, nor is it likely to be for sale. Tell him to forget it. Now, best you get off our property; we got work to do."

The conversation was becoming personal for Rowdy Hanson. That never happened. He, himself was never threatened. To be talked to that way by this grubby miner was more than he could reasonably accept. He was perversely proud of the fact that no one ever talked back to him. He enjoyed seeing men cringe before him. His self-control was never allowed to slip.

Big Mike wouldn't like him challenging this man by himself, but Rowdy's pride was on the line.

"Mister. Ya need to keep a civil tongue in yer head, else I'll lay yer sorry carcase across one of them mules and haul ya down the hill, dead or alive. It don't matter none to me."

"You figure to be man enough; you just step right up and have at it."

Rowdy wasn't a fast gun man. He was more of a careful, methodical gun man. Startled at the challenge, without looking, he slid his hand off the saddle horn, keeping his eyes fixed on Zac. He pushed his cow-hide vest aside and laid his hand on the Colt, not lifting it, just touching it. Usually, the threat alone was enough to back his words when dealing with miners, few of whom were fighters.

He took a quick glance at Dominik and Lem, assessing the threat, before sliding his eyes to the tent doorway where Phoebe was standing. He saw nothing to concern him.

But when he looked back to Zac, scarcely a second later, he was staring into the muzzle of the Henry. It stopped him. It stopped him cold. He felt a chill pass through him. To let someone get the drop on him was unheard of. It wouldn't happen again. He would see to that. But for now, if he was to live out the plans he had for his old age, caution was called for.

He slowly lifted his hand from the Colt and placed it back on the saddle horn. With his eyes locked on the cold, staring eyes of the gun wielding miner, he carefully turned his gelding, readying for the ride back down the hill.

"Ya need to reconsider. Our next visit won't be just me."

The three miners and Phoebe stood silently, watching the horse slowly amble down the steep grade.

Dominik was the first to speak.

"What is? What is this buy mine? Dominik not understand."

"C'mon, partner. Let's go see what the cook has in that pot. I'll explain it to you."

CHAPTER TWENTY-FOUR

Big Mike did not take Rowdy's news well. He could hardly remember the last time anyone had defied him. His first impulse was to call in a few other thugs and ride up there himself. A show of force usually turned the trick for even the toughest mine owner.

Instead of jumping to his first impulse, he asked, "Who all's up there? How many?"

Rowdy shrugged, trying to appear nonchalant.

"Didn't examine the mine tunnel. Any men working the face couldn't be seen from the opening. What I saw was two white men and two blacks. Nigras. Man and woman. Fine look'n woman, Nigra or no. One white, he done the talk'n. Mighty quick with a Henry rifle. 'Spect it might cost some flesh to dig them out."

Big Mike sat silently, studying Rowdy. He had never seen the man show doubt. He'd have to be cautious on this one. He trusted Rowdy's judgement. Had never known the man to be wrong.

A few more seconds of silent pondering led him

to a new thought.

"Good look'n woman, you say? The kind that might get her man's tail in a twist if she was to be took on a visit to town?

"Say a couple of you was to kind of invite her here? Catch her when she's loading up with camp supplies or at a dress store or something like that? Nigra? No one in town is going to get too upset. Mostly folks are content to leave those people to their own ways."

Rowdy had few morals. Most of those he had been raised to hold dear, were broken and cast aside years before. But he had never given up on respecting a good woman. He wasn't about to change that for Big Mike or anyone else. And he had no reason to believe the beautiful Nigra up at the camp wasn't a lady. He'd give her that until he knew differently.

He took a hard look at Mike to see if he was serious, knowing the man would push too hard one day, and people around him would be hurt. Rowdy didn't want to be one of those people. The fool thought he was above the law. Rowdy knew that when the chips started to fall, no one was above the law. He had skirted many a law himself and outright broken most of the Commandments he could remember, but he was sure he knew when to quit. When to back off.

Some years before, Rowdy had been enjoying a quiet drink at a back table in a small establishment up in Montana when the local folks reached the limit of their patience. He took the experience as an example of what could happen.

A rancher rode into town with three rustlers tied securely on their saddles, shot up a bit but alive and badly frightened.

Rustling had become a serious problem the previous winter, when the cold and piled-up snow kept too many ranch riders close to their bunkhouse stoves, leaving the range open to independent operators. These three were the first rustlers to be caught that spring.

Two other ranchers were in the saloon. At a shout from the street, both had walked outside to see their neighbor with three led animals.

"What ya got there, Straun?"

"Found these three on my high plateau range. Built themselves a small corral some time back, looks like. Had a nice little gather they was work'n over. Had them a lean-to shack. All set up to stay awhile. Most of the corralled animals were mine but there were a couple of 'Gate Post's' and three 'Triple D's'. Couple of others."

Straun only named the animals that belonged to the other two ranchers.

Without saying a word, one of the men stepped onto his horse and loosed his catch rope.

"Bush behind the livery's as good a place as any."

He reined his horse that way, and Straun followed, leading the three seized riding animals, each with a terrified man securely tied to the horn in front of him.

The other rancher followed along, walking with a dozen or more town men who had come from the saloon.

It was all over in a matter of moments, all quick and efficient.

The rancher's interests were satisfied when the rustlers were dealt with, but the townsmen decided it was as good a time as any to clean up a few nagging problems.

Two crooked gamblers were dragged down the street, followed by one thief the sheriff had locked away in the flimsy jail. It was all taken as a good night's work.

Rowdy stepped onto his horse and left town by a back road, as soon as the first bunch started to walk to the livery. He abandoned his bedroll and carpet bag in his hotel room, counting it as a good bargain against his life.

Now, all these years later, he thought perhaps the time had come again.

Big Mike was still staring at the ceiling, his thoughts going around into ever more dangerous territory. Rowdy took another look at him and turned to the door, locking eyes with Gertie. Rowdy had always frightened her, although she had never been threatened by him, verbally or in any other way.

Somehow, he didn't need to say anything for her to recognise the depth of his potential violence. She swallowed heavily and reached into her pocket, lifting out a gold coin. Without even looking at it Rowdy felt it drop into his hand. He continued holding his hand out, his eyes firmly locked on Gertie's. She pulled out two more coins and dropped them into his waiting palm.

Rowdy closed his fist, nodded just slightly, and stepped to the door. Gertie exhaled a long-held breath when the door closed behind him.

Without speaking to anyone, Rowdy stepped aboard his gelding and rode directly to the bank. He closed out his account, placing the substantial withdrawal into a leather sack he carried in a saddle bag. His next stop was his hotel room. It took no more than five minutes to stuff his spare clothing into a carpet bag, pick up his rifle, and head to the street. A couple more minutes to tie everything onto the gelding, closed out Rowdy's connections with the town of Idaho Springs.

Without seeming to rush, and with no desire to draw attention to himself, he reached the edge of town, joining the constant passage of wagons and riders making the downhill trip to Denver. From there, the whole country lay before him. He would decide his next direction as he rode along. He had never liked cold country anyway. Perhaps Santa Fe would suit him for a while. Or out on the west coast, in the sunshine.

It was two days before Big Mike admitted to himself that Rowdy had loaded up and left town. His anger threatened to explode, but he held it in. Watching it all, Gertie was more frightened than she had ever been.

Mike glanced her way and said, "See if you can find Hammer. Tell him I want to see him right away."

The relieved woman left the room, intending to push her absence into several hours if possible. No matter what some people thought of her she wasn't about to go from saloon to saloon, looking for Hammer. She wasn't a saloon girl and she wouldn't be offering any fodder for the gossips to chew over. It was bad enough that she was saddled with keeping company with Big Mike in his office above his drinking establishment.

Going down the stairs from Big Mike's office

into the saloon, she glanced around the dim room. At a back corner, idly playing solitaire, sat Shrug Glover.

She completed her walk down the stairs and approached the card player.

"Big Mike wants to see Hammer. Do you good in Mike's eyes if you could find him and bring him here."

Shrug nodded and stood. Without even stacking the cards, he eased past the table and the woman. Gertie and the bartender watched him leave and then grinned at each other. The bartender had, months before, told Gertie that if she ever needed help, to talk to him. She remembered that but held the offer in reserve.

CHAPTER TWENTY-FIVE

The deep gray, overcast sky, and the chill in the early morning air, were sure signs that summer would soon be a memory. Summers were short in the high country in any case, and the winters were long, cold and snow laden. The others hadn't mentioned the matter openly, but Zac knew neither Lem nor Phoebe had ever faced such as what the high up Rockies could throw their way.

For himself, he'd hoped the bone-chilling temperatures experienced during the war were the last he would ever see.

He had no idea how Poland stacked up for weather. Dominik never mentioned weather, good nor bad. It was as if his whole life revolved around rocks. Zac couldn't blame him. Rocks that yielded gold were difficult for a man to drag his eyes from.

A week after the visit from the hard-nosed rider who demanded they come down to talk with someone named Big Mike or some such thing, there was a need for supplies. There had been no trouble at all with the merchants of Idaho Springs because of the color of Lem or Phoebe's skin. If a person had cash money, the merchants were happy to make the sale.

There were actually a goodly number of Blacks in and around the mining town, but most of them were labourers in the mines. There were a couple of black cooks in the big restaurant in the hotel and several women working as maids, either in hotels or private residences. Few, if any, were mine owners themselves.

For safety, Zac had always accompanied Phoebe when she did their shopping, but after several trouble-free trips he saw no danger with Lem going in his place. He and Dominik stayed with the hammer and steel, ever taking the mine deeper. They were in the process of turning the dimly lit tunnel thirty degrees to the right as they followed the valuable seams.

The shoppers had been gone perhaps an hour and a half when Lem whipped the panting and sweating mules onto the mine site. Frantically leaping from the wagon seat, he charged into the tunnel, shouting, trying to get Zac's attention over the ringing sounds of the hammer hitting steel.

Zac finally heard the call and lay down the hammer. The two drillers turned to Lem, wondering what all the shouting was about and why their friend had returned so soon.

Out of breath and almost out of control, Lem hollered, "They done took her. They took my Phoebe. Two men. Right offen the street. Jest grabbed her and threw her inta a buggy. Laugh'n and jok'n like it was great fun. Whipped thar animal around and drove off down the road. I follered as fast as I could run. Saw where at they took her. Dragged her inta that saloon that lies a bit outa town.

"I was gonna run inta the building to git her but a man on the sidewalk, he stopped me.

"'You run inta that thar saloon fella, they gonna make yo dead. They's wait'n fer ya.'

"That's what the man told me, and I believed him.

"I hadn't no gun and I shore be no help to Phoebe if'n I be dead. I come back ta git my rifle, 'n' go git Phoebe from them men."

Zac glanced at Dominik, seeing both the fear and the determination in the man.

"You stay here. You get your gun and go to the tunnel mouth. Stand guard. I'll be back."

Turning to Lem he said, "You give those mules a good breather then get yourself back down there."

Zac ran past Lem, picking his Henry off the pegs as he ran. He threw a saddle on the gelding and was off down the trail in a matter of minutes.

Halfway down the hill the sky opened with a chilly, fall rain. They had all been watching the sky during the morning, trying to judge the possibility of making a supply trip without getting wet. It appeared that they missed their guess by a couple of hours.

Zac let the horse run, allowing the gelding to judge the footing and the obstacles. He was at the isolated saloon in less than a half hour.

Pulling up before the remote saloon, he bailed off the animal before it was fully stopped. With a quick look around, Zac leaped onto the boardwalk and crashed through the swinging doors, the Henry, as always, leading the way. The room was empty except for the bartender who stood behind the bar, his big hands in full display, fingers spread out over the countertop, showing no threat.

The lower floor of the building was one large room, divided only by a wide set of stairs.

The bartender stopped Zac with a quiet word, as if he didn't want anyone else to hear.

"You climb those stairs fella, you best go shoot'n. They're wait'n for you."

After surviving three years in the cavalry Zac never dreamed that his most dangerous moments might come in a saloon in a small mining town in the west. But there was no stopping him. He took the stairs two at a time, three jumps to complete the six steps to the landing. A left turn and then nine more steps would take him to the second floor.

With the pound of his feet on the bottom steps, a scruffy looking man rose from a chair beside the office door and charged to the top of the stairs. He held a Colt pointed in Zac's general direction, but he hesitated.

'Fool. Never hesitate, if you're going to do, then do it!' thought Zac as the Henry belched its tune. The man grabbed his belly, folded forward and rolled down the stairs. Zac ignored him as he charged up the remaining steps. The Colt slid to the top step and then bounced down to the landing.

Zac grabbed the newel post, using it as leverage as he rounded the railing. There was only one door. With three quick steps Zac laid his heavy boot on the flimsy wood, right beside the doorknob. The door crashed open, swinging wide and bouncing off the wall. It then sagged sideways and hung there, held up by the bottom hinge only.

Two Colts hammered lead towards him. If he

hadn't kept moving, there was no doubt he would have fallen. Shooting from the hip as he so often did, Zac took the man behind the desk first, only because he was closest. Big Mike slammed against the back wall with two pieces of lead in his chest and belly, before falling forward onto the desk and then sliding to the floor.

Zac turned only slightly to his right and shot Hammer Slake, whose lead had already taken a chunk out of Zac's upper leg.

Zac staggered a bit with the pain and shock of the wound, but he didn't go down.

The shot from the Henry had gone true, but Hammer was still standing, trying to bring his Colt back into line. He didn't make it. Zac's next shot ended the game for him.

Behind him Zac heard two other guns belching. He turned to see another thug holding a smoking weapon at arm's length. But now it was pointing at the floor. He had no idea where the shooter's slug had gone and there was no need to shoot him again. He was already bleeding heavily, and his eyes were closing in pain. He was out of the game, but he was alive.

As he watched, fire and lead escaped from Phoebe's reticule. The shooter fell to the floor. The man, near death, made one more attempt to raise his gun. He looked hatred at the black woman he had laughingly grabbed off the street such a short time ago.

Phoebe lifted the pistol from the reticule, bent a bit, pointed the weapon carefully at Shrug Glover's head and pulled the trigger.

"That should do it," thought Zac.

It was not clear at all what was going on with the kidnapping. He had no proof of who any of these men were, although he guessed that the one behind the desk was Big Mike. Until then, no words had been spoken.

Zac turned to Gertie, the Henry following where his eyes led it.

"Who are you? And how do you fit into this thing?"

Gertie was terrified and frantic, ready to plead for her life.

"Please don't shoot me, sir. I was kidnapped too."

She pointed at Big Mike, whose lifeless body lay behind the desk.

"I'm glad to see that animal dead. I just want to get out of here and somehow find my little boy."

There was no time to discuss the woman's plight, so he simply said to Phoebe, "Watch her."

CHAPTER TWENTY-SIX

Zac never was one to leave a job half completed. He knew someone would have to gather up the bodies and haul them out. He decided to help them along. Or perhaps he didn't really think at all. Perhaps his actions were more of a demonstration of his anger.

In any case, some physical activity might help his rushing adrenalin and throbbing nerves to settle down.

Grabbing the man closest to the wall by the collar and the seat of his britches, he lifted him to knee height and headed for the window. A quick swing back and then forward sent the man sailing through the window, spreading splintered glass in all directions. The body bounced off the roof that covered the boardwalk before thumping into the mud of the rain-soaked road.

A woman screamed and two horses at the tie rail broke their reins and trotted away.

Zac then went to the man behind the desk, dragging him across the floor. Big Mike proved to be a heavy burden, but Zac picked him up with only the slightest struggle and flung him out the window. Some trim boards and a few shingles from the boardwalk roof broke free, fluttering through the rain, to fall on top of Big Mike's crumpled form.

The foolish woman screamed again. Zac saw a small ring of rain-soaked faces looking up at him. It would ever be a mystery to him how folks were so drawn to someone else's misery, and just had to come see, even on a rain-wet, miserable day.

As he went for the third man, Phoebe grabbed one arm, waiting for Zac to grab the other one. Together they dragged the corpse to the window. Phoebe, as strong as a lot of men, held onto the arm and then clutched one pant leg. Zac closed his fist around the cloth of the other leg. Together they sailed the man out the window, and down to the road.

This time the gathered onlookers were silent.

Zac had spotted the open safe behind the desk. He stepped that way and bent to look.

Heavy footsteps pounded on the stairs. Phoebe turned to the door, her reloaded pistol up and ready. The rain-soaked face that showed in the broken doorway was black, displaying deadly determination.

Lem pointed his double barrel shotgun into the room, looking around the small space as he entered. Phoebe rushed to him and folded herself into his strong arms.

Gertie held her cowering position against the wall, saying nothing, not so much as moving.

Zac spotted a carpet bag folded up and jammed between the safe and the bookshelf beside it. He tugged the bag out and stuffed everything from the safe into it. He then went through the desk drawers, finding nothing of interest.

Standing, with the carpet bag tucked under his arm, he said, "Let's get out of here."

Lem led the way with the shotgun held ready.

Phoebe still held her pistol. As they neared the top of the stairs, she dropped the weapon back into the leather reticule.

Gertie stepped to where Phoebe had shot Shrug Glover. She bent to pick up his fallen Colt. Zac took note but didn't try to stop her.

On the stairs Zac told Lem to let him go first. He wanted to take a good look at the street before venturing out.

The man lying crumpled on the stairway landing wasn't moving but he was alive. His dying eyes followed as each one walked past.

Zac bent a bit, looking the man in the eye.

"So, what about you?"

Gertie nudged Zac aside.

"I'll show you what about this piece of trash."

She pointed the Colt she had grabbed upstairs. The wounded man's eyes opened wide in terror.

"Call me 'cheap', will you. Think I'm trash, do you? I'll show you trash."

She squeezed the trigger twice, hitting the man in the chest both times. The hammer fell on an already fired casing with the third pull. She dropped the gun and finished the walk down the stairs.

Zac was too startled to stop her. But then he thought, 'kind of wraps up this little adventure'.

Zac went to the front window and glanced up

and down the street. Seeing no threat, he called Lem to help pull the man off the stairs. Lem passed the shotgun to Zac.

Needing no help, the deeply angered former slave grabbed the back of the man's collar, bumped him down the steps and dragged him to the door.

Pushing the door open with his Henry in one hand and the shotgun in the other, Zac led the way from the building. Lem dropped the corpse unceremoniously on top of the other three. The rain had turned into a miserable downpour. Most of the curious folks looking on tried to huddle under the boardwalk overhang. The wise ones had already left to find a safer and drier location.

The wagon was close by, the mules tugging at some grass growing along the dirt track.

Zac said, "Lem, get the women out of here. You're going to get wet, but don't stop until you're at the mine."

He tucked the carpet bag under the seat.

"Keep this safe. And as dry as possible."

With Phoebe and Gertie both settled onto the wagon seat, Lem whistled the mules into action.

Zac turned and re-entered the building. The bartender was still standing behind the bar, as if he was too startled to move, or perhaps he didn't know what to do.

"Is there money in that cash drawer?"

The bar man nodded, fear and wonder showing in his every move.

"You going to take it?"

"Everything I want from here I've already got. Take it and git."

The beer slinger emptied the cash drawer into his pockets, picked up a small metal box, which Zac figured also held money, lifted two bottles from the stock of good stuff under the counter, and fled the room through the back door.

Zac lit a lamp that was sitting on the end of the counter, ready for the evening's needs. When it was aflame, he tossed it against the back wall and reached for another. With three broken lamps spreading their flaming kerosene down the walls and across the floor, the tinder dry wood was catching nicely. There was no chance of putting out the fire, but the rain, plus the distance from the next building would protect the town.

Zac went outside, mounted his gelding and turned to leave, just as the overweight sheriff puffed up the walkway, sided by two deputies.

Trying his best to sound official and in control, the lawman sleeved the rain from his face and hollered, "What's going on around here?"

Zac was tempted to simply ignore the man. Instead he pulled the gelding to a stop and said, "Just doing your work for you, Sheriff. Freeing two kidnapped women. You weren't here so someone had to do it."

The two men looked at each other. The sheriff glanced at the corpses and then at the smoke coming from the saloon door. He swallowed audibly but said nothing.

"Anything else you want to know, Sheriff?"

The sheriff ignored him, so Zac booted the gelding into action, riding to catch up to the wagon and its three passengers.

As he turned to follow the wagon up the hill, Zac heard the clanging of the big brass fire bell from somewhere in town. He thought, 'let it burn'.

On the long trail up the hill Zac's emotions went through the same drained, yet exultant turmoil he had felt after each battle; weary beyond description, yet overjoyed at being alive, when many were not so fortunate.

He could never be sure which emotion would push its way forward most forcefully.

CHAPTER TWENTY-SEVEN

Zac rode his worn and wet gelding onto the mine site just one hundred yards behind the wagon. Opening the corral gate, he ushered the animal inside, pulled the saddle and bridle, and closed the gate behind him. The sweating around the bridle bit and the leather of the saddle, in spite of the rain, signaled the hard use the animal had seen. In normal circumstances, Zac would have treated the horse to some kindness, but these weren't normal times. The animal would have to make out the best he could.

Zac stowed his rigging in the lean-to shelter, lifted the Henry from the scabbard, and started walking slowly up the grade, past the mouth of the mine. Dominik stood at the mine entrance, alert and ready for trouble, his rifle leaning against the rock wall beside him. The others were huddled inside the tent while Lem worked to get a blaze going in the sheet iron stove. They needed some warmth.

Zac didn't look their way, simply staring ahead as he walked.

Phoebe turned her eyes from Lem and noticed Zac walking away. Concerned, and aware of his severe mood swings, she made her way past the others, stepped to the bottom of the hill and watched as he climbed the small grade, disappearing over the top.

She was tempted to go after him, to bring him back. Instead, she prayed a short prayer for his wellbeing and headed back to the tent. She couldn't conceivably get any wetter than she already was, and she was shivering like a scared pup. To get out of the rain seemed like the thing to do.

The thought crossed her mind that, even though she had been rescued from Big Mike and his thugs, she was still facing her own high emotions. How much good could she be to Zac or anyone else at that time.

Even slavery hadn't hardened her to the trauma of being taken hostage by gun wielding men. And then, to think that she had killed a man. A white man. How could that possibly be?

Lem would soon have some heat radiating from the stove and filling the tent. She was warmed a bit just with the thought of crackling pine logs.

Dominik went to the lean-to and dug out a couple of dry towels, passing one each to Phoebe and Gertie.

Phoebe sat as close to the stove as safety allowed. She couldn't get her mind off Zac. After witnessing his single-minded, incredibly violent, non-stop action in Big Mike's office, doing little more than flinching when he was shot himself, she saw the man in a completely new light.

In Big Mike's second floor office Zac was no longer the friendly neighbor who returned home from war and was now looking for a path forward. He was the complete warrior. Nothing less.

In the short battle that morning he stood tall, facing the enemy, not backing down until all was completed. Until all his enemies were dead and silenced.

Phoebe had been shocked by Zac's actions outside the general store in the little village on the trip west.

Although she was sure those two men were grievously injured, this morning the situation went a step further. The men at the saloon were dead.

To think that this quiet, composed man, their friend, had faced life threatening circumstances like he had that morning, for three years, and more, was beyond her comprehension or imagination.

When Phoebe tried to envision the pain from the loss of his family, on top of the battle scars, she couldn't add it all up, leaving her with no notion of what would ease the burden on Zac's heart.

During each battle his cavalry troop had ridden into, Zac had experienced exhilarating highs, adrenaline pumping full strength through his system. After the battle he suffered through debasing lows.

There was no easing off; he was high and then he was low. For at least the past year he had been unable to stake out the middle ground.

Towards the end of the war he wasn't always sure he would survive the lows. He seemed to be dragged lower with each event and stay low longer.

The morning at the saloon was a battle like no other he'd experienced. With the life of a partner and close friend threatened, as well as the work they had put into the mine, his rush to combat had him acting like a madman. He realized, on reflection, that his actions were without a plan, except to kill and destroy the enemy. His fervor for battle would tolerate no other outcome.

But now, with the battle won and the enemy forever put aside, what was to become of him? On the one hand, he faced battle with an assurance brought on by experience. On the other hand, his every thought, his every nerve and emotion cried out, 'enough, no more'.

Climbing the gradual, rocky grade behind the mine, and acknowledging that the risk to him and the partners was behind him, he could feel the last of the adrenaline seeping away. He could sense his muscles relaxing to the point where he wasn't sure they would hold him up. His mind, sharp in battle, was becoming blurred with uncertainty, now that the battle was over.

The old, familiar, overwhelming sadness threatened to draw a black cloud over his life.

Already rain soaked, he ignored the continuing downpour as he climbed the rocky grade of the rough trail. He was not really going anywhere. Just away. He only wanted to be away. To be somewhere else. To be alone. To be at a place where there were no questions to answer.

Maybe he only needed to be alone for a little while. Perhaps forever.

Zac knew he couldn't place the burden of his troubles onto his partners. They didn't deserve that.

Why go on? It's true the mining partnership was

producing gold. His bank account grew after each load was taken to the hammer mill. But he had no use for the money. There was no one he loved. No one who loved him. His wife and daughter were murdered. His parents were murdered. He doubted he could ever love again or would even wish to.

What was keeping him here on this troubling earth? What was God doing with him? Perhaps God would soon take him out of his misery. Or should he help the Lord along with that?

Suddenly his thoughts scared him. What was he thinking? Or was he thinking at all? Was it all just self-pity? Did he actually just consider taking his own life. Surely not! He wasn't that out of control.

He still believed in God. But did God still believe in him?

He couldn't recall the details, but he remembered something he read long ago, about a man wrestling with God. Somehow, all night they wrestled. That didn't seem to make much sense, but it was written in the Scriptures. How can a man wrestle with the Creator God? Perhaps it was symbolic. Perhaps it was a metaphor. Or perhaps God was saying, "You can't win fighting Me. Give in. Trust. Let Me take control."

It seemed as if he couldn't control his mind. His scattered thoughts rambled, even as his feet wandered over the rocks, nearly tripping on the small brush that grew from the cracks.

Zac found himself wishing that somehow, perhaps by sheer force of willpower, he could be back to who he was before the war. But he knew it didn't work that way. So, he continued walking, shuffling really, wishing his hours and years away.

***

Huddled under the tent, more or less protected from the cold, fall downpour, the miners and their new female guest sat in stunned silence. Neither woman ever expected to kill another human being, or to witness the violence of others. Phoebe especially was shocked that she had shot and killed a white man. Of course, that man was intent on shooting Zac, and she would have probably been next. She couldn't allow that to happen. She also knew it was something she could never talk about.

After her capture and the reckless buggy ride to the office above the saloon, Phoebe had been fiddling with the little silk handkerchief in her reticule. Trying to remember some of the things Zac had taught her and Lem, she tried to create a mild distraction. Wanting the men to become at ease with her opening and closing the leather bag, she sniffled and feigned weeping. With the bag hanging from its drawstrings on her left wrist, she reached in with her right hand, pulling out the small square of cloth. She wiped her eyes and sniffled some more, then put the handkerchief back into the bag. She repeated this whole charade several times during the long wait for Zac or Lem's arrival.

The big man behind the desk kept telling everyone to be patient. The men they needed would be arriving soon. They would be arriving with their hats in their hands, pleading for the release of the black woman, offering anything Big Mike asked for. Then the Freedom Mine would be his.

Big Mike sat behind his desk, smirking, first at

Phoebe and then at Gertie. Although he was seated comfortably, he insisted that everyone else stand.

By the time they heard the unexpected shots on the stairs, and a bare moment later, jumped to attention as Zac burst through the door, the men were no longer paying any attention to Phoebe, or her actions.

The wait had been long. During that time their minds wandered, and their vigilance waned.

When the door into Big Mike's office burst open it was immediately obvious that the attacker didn't have his hat in his hand.

Nor had he come to negotiate.

Instinctively, Hammer Slake lifted his filthy hand from Phoebe's arm and drew his Colt, looking for a target. But Zac never stopped moving. The slow-witted thug hesitated, trying to take careful aim at the moving attacker, at the same time wondering if that would be Big Mike's wish.

As the first shots were sounding in the room, Phoebe reached into the reticule again, only this time she didn't take hold of the handkerchief. She placed her hand carefully around the small pistol, and just as Zac had instructed, she shot through the leather bag.

Her hand, inside the bag, was only inches from Hammer's chest.

Her first shot entered the guard below his rib cage, on his right side, traveling up and out, under his arm on the opposite side. His shooting arm dropped, pain and shock causing his finger to tighten on the trigger. The bullet drove into the floor at their feet.

He turned slightly towards Phoebe, a pain filled,

startled look on his face, wondering where the shot had come from. He couldn't imagine a black woman would know how to use a pistol, or even have one.

She raised the reticule a bit and pulled the trigger again, looking him right in the eyes. Her adversary slowly crumpled to the floor and lay there, looking up at her unbelievingly. Taking her time, but determined to finish what she'd started, she lifted the pistol from the bag, pointed it carefully at the thug's head and squeezed the trigger.

The shooting in the room had ceased by the time Phoebe triggered off her last shot.

Now, sitting beside Lem, in the shelter of the tent, thinking of what she'd done, Phoebe shuddered, burying her face in her hands.

Looking back over those actions, it was as if someone had been acting it out in a play. Someone else. Not her. It couldn't be real.

But it was, and she trembled at the thought.

Lem, never before feeling free to make a public show of affection towards his wife, pulled her a bit closer and held her in his strong arms.

Gertie hadn't said a word since their arrival except to answer when Lem asked her name.

Dominik was totally befuddled by the happenings. He sat silently, wondering at the whole matter. But he still held his rifle, the butt resting on the floor between his feet. He watched the trail and the hillside, between glances to the mine entrance and then to the other three in the tent.

Phoebe was not quick to assess the situation. Her mind was still focused on the battle and what they would do if someone should sweep up the hill with a counterattack. Without Zac it would be up to Lem and herself. Perhaps Dominik would take a hand. Gertie may or may not; Phoebe couldn't judge that.

Lem hesitated but finally said, "I'm think'n we men could make-do in the mine for a bit or maybe in that sleeping shelter, side us here. We's all pretty wet wit da rain. The ladies would brobly enjoy to dry theirselves off and change der clothes. Could be Phoebe got somth'n Miss Gertie could wear, what's dry."

Dominik jumped to his feet. "Sorry ladies. Dominik not tink of that."

Lem took a couple of steps towards the entrance of the tent and stopped. Turning around he asked, "Gertie, do you still have dat Colt?"

"No. I dropped it on the floor back at the saloon. It was empty anyway."

They were all content to have this stranger un-armed until they knew who she was and how she fit into the whole thing.

Dominik, who hadn't spent any time in the rain except to run from the shelter of the mine to the tent, went back to the mine, but not to work. He pulled an empty wooden powder box far enough into the tunnel to protect himself from the rain, sat down, and lifted his carbine onto his lap.

In thoughts and actions, he was a long way from the little farm outside Krakow, Poland.

Lem went to the animals, brushing them a bit more and taking them again to water. There was no shelter from the rain for the poor beasts. A feeding and a time of rest would have to do for them.

Phoebe sorted out a change of clothing for Lem, laying the items on a chair, ready for him.

With the animals dealt with, Lem bundled the

dry clothes into the sleeping lean-to, along with a towel. In just a matter of minutes, he was dried off and feeling close to normal again. He ran for the mine entrance, holding the towel over his head, spending as little time in the rain as possible.

Phoebe stoked up the fire in the sheet metal stove and made coffee. After the two women were dried off and clothed again, they worked together to get the evening meal started.

Phoebe was still recovering from her shock of the morning's events.

Gertie was silent except for some sniffling and, occasionally wiping a tear.

When the coffee was hot, the men were called back to the tent.

They nursed their coffees as long as they felt they could. No one had much of anything to say.

Zac's absence was starting to wear on them. Finally, with the decision made that no mining would take place this day they went their separate ways.

Phoebe showed Gertie to the lean-to.

"This is where Zac and Dominik call home. They won't mind if you stretch out for awhile. An afternoon snooze will do us all good."

Phoebe, herself, then took to her bunk.

Lem took his place on the shipping case inside the tunnel mouth, his rifle across his knees. Dominik went back into the mine to break small rocks into smaller rocks, hoping to find valuable ore. He added a chunk or two of promising looking pieces to take to the assayer's office.

Just before sunset, Zac returned. He offered no explanations, and no one asked.

CHAPTER TWENTY-EIGHT

Phoebe and Gertie had set aside a plate from the hot meal they prepared earlier. Sitting in his saturated clothing, Zac ate a bit and then pushed his plate away. He waited until he had Gertie's attention and then pointed a hard, not altogether trusting look at the woman.

"Alright, young lady. Talk to us. You told us a bit back at the saloon. Now we want the whole story.

"Who are you? How did you get caught up with that bunch of criminals? What's this about having a lost son? What are we supposed to do with you?"

After her short nap, Gertie had regained most of her poise and confidence. As much as Big Mike hadn't shamed out of her, anyway. She looked around the table and started to tell her story.

"First, I must thank you. Thank you all."

She seemed to catch her breath while the others waited patiently.

"Although I'm sorry you got dragged into that mess, and I'm certainly saddened that you took a bullet in your leg, Zac, I'm not in the least sorry that Big Mike and those others are lying dead in the rain. Except for one thing."

Phoebe jumped into the conversation with a startled expression.

"Zac, I forgot you got shot. You never said anything. How bad is it? I've got some salve and clean bandages. Where were you shot? Let's get a look at it."

Listening to the woman's non-stop questions, Zac found a chuckle somewhere inside him, in spite of the day it had been.

"It's not much and it's not anywhere you're going to be administering your salve on. You lay out the salve and a bit of bandage. I'll get to look'n after it, bye 'n' bye."

After Zac and Phoebe had a short staring match, as if to decide the final authority on wound treatments, with Gertie swivelling her head from one to the other, Phoebe bobbed her head and said, "Yas'm, Massa. I's jest gonna do as Massa say to do. Massa most alays right. Yass'r. Dat da trut. Phoebe ala's list'n ta Massa."

The looks on the faces of the others around the small table ranged from startled to wondering. Zac burst right out laughing. He hadn't laughed in many days. The sound bothered him.

Lem was not amused.

"Phoebe you quit wit dat der slave talk. You no slave. Old Missus Watson, she hear you talk dat slave talk, she come right back from de grave and she lay a haunt on you. Dat woman, she teach you right talk. No more slave talk. You hear me, woman?"

Phoebe said nothing.

Zac studied Lem, never having heard him speak to his wife with anything but gentleness before. But his short speech on Phoebe's slave talk left no room for discussion.

Gertie waited for her rescuers to sort out whatever it was that was troubling them, but finally decided to continue with her story.

"It all happened about six months ago. My husband was killed in a mining accident a few months before that. I was alone with our little boy. He was a year and a half old. I had no money and nowhere to go. What little family I have are all back east. I didn't know what to do.

"I don't know how Mike even knew I existed, but somehow, he did. When I was becoming desperate, he sent one of his goons to escort me to his office. They really gave me no choice, but I half welcomed any opportunity that would give my son and me some security. I left the baby with Missus Grady, who owned the boarding house where I was staying. Good woman. She did her best for Bucky. His real name is Andy but one way or another, he got stuck with Bucky.

"Mike seemed the real prosperous gentleman when I first met him. What I didn't know was that while he was wooing me at the hotel restaurant, his goons were at the boarding house, kidnapping Bucky. They simply pushed Missus Grady aside and grabbed the baby. With Missus Grady screaming and running after them, they piled into a buggy and raced away. I have no idea at all where they took the baby or what's become of him in the months since. I spend all my waking moments and much of my nights wondering, worrying and praying for my little boy.

"After Mike knew his men had the baby, his character totally changed. He made it plain that unless I, as he said, 'decorated his life' and his office and home, I would never see my son again.

"I thought I was desperate before. I didn't even know what desperate was until they took my little boy. So, I 'decorated' Big Mike's life, hating every minute of it, and looking all the time for a way out. But I soon found out that even if someone knew where my boy was, they weren't talking about it. Mike's goons were bought and paid for, even though they were terrified of him. One of Mike's boasts was that no one ever quit him. Then he would laugh and say, "They wouldn't dare"."

The group sat silently, soaking in the story. Zac found that he wanted to believe Gertie, but he wasn't prepared to take her completely at face value. Not yet, anyway. But it had been an exhausting and troubling day, so he held any questions he had for another time. They all needed to get some sleep.

Zac stood and stretched. "Y'all need to get some rest. Gertie, you can take my bunk in the lean-to. It's dry and shelters you from the wind. Dominik will be taking the other bunk but that doesn't give you anything to worry about. Just relax and get some sleep. You and I will be riding first thing in the morning."

Gertie looked up from the table when Dominik said, "No, no. I'm no sleep in bunk. I go to mine. Maybe watch for riders. Maybe sleep some. You take sleeping place for yourself."

Gertie simply nodded her head and rose from the table. She and Phoebe had spread their clothes out where the heat from the sheet metal stove could work on them. Gertie turned hers over so the other side could dry, and then ducked through the rain to the lean-to.

Dominik went to the mine, while Lem stretched out on the bed in the back of the tent, fully clothed and with his rifle and shotgun close to hand.

Zac pulled the carpet bag of documents out of the corner they were stuffed in and laid it on the table. Phoebe rushed to remove the used supper dishes to give him room. She then lighted a lamp and set it close to where Zac was laying out the various documents. She seemed to have forgotten about his wound. Or at least allowed the matter to pass.

Tired, but curious, Phoebe sat down and watched as Zac glanced at each document before placing it on a stack of similar items. A few that were of particular interest, Zac passed to her. She read silently, with only her occasionally raised eyebrows or a rapid intake of breath indicating surprise.

Zac drew a large, brown paper envelope out and opened it. He gasped, reached in, and lifted out a bulky wad of paper money. Another brown envelope duplicated the result. Zac didn't take an accurate count but a quick shuffle through one pile of bills was enough for him to say, "That's a lot of money."

Phoebe nodded in agreement, before speaking. Somehow, with the rain still falling, the darkness of night fully on them, Lem sleeping a few feet away and Gertie sleeping close by, she sensed the need for stillness.

She could only look up at Zac and quietly say,

"More than I ever saw before."

She was getting over her annoyance with Zac. There had been no more slave talk. But he still hadn't attended to the bullet wound.

A few more documents followed. Zac leafed through them one by one, then leaned back in his chair. He motioned towards the stack of papers and spoke quietly.

"These are all related to mines throughout the valley. It appears that Mike either owned these mines or he somehow had control, and the mine owners were paying him a cut off the top. The guy was a crook to the core.

"He abused women and kids. He bullied his own goons. He stole from the miners. Whatever else he might have done we have no idea. What a great citizen."

Phoebe wiggled a single sheet of paper out of the pile, thinking it looked different. It didn't have the legal, printed format of the others. She studied it for only a few seconds before saying quietly, but excitedly, "This is the name and address of the people who have the baby. Only there's three names here. Do you suppose he kidnapped three children?"

Zac had no answer, of course. He looked at the document before carefully laying the paper aside. His mind was whirling with possibilities while he placed the remainder of the documents into the carpet bag. He counted out some bills and placed them aside also. The remainder of the money went back into the envelopes and then back into the bag.

With the table again clear he slid the sheet with the names on it towards Phoebe.

"How would you like to make a copy of this and

put it carefully away? Then you had better get some rest."

He stood, stretched, picked up his Henry and said, "I'll go keep Dominik company."

Phoebe dared a comment, fearing a bit how Zac would respond. "You haven't changed into dry clothing yet nor bandaged that wound."

"I'll take a towel and my dry clothing to the mine. I'll be fine. Thanks for your concern." ·

Phoebe took that as a truce between two friends.

Back in the mine, Zac and Dominik carefully buried the carpet bag under a large pile of ore. The ore wouldn't be moved until it was time for another trip to the mill so it should be safe enough.

CHAPTER TWENTY-NINE

All seemed to be still after the shooting at the saloon. Zac saw nothing that threatened the Freedom.

Although he and Dominik took turns sleeping and watching, the mine had no unwelcome visitors during the night. In the morning everyone was still a bit on edge, but they decided to go back to work, stopping occasionally to take a long look down the trail.

Zac and Gertie were rigging out for a ride to town. Zac hadn't told her about the name and address on the sheet of paper. He wasn't sure why. Perhaps it was because he still didn't totally trust her, or fully believe her story.

The rain had slowed down to a light drizzle but the black clouds in the west warned that the storm may still have a surprise or two waiting for them. It wasn't unheard of for rain to gradually turn to snow at this time of year at this upper elevation.

Zac saddled the gelding and led him to the tent. He held a stirrup for Gertie. He didn't want the woman to be behind him where she could possibly reach one of his weapons. Or produce one herself that she hadn't owned up to carrying.

"Get in the saddle. I'll ride behind."

Gertie, wearing Phoebe's slicker, over a split skirt and a blouse, gave him a questioning look, then lifted her foot, while Zac guided her shoe into the stirrup. When she was seated, he swung up behind. The horse was rain-wet, but Zac ignored the situation, soaking his pants through within seconds.

With Zac holding the reins, and Gertie hanging onto the saddle horn, the animal moved out onto the familiar trail.

Nearing town, Zac asked, "Do you have any money?"

"Some. Mike always liked me to have some gold coins in my dress pocket. He found it to be great sport to demean his crew by having them hold out their hand to me for a bit of payment. I have about one hundred dollars left. I guess it's mine now."

Zac had no response on the reason for the coins. He simply said, "It's yours. We'll find you a horse to buy in town. We can't ride double all the way to Denver."

Gertie turned as much as she could to look at Zac. "Why are we going to Denver?"

"Because I found a sheet of paper with a name and address on it in that pile of stuff. It looks like it might be where your baby is being held."

Gertie started to cry, blubbering out, "Oh God, I pray that's true."

They dismounted at a livery with a small corral of sale horses close by. Zac walked into the corral, gently nudging animals aside to isolate a small bay gelding he judged to be the best of a poor lot. The hostler watched from the shelter of the barn door.

With the gold fever in full swing and people coming and going, the livery owner was not in a bargaining mood.

"That's a good horse, there mister. Climb on and see for yourself if'n you wish. Horse, saddle and the rest, fifty dollars, and good value at double that."

The hostler gave Zac a half minute to study the animal before saying, "You can stand there on one foot and then the other all day and into the night if you wish. It'll still be fifty dollars when you decide to buy."

Riding away, each on their own animal, Gertie said, "That's a lot of money for this horse. And I can already tell you this ain't much of a saddle. or much of a horse, comes to that."

Zac ignored her comment.

"Can you show me where Mike lived?"

In annoyed silence Gertie led Zac to a small residential area one half mile into the hills. She pulled the newly purchased horse to a stop in front of a small house, pointed and said nothing.

Zac dismounted and tied his gelding. Turning to Gertie he held out his hand as if to say, 'well'?

"I don't want to go in there. There never was a single good thing happened there."

"It don't really matter about any of that. We have to take a look. Now get your feet on the ground. We're wasting time."

The door was locked but Gertie had a key. There was no sign of disturbance inside. Zac walked through the four small rooms, flipping window curtains back to look behind them, lifting mattresses, opening drawers. He found nothing he wanted.

Finally, he spotted a small safe tucked behind an overstuffed couch in what would pass as the formal sitting room. He pulled the handle but the safe was locked.

Without bothering to look at Gertie, he asked, "Do you know the combination?"

She was slow to answer but finally Zac heard her quiet, almost embarrassed, 'yes'.

"Seems you know a lot for someone who was supposed to be a captive."

"You're judging me awful hard, mister. But I don't care about any of that. In the past few months I've found there's nothing I care about except finding my baby. So, you think whatever will make you happy. Just get me to my baby.

"But if you're looking for a bit of truth, I'll tell you. I found the combination on a scrap of paper Mike was using as a bookmark. I tried it and it worked. I put the paper back and never touched the safe again.

"Go right to six, back left to twelve, back right to eighteen. Take your look and let's get out of here."

Zac twisted the dial on the simple locking system and pulled the handle. The safe opened to reveal a few more papers and another wad of money, plus a small sack of gold coins. On the bottom shelf was a small ,32 cal. pistol and a box of shells. He settled back on his heels, deciding what to do.

Finally, he said, over his shoulder, "Can you find a sugar sack or something to put this in?"

Standing beside their riding animals after locking up the house he held the gun out to Gertie, with the box of shells.

"I unloaded it. Don't re-load it until I tell you to. I'll trade you for the key to that house."

Gertie looked suspiciously at him but finally reached into a pocket and passed the key over.

Zac stowed the filled sugar sack in a saddle bag to keep it dry. He had placed the small pouch of gold coins into his pocket.

Riding through town they made one stop.

Zac swung down in front of a lawyer's office.

"I'll not be long. You can get down and take shelter from the rain if you're of a mind to. Now understand me; I'm not holding you here. If you decide to take off on your own, I'll not come looking for you. I'm here to help you. You can believe that or not."

With that, he swung up onto the boardwalk and entered the office. The tiny room made a warning bell on the door unnecessary. There was one desk and two chairs for visitors. Behind the desk sat a young man, thin and pale, and frail looking. On the wall behind the desk were two framed diplomas. Zac couldn't read them from where he stood but he assumed they were college law degrees.

"Sign on the door says, Gomer Radcliff, Lawyer. That you?"

The slight-built man made no attempt to rise or offer to shake. "That would be me. What can I do for you?"

"Isaac Trimble. Folks call me Zac. I'm looking for an honest lawyer. Do you qualify?"

A slight smile broke out on the thin face.

"Ma would be ashamed, and Pa would take me out back and lay on a whoop'n, or try to, if I couldn't give a positive answer to that question. Yes, Zac. I'll claim honesty for myself, although I'm not too sure that's the road to fame and wealth in this new western frontier. Some days even ill-gotten gain could tempt a hungry man. Now I'll ask again. What can I do for you?"

Zac thought long enough to confirm his original plan. The plan that brought him to this office.

"Have you heard the name Big Mike Mullins?"

The question caused Gomer to lay his pencil down and lean back in his chair.

"I'm assuming you're referring to the late, the recently late, Mike Mullins. I can't say as I ever met him, but I've seen him around. His reputation is familiar to me as well. How does that tie in with your visit this morning?"

To confirm his original decision to trust this man, Zac gave him another hard study, before proceeding.

"His personal and business papers have fallen into my possession. I'm not totally sure what to do with them and I can't take the time today to go into it with you. I have a prior commitment in Denver. I'll be gone a couple of days.

"What I think needs to be done is for you to visit the local banks. Find out if Mike had an account in any of them and then get that bank's agreement to hold the account untouched until something can be done with Mike's estate. There is a considerable amount of money involved, both in cash and property. I'm thinking there will be several miners challenging his holdings.

"Mike owns a house in the south end too. It might be good to somehow seal that up too until things settle down."

As Zac talked, the pieces fell together in the lawyer's mind. With a smile he said, "My understanding is that his office is no longer of concern."

Zac grinned in return.

"Well, it seemed like a good idea at the time."

The lawyer returned to business.

"Where are these papers and what do you intend to do with them?"

"The papers are in a safe enough place. You'll see them soon, after I come back up the hill."

Zac laid some coins on the desktop.

"In the meantime, will that get you working?"

Gomer shuffled the coins with his finger.

"Fifty dollars? Most lawyers don't make that in a month in this burg of a village, or in Denver either, far as that goes. Yes, I'd say that will get me working. You have to understand though, there is a limit to what I can do. Even with you having the papers, I must still seek the court's approval to act as a trustee of some kind. We don't know at this point if Mike left a will or has any family."

Zac turned to the door.

"You sort that out. I'll see you in a couple of days."

He didn't give the lawyer time to respond before he pulled the door closed.

Zac and Gertie hadn't ridden more than fifty yards when a voice from the sheltered boardwalk hollered out. "Morn'n Zac. Wet to be rid'n."

Zac pulled to a stop, glad to see the powder man.

"Wiley. Great to see you. And seeing you gives me a thought. We've gotten into a bit of a situation. I think it's over, but I can't be sure. I'm going to be away for a couple of days. Do you know of two or three boys that could be trusted to stand guard at the mine while I'm gone? Not to guard the mine, but to keep the people safe. I'm happy to pay them, and Phoebe will keep them well fed."

Wiley grinned up at Zac, who was still aboard his gelding.

"You somehow imagining that I don't know what you're referring to? Son, it's all over town, so you can put any hopes of secrecy out of your mind.

"Sure, I'm thinking I can round up a man or two that would rather sit on a chair with a shotgun over his lap, than swing a hammer. More than just a few of those around. I'll send a couple up later today."

Zac nodded in relief. "Well, I'm thanking you, Wiley. The sooner they get there the better, I'm thinking. You might find time to take them up and introduce them to the others. If they just show up, they may not be welcomed."

"Leave it with me. The Freedom's one of my better customers. I've got to take care of you, or how will I pay my rent next month?"

Both men laughed and with a casual wave of his hand, Zac kicked the gelding into action.

Gertie looked at her escort.

"Is there anyone in town that you don't know?"

Zac ignored the question, tugging his hat brim down tightly as the rain picked up.

CHAPTER THIRTY

It was evening before the wet and weary travellers found a hotel in Denver. The constant complaints from Gertie about the scatterbrained horse and the old saddle the dealer threw into the deal had caused Zac to fold his thoughts into himself. If it wasn't for the baby they hoped to find, he would have turned for home, leaving the complaining woman to her own devices.

If he ever needed proof of his reaction to petty nagging, and self-imposed stress, this day had provided it in quantity.

The hotel clerk passed each of them a key and confirmed that the restaurant was still open. With the horses cared for, the rooms secured and a good meal behind his belt, Zac was done for the day. It felt as if he hadn't had a good night's sleep in weeks, although it was really only a couple of days.

He was weary of caring for Gertie. He suspected she felt the same about him. Hoping to end the troubling day on a more positive note he said, "We don't have to get up with the sun tomorrow. That is, if the sun ever shines again. You take your rest. I'll look for you at breakfast when you get there."

With no further words he climbed the stairs and disappeared down the hallway. Gertie watched him go and turned to the clerk.

"Is there a chance you could find some hot water? I'd sure enjoy a bath."

***

After a night's rest and a leisurely breakfast, it was nearing mid-morning before they were in the saddle again. The miserable rain continued to fall.

Wondering how to proceed, given that the matter with the children started in Idaho Springs and had now led them to Denver, Zac finally decided it was a bigger matter than the local law in either town could handle.

With his decision made, he asked the hotel clerk for directions to the federal marshal's office. It turned out it wasn't difficult to find in the small, but rapidly growing town.

Zac stomped some mud from his boots onto the boardwalk and whipped rainwater off his pants with his hat. He studied the sign on the door for just a moment.

'Rocky Haubner, Deputy Federal Marshal', it read.

He opened the marshal's door and stepped inside.

"Close the door. I purely don't care for a rainy day."

Zac looked at the man behind the desk.

"Well, if I had the say-so, I'd order the sun out

for you. You and me, both. But I don't, so you're just going to have to put on your slicker and come for a short ride in the rain with me. Got a situation that needs the law's input."

The lawman looked up from the stack of wanted posters he was thumbing through.

"You've got to be funn'n me. This'n ain't no kind a day ta be out'a doors. I was kind of figuring on send'n a note around town for no one to shoot anyone until the sun comes back. Just so's I could hole up here beside that pot-bellied stove. Why don't you just forget it, whatever it is. Come back when the rain stops."

Zac stepped to the coat rack and lifted off a slicker and hat. Dropping them on the desk, he said, "Now's the time. Let's go."

"Aw'right, aw'right. What you gett'n me involved in?"

"Might be a kidnapping. Might be a false lead. Thing is, we won't know for sure if you don't step it up. If it's what I think it is, our people won't be sitting, drinking coffee, while they wait for you to show up."

Zac and Gertie waited while the grumbling marshal saddled his riding animal, then Zac told him who they were looking for.

"Do you know a man named Faulkner? Gus and Esther Faulkner?"

"I know them. What's up with them?"

"Just take us to their place and we'll find out."

The marshal wasn't happy, but he led out. A short ten minutes later they pulled their horses to a halt as they heard a man shouting.

"Hei-aw, hei-aw git up there you bronks."

They watched in wonder as the man whipped the team with the loose reins, while a woman hung onto the seat back, as if she was afraid of falling off. The wagon skidded on the muddy trail leading from behind the house, turned sharply to the right, and lined out onto the town road.

Gertie heeled her horse out of the way while Zac and the marshal held fast to their positions. With their arms in the air they signalled 'stop'.

For just a few seconds the indication was that the driver had no intention of stopping. The look on his face said that he might just plow right through the riders. But when Zac pulled the Henry and sighted it at the wagon, the driver pulled back on the leathers. Slowly, the wagon ground to a halt.

The marshal hollered from where he was seated on his frightened gelding.

"You gone mad, Gus? That ain't no way to treat a team, nor a wagon neither, come to that. I'm guess'n you ain't head'n out fer a picnic down ta the river, so might be you should tell me jest wher ye were head'n fer."

Gus offered no explanation.

Zac convinced himself that the man looked guilty of something, but that might have just been his imagination.

The marshal said, "How about if'n ye were ta drive that wagon back inta the yard and we'll all have a little meet'n in the house, outa the rain."

Gus knew he was defeated. Just a few minutes. That's all he had needed. Just a few more minutes. But the news from up the hill hadn't come his way until after breakfast, this same morning. One of Big Mike's lesser followers came by the house with the news. The man was on his way to Fort Dodge. He seemed to be in a bit of a hurry.

Gus and Esther had jumped right into their get-away plan, moving as quickly as possible. They knew this day was likely to come, sooner or later. They already had the wagon loaded with the gear for the trail. All they had to do was grab some clothing and harness up.

Cheyenne was their goal. They would see what happened after they reached that first stop. Maybe they would head back east. But that probably wasn't going to happen now. So close. So close. They had almost made it.

If Big Mike wasn't already dead, Gus would kill him himself next time he came his way. How had they ever allowed Mike to get them involved in this nonsense anyway? Well, of course, it was the money, and the escape from the tedious toil of the mines. But, overall, it was a stupid decision, a plan that was doomed to failure. And who knew what was going to happen now?

CHAPTER THIRTY-ONE

Gertie ran her horse to the front of the house and bailed off into the mud. She was running up the stairs when she heard Zac hollering.

"Hold up there, Gertie! We don't know what's in there. Wait, let me go in first."

Gertie paid no attention, even though she knew Zac was right. But her little boy was supposed to be at this address. Nothing was holding her back now that she was here. She didn't stop running or bother answering Zac.

She pushed the door open and entered. A few seconds later she screamed. Zac was only ten steps behind her. He rushed into the house to see Gertie crumpled on the floor with a child enveloped in her arms. Both Gertie and the child were crying and clinging to each other.

The little boy was saying, "Mommy," over and over.

Zac squatted down beside the pair.

"Is that your boy? Is that Bucky?"

Between sobs Gertie managed to get out, "This

is my little Bucky. My sweet little boy."

She held him away from herself at arm's length, seemingly examining every part of him.

"My, but you've grown. What a big boy you've become."

When the little fellow reached for her, she folded him back into her protective arms. She was smiling and half-laughing and crying, all at once, with great tears swimming down her cheeks.

Zac was left in no doubt of the genuineness of her claim.

The stomping of boots on the back porch and the opening of the rear door announced the arrival of Gus and Esther Faulkner, followed by Marshal Haubner.

Rocky Haubner ushered the pair into the family room and pointed to the couch, a few feet from where Gertie and her baby were still sitting on the floor. He stood close to the pair, almost hovering over them, forcing them to tip their heads back to see him.

He started to say, "All right, you two, let's..."

Zac arrived from the back bedroom with a child holding each of his hands. A little girl was black. The boy was white.

"Looky here, what I found."

Rocky was speechless. He looked at the children and sputtered. Finally, he pointed at them and turned his eyes back to the couch, where the two escapees were sitting.

"Two more! Three kids! Is that all or are there more in the cellar? Of maybe in the attic? Or how about the barn loft? Come on, speak up, you two. What's going on? I need the whole story and I need it now."

It turned out to be a sordid tale of kidnapping and forced business partnerships. Of doing anything for money and power. Of desperate parents bowing to Big Mike's every whim on the promise that their children were well cared for and would one day be returned to them.

Zac had no real interest in the other two children. Although it satisfied him greatly to see them safe and the miscreants huddled in fear on the couch, he was content to leave the matter in the hands of the authorities.

He bent and picked Bucky from Gertie's arms.

"I'll hold the boy. You go find whatever clothing and what-all you'll need for a long trip. Gather it quickly and let's get out of here."

An hour later they stood under the shelter in front of the stage station. Gertie had a ticket to Santa Fe folded carefully in her pocket. The stage wasn't leaving for another two hours.

Zac walked into the stage station and asked for an envelope. Turning so no one could observe his actions, he tucked the money he had peeled off the bundle of bills, back at the tent the night before, into the envelope. He placed the envelope into his pocket before walking up close to Gertie. Her took her by the elbow and ushered her away from the others who were gathering for the stage.

He lifted the small bag of gold coins from his pocket and pressed it into her hands. Quietly, so no one else could hear, he said, "Let me hold the boy. He'll be fine with me for a short while. You get yourself down to that general store and buy some nice clothing for the two of you. There's more than enough in that sack to cover it.

"You probably already know this, but I'll say it anyway. You're a beautiful young woman. I'm sure that's what caused Mike to choose you over others.

"You don't have a husband along with you, but you have this child. Folks are going to judge you on what they see. If they see you dressed poorly, they will assume the worst. You need to dress and act the lady, if you expect to be accepted as a lady.

"You set a good appearance; you can demand respect. Those wet and wrinkled clothes won't do it. Nor will the boy's clothes. Go spend some money and see if there's somewhere you can change at the store. Throw away the stuff you're wearing now. You do that quickly and we'll still have time for lunch. By then it will be stage time."

At the hotel, with lunch spread before them, Zac reached into his pocket and pulled out the envelope of money. Glancing around the room to see who might be watching, he held it out to Gertie under the table.

Whispering, he said, "There's about three thousand in that envelope. You take it and care for it. Don't let anyone know you've got it. That's enough to get you wherever you decide to go, and to give you a new start.

"If I was you, I'd not stop in Santa Fe. It's too close. Someone may see you there and your nightmare could start all over again. But from Santa Fe you can find a road that'll take you in any direction you decide to go. And don't tell anyone the kidnap story. You never know where one of Big Mike's thugs might show up. You need to disappear for a while, maybe even change your name.

"Go wherever you wish but make it far away. It's my belief that if you demand respect, you'll get respect. Go far and make a new life. A good life."

As an after-thought he said, "My friends and I wish you every success."

Gertie took the envelope. She fingered it a few seconds, thinking. Finally, she said, "I suspect this is from Mike's safe. But that's dirty money. I appreciate your thoughts but how can I start a new, clean life with dirty money?"

"There's no such thing as dirty money, Gertie. Money has no life of its own. It isn't the money that's dirty. It was Mike himself, and those around him. You take the money and spend it carefully. And you leave the guilt to Mike. He'll have to answer to God for all his dirty deeds. Now, come on, we'll miss that stage if we don't get going."

Another woman with two little kids got on the stage, followed by two men who were clearly peddlers; travelling salesmen. They plopped down on the rear bench, pushed their sample cases under the seat and leaned back, as if this was a normal, tedious part of making a living.

Gertie shocked Zac by throwing her arms around his neck and kissing his cheek.

"Thank you, Zac. I know this has been a nightmare for you and your friends too. I'm so grateful for all you've done. And I'm beyond happy to know that Phoebe won't be facing what I lived through all those months. I promise to pray for each of you.

Stay safe. God Bless."

With that she stepped onto the stage. Zac passed the baby up to her and closed the door. The driver cracked his whip, let out a totally unnecessary yell and the stage rocked into motion, throwing mud in all directions.

Zac turned to his horse. He mounted but didn't put the animal into motion. He sat there watching until the stage was lost around a bend in the trail. The rain was still falling.

CHAPTER THIRTY-TWO

It was early afternoon. Zac was relieved to have Gertie on the stage and away from the need of any more assistance from him. He was also exhausted from a series of poor sleeps. He'd hoped the hours in the hotel bed the night before might prove to be sufficient but it wasn't. He feared his weariness was affecting his judgement. And he had become mortally tired of the rain.

He felt himself slipping. If there was anything at all to be thankful for in his dramatic mood swings it was that he usually felt them coming on. Sometimes he was able to counteract the darkness by busying himself in some project or pursuit, but usually all he could do was put himself into a position where the pressure would be the least harmful.

Riding slowly along the muddy street of Denver, leading the animal Gertie had purchased, he thought longingly of a warm bed and sleep filled oblivion. Almost of its own volition his gelding turned into the livery barn. Zac let it take the lead.

With the animals housed, wiped down and fed,

he waded through the mud to the hotel. Within minutes he was shed of his wet clothing and rolled in the blankets. Sleep took him almost instantly and held him for hours, not loosing its grip on him until the twilight of early evening. He struggled into his still damp underwear, wiggled into his shirt that seemed to want to stick to the damp underwear, and stood up to pull on his canvas pants. The wet socks were discarded. The boots accepted his feet only after he stamped several times on the floor. He was dressed, but he felt clammy and chilled.

Walking down the stairs at the hotel, listening to his feet squish in the wet boots and feeling the damp canvas pants slide up and down his legs, he thought, "I'm not too bright. I've got money in my pockets and these clothes need throwing away, even if they were dry."

He found a general store a block from the hotel. Within minutes he was loaded down with a wrapped package of new clothing, with a pair of boots laid over his shoulder, hanging from the tied-together laces. Draped over his arm was a bulky, sheepskin lined coat. He had never seen anything warmer. He had to have it.

Another few minutes in his hotel room had him decked out in the new duds, with his feet comfortable in the lace-up boots.

He left the pile of wet clothing on the floor and descended to the hotel foyer, where he decided he was hungry. Not fully trusting of the world, he had slung his saddle bags over his shoulder and picked up the Henry.

An hour later, fed and with one drink to get his blood flowing, he stood in the hotel foyer, watching the never-ending rain. The street was empty, everyone having found a better place to spend their evening. He felt rested but could still sense the battle to come with his inner darkness. He hated this whole thing that had become such a living part of him.

His mind drifted to the mine and his partners, and his responsibilities. He thought of the winter coming on and wondered how the group would handle the snow and cold. The tent wouldn't do; that was beyond question.

Then there was the carpetbag full of Big Mike's papers. What would the lawyer have to tell him about that? Was that going to distract him from the mine?

He stood at the window like a statue. The most of an hour went by before he noticed the rain dwindling off to a mere shower, then stop altogether. He stepped out of the hotel onto the boardwalk. Several men joined him, all of them studying the sky.

As they watched, a warming, friendly breeze arose over the mountains, blowing from west to east. The solid gray sky overhead broke into scattered overcast and then into individual clouds, all of them racing across the sky as if they were chasing each other.

Before long, the final rays of the sun, now hidden totally behind the mountains, but reflecting off the snow caps, and turning the edges of the small clouds to a yellowish-red color, cast a slight brightness to the sky.

The streets were still a swamp of mud and most folks' clothing was damp and sticking to their bodies, but if a person judged only by the sky, it had been a beautiful sunny day with the promise of another like it to follow.

A man standing a few feet away waved his arm at the sky and grinned at the men standing near him.

"Welcome to Colorado, fellas where almost anything can happen and most likely will."

Zac had spent many nights on patrol during his time with the cavalry. He found that he didn't mind night riding at all. In fact, being wrapped in darkness, away from prying eyes and those who might try to take advantage, was often a comfort to him.

He felt as rested as he was likely to get, knowing that returning to the hotel bed would mean hours of tossing and rolling, waiting for the dawn. And the unwelcome dreams.

Lately it seemed that he was often moving in a specific direction even before he consciously made the decision to step out. He didn't want to live his life on impulse, but on the other hand, when the darkness descended on him his considered decisions were suspect anyway.

So why not just go where his footsteps took him? Perhaps something inside, some inner drive, dare he say some leading from the Lord, was moving him forward.

Zac didn't understand any of that, any more than he understood where his darkness came from or where it went when it decided to give him a few days rest from the oppression.

These disjointed thoughts rambled through his brain as he stepped gingerly through the mud to the livery barn, trying to damage his new boots as little as possible. He hadn't really decided to step off the boardwalk. He simply found himself in the center of the mud and waste-clogged trail and could see no reason to turn back. His saddle bags were draped over his left shoulder and the Henry hung from his right hand. There was nothing but old clothing and worn-out boots left in the hotel room.

The hostler wasn't anywhere to be found so Zac weighted a paper five-dollar bill under a rock on the padded nail keg the old man usually sat on. It was overpayment for the couple of days boarding, but the man was a help with the horses. Zac didn't figure the fella had any more income than he needed for surviving day to day. It wouldn't hurt to show a bit of gratitude.

With both horses saddled, Zac mounted his gelding, leading the second animal. He had offered to pay Gertie for the horse, but she wouldn't hear of it.

"Take it and re-sell it if you want. Or keep it. And if you see someone with a big enough fire burning, throw that wretched saddle on the blaze and know that I'm grateful to be free of the thing."

Zac had more money in the bank than he ever dreamed possible, but he knew he still wouldn't be able to bring himself to discard the old saddle.

The struggle of providing for the family on fifty acres in East Texas had left an indelible impression on his mind, first as he watched his parents nearly work themselves to death when he was a child, and then he and Maddy on their own land.

He would keep the saddle.

The clouds and rain seemed to have moved on. The night wasn't warm, but it was pleasant enough. Wrapped in his new coat and clothed in dry pants and shirt, he was prepared for the hours on the trail back to Idaho Springs.

CHAPTER THIRTY-THREE

The night and the trail were both long, but Zac contentedly let the gelding choose its own pace. He allowed his mind to wander, thinking of the gold mine and his new friends, and the wealth they were each slowly accumulating. He had no fixed opinion on what they should do next, but he was certain the operation was becoming larger than what the four eager partners could manage on their own.

Dominik was firm in his opinion that there was a range of other minerals they were ignoring in the search for gold. If the latest assay, ordered just a few days ago, confirmed that, they would have other decisions to make. It was obvious that even with the early profits, which were large numbers for people who had started with so little, they didn't have the capital to expand operations or include other mining methods.

With Dominik being the only one who understood any of the mineralization details, Zac and Lem were a bit lost and unable to contribute much to the decision making.

Phoebe, seemingly content with tent living, was working as hard as the men. Keeping everyone fed in the primitive conditions was no small task.

Back at the beginning of the venture, Phoebe was sure she could keep all their clothing and bedding clean, along with her other tasks. At least, she was determined to try.

Around mid-morning on the first wash day, Zac had walked into the tent, hoping to find a cup of coffee. The exhausted woman was brushing hair out of her eyes as she stretched to relieve her sore back.

They had no rope to string out for a drying line. Phoebe had wet clothing draped on every surface, with a tub-full yet to be washed. Zac took a quick look and started to laugh. He had seldom seen such a hopeless situation. No one person could do all that had to be done.

Phoebe took exception to his laughter and was working up a response, struggling between her slave upbringing and her still-respectful freedom.

Zac said, "Phoebe, I'm thinking y'all need to finish what you've started here, but that'll be the end of it. From now on this will all go down to the laundry in town.

"As for lunch, how be if I send Lem in to put a meal together. He's pretty handy around the pots and pans. Would that suit y'all?"

Phoebe was so tired she could hardly speak. Again, she brushed hair from her eyes with the back of her hand and nodded.

"Send him along."

Zac chuckled again at the memory.

Whiling away the hours of darkness as the horse

plodded its way towards Idaho Springs, Zac was encouraged and lightened by this reminiscence. So much had happened. It almost felt like many months had gone by but in reality, it was only weeks.

It's true that it was weeks of brutally hard work, but none of them had shied away from the toil, nor had there been any complaints. And the results had been spectacular, at least in the eyes of these amateur miners.

His thoughts took a darker path as his mind turned to Big Mike and his kidnapping of Phoebe. How badly that might have turned out shook him to the core.

He hadn't hesitated, nor did he really have regrets, for he had done what was necessary. But the fact was, he had killed again; willingly, eagerly, he had killed the kidnapper.

In every ounce of his being, he wished to live a life of peace; to be left alone. He had done enough violence; he wanted no more. His mind and his emotions were constantly on a razor's edge. He needed peace to allow time for the memories to fade and for his troubled soul to heal.

But Big Mike had challenged him. Challenged them all, really. Using Phoebe as a pawn, the big man had thought to see the mining group fold, and pander to his demands, as others had done.

But Zac wasn't the folding kind, had never been, even before he put on a uniform. If Mike had been a better judge of character, he would still be alive.

The dark thoughts, as dark as the night around him, were threatening again. To reverse his mind's direction he started to sing, hoping to cast a different light on his soul. There wasn't one person in the whole world who had ever asked him to sing. Not twice anyway. But the horses didn't seem to mind and there was no one else around, as far as he could see through the dark. So, he sang.

Mostly what he knew were hymns. Oh, he knew a few ribald tunes from his army days, but he was better off to set those aside. He sang one hymn after another. When he couldn't bring all the words back from memory, he hummed the tune until he stumbled onto the next familiar lyrics. He sang until his throat could produce no more sound.

He was starting to fight a largely losing battle with his darkness of soul until he saw a few random lights in the distance, indicating the outskirts of Idaho Springs. Forcing his mind and his body into a better direction, he sat up straighter in the saddle, realizing he had been slumping. His old cavalry officers would have drilled him unmercifully if they had seen that on the parade square.

As Zac rode into town, the sun was starting to peek over the horizon. More lights were coming on and a few people were moving about. Zac realized that he was hungry again. Perhaps that was a good sign. In his darkest times he didn't think of food, sometimes going for many hours without even a sip from his canteen.

He had only eaten in town a couple of times but there was a fondness in his mind for the little hole in the wall eatery where the partners had met Dominik.

After caring for the horses, Zac made his way to the little eatery and went in. The same woman was serving the busy tables. She showed no sign of recognition. She simply called to him over the heads of the men at the next table, "Flapjacks or eggs?"

It seemed she was holding to her belief in a simple menu.

"Eggs."

With his belly full and the horses rested, he tightened the cinch on the gelding and mounted, wishing to be home, at the mine. But first he would see the lawyer, if the man was this early to work.

There was a light showing in the little office, so Zac tied the animals and pushed the door open.

"Wasn't sure you'd be working this early."

Recognising the voice, Gomer Radcliff didn't bother looking up. He continued to peruse the document lying before him, with his forehead resting in the palm of his left hand, his pencil entwined in the fingers of his right hand. Judging by the crackle in his voice he wasn't fully awake yet.

"I wouldn't be here this early except for this can of worms you loaded me down with. I'm hoping you aren't bringing more work with you. I might be the rest of my life sorting this one out."

Zac didn't bother responding. Instead he asked, "What's happened so far? Did you find any accounts for Big Mike?"

"I found two accounts. The banks sent messages down to have their Denver head offices search their records. We'll know on that by and by."

"Did the banks agree to hold the funds?"

The lawyer leaned back and smiled, like the cat that caught the canary.

"Better than that. I got the judge to sign off on a court order sealing the accounts. No one can touch them until the court has its say."

Zac was surprised but pleased.

"And how exactly did you manage that?"

"Normally, my gold mining friend, my natural instinct towards modesty would prevent me from any hint of self aggrandizement. There's bigger and stronger lawyers all over the country, but if you were to take a close look at those framed diplomas on the wall behind me you would see the words, in small print, 'With Honors'.

"That means I have every right to expect intelligent things from myself. My dear old father, who was a smallish man himself, told me often that if you can't compete in brawn, you can still beat them with brains.

"So I carefully prepared my arguments with all the evidence at my disposal, which by the way, is exactly zero, and with wit and wile I convinced the judge that you were on the side of the angels and that my sole purpose was to see that right was maintained. As convincing as all of that was, it was also convenient that I play chess once a week with the judge."

Zac stood wondering what all the words boiled down to as Gomer Radcliff entertained himself, enjoying Zac's puzzled look.

When the lawyer felt Zac was ready for more news he continued.

"I accomplished another thing as well. You are now the official, court-appointed trustee of all things pertaining to one Mister Mike Mullins.

"And I, sir, am appointed to handle all financial transactions in this matter, receiving my directions from you, of course. My one regret is that the deceased saloon and office no longer have value. I know of no one at all who would part with good money for a burned-out shell. Mind you, the out-house still stands, so there's that."

Zac felt his knees go weak. He stepped forward and flopped into one of the chairs facing the lawyer's desk. He sat silently for a half minute, searching the face of this lawyer he had hired, and wondering what the penalty would be for throttling the man.

"Why in the world did you do that? I've got a mine to work and partners to stand beside. I've got responsibilities. I can't be running around trying to sort out things I know nothing about. And any-way, since I'm the one who ushered Big Mike out of this troubled world and into the next, some might see a conflict of interest."

Lawyer Radcliff smiled.

"It can all be dealt with. And my bet is you will understand it all by the time you've completed the task and things are settled."

"What about if I hired a different lawyer and you were to tell your chess playing judge that I've threatened your life if he doesn't pull back on his decision?"

"Aww. You're not going to do that. In fact, you don't really want to do that. This is a chance to help the poor and needy, the downtrodden and abused. Just the way you helped that other woman in the process of helping your own partner. Only now, you get to help the miners who had their property either stolen or compromised.

"It's what you do, my friend. It's who you are."

Zac had no words. The lawyer's wordy rambling had tied his mind in knots. He should have had his eggs and gone back to the mine. In fact, that's ex-actly what he was going to do. The sooner, the bet-ter. He needed to think this all over. He rose from the chair and in three steps was at the door. As he started to pull the door closed the lawyer hollered after him,

"Bring those documents in."

Zac ignored him.

As he swung onto the gelding he said, "Now that's a fine fix we're in."

The gelding seemed to have no response.

CHAPTER THIRTY-FOUR

Zac led his two horses into the corral at the mine and worked them over just a bit before closing the gate and heading to the tent.

Phoebe was standing in the tent doorway, watching. She greeted him with, "So, you've either been at the hotel in Idaho Springs or you've been riding all night." She left the unasked question lie right there.

Zac's weary grin answered the question for her.

"Got any coffee left?"

"Sit yourself down. I'll get the other men. You can tell us all at once."

With the four partners settled around the new table, each nestling a cup of hot coffee in their hands, a welcome bit of heat on this fall morning, Zac went over the highlights of his trip to Denver. He didn't figure they needed to know all the small details.

When he was finished, Phoebe had a comment and a question.

"So, Gertie has her son back and is on her way to

Santa Fe. That completes what you started to do for her. But what about those other two kids? You say one of them was black?"

Zac picked up on the question wrapped carefully inside the other question. What Phoebe was really asking was, "What do you plan to do about the other kids?"

He hadn't really planned on doing anything about them. He didn't want anything to do with solving another kidnapping, nor of finding the parents for the captured kids.

"I left them in good hands. I expect the law or the lawyers or the courts, or someone will sort it all out."

Phoebe often held her thoughts back. It wasn't long ago she was referring to Zac as Mr. Isaac. To come right out with a bold confrontation was more than she could contemplate. Still, she felt strongly about the kids.

"I hope your faith in the law is justified."

She dared say no more, but she was clearly doubtful of the ability of the law to handle the delicate matter of kidnapped children. Especially a black child.

After a few moments of silence Zac said, "There's more. I saw the lawyer in Idaho Springs on my way through this morning. He's got a court order protecting Big Mike's bank accounts until the matter is sorted out. He's also had himself appointed as financial controller over the whole mess.

"The problem is though, that he went and got me appointed as trustee of Mike's estate."

Dominik looked puzzled.

"What that mean, this trustee?"

Lem and Phoebe bent a bit closer, waiting for the answer, as if they didn't understand it either.

"It means that I'm the one who is supposed to sort the whole mess out. The lawyer will help, of course, but it will still be a lot of work. And if some of the old mine owners have left the area the matter may never be resolved."

When nothing was said by the other three partners Zac continued.

"It sounds like a lot of work and time to me. Time I won't be any use to you around the mine. Perhaps if I talk to the judge, he'll remove me and put someone else into the position."

Phoebe was quick to answer.

"No. You're the right man. Especially for those kids. I'm thinking the kids are from Idaho Springs. We should ride back down there and bring them here until we find their parents."

Zac shook his head, as if he hadn't heard correctly.

"We? We have a mine to work. How do you figure there's any 'we' involved in this? Are you planning on walking the streets or knocking on doors, asking folks if they've lost a child?"

Phoebe took a bold approach.

"No, what we're going to do is hire some workers to help you men pound rock. You're all working yourselves nearly to death and there's no need of it. We're making a profit. To spend a bit of it on workers sounds like good business to me.

"Dominik says we should be starting a second cut to follow the seam that disappeared into the wall. He's chipped around for a foot or more. He figures the quartz keeps on going.

"We should hire four men. With Dominik studying the rocks, and Lem helping me with making meals, the mine work will go just fine."

The three men studied Phoebe in silence. Clearly, she had put some thought into the matter.

Zac shook his head, studying this former slave, wondering what other thoughts might be forming themselves in her freed mind.

"And what plans do you have for me, except solving all the problems Mike's demise left the community with?"

Phoebe smiled, as if the answer was so obvious, she couldn't understand why Zac couldn't see.

"Why you and I are taking the wagon down to Denver in the morning. We're going to get those kids before the do-gooders ship them off to some home for orphans or some such."

The light went on in Zac's mind. Lem and Phoebe had two little boys stolen and sold off. They had not been seen since. And neither of the former slaves had fully recovered from the terrible loss. When Zac mentioned that one child was black, Phoebe's heart was struck with the need to do something.

Zac rose from the table and left without a word. He walked to the mine entrance, where the two hired men were stationed, alternating their time between resting and standing guard.

Dominik and Lem followed him to the mine. Zac stood on the tailing pile and spoke to the guard on duty. The second man was apparently taking some rest in the sunshine.

"We haven't met. I'm Zac, one of the owners. What do they call you?"

"Toby Klassen. My partner is Taylor Rooney."

"Give Your partner a call. I need to talk to both of you."

With the two men facing the mine owners, clearly wondering if their guard jobs were finished, they cast their eyes from one man to the other.

Zac asked, "What are we paying you fellas?"

Phoebe had quietly walked up behind the partners.

"We're paying them a dollar a day and feeding them their noon meal. They're here at seven in the morning. They go home at six in the afternoon."

Zac looked at her and then back to the guards.

"And what's the going rate for a hammer and steel man?"

Toby answered, "Dollar and a half, ten-hour day. Six days a week."

Zac glanced at his partners and then turned to Phoebe.

"What do you think, Phoebe? You've been considering this already."

Phoebe spoke directly to the guards.

"No other mine lays a meal on. How does the dollar and a half, with your noon meal included, sound to you? You go back on the hammer and steel. I don't think we need guards now. We'll hire two more men. You'll alternate between hammer and steel or shovel and wheelbarrow. You'll do what has to be done."

Toby and Taylor looked at each other and shrugged. Again, Toby was the spokesman.

"We figured this guarding wasn't going to last. We'll take the other job. We could bring a couple of good men up too, if that would help you."

Zac nodded, "All right, you bring two more men

in the morning. Finish out the day the way you are. Tomorrow you're on the hammer."

Phoebe had one more thing to say.

"We'll trust you men, until you prove that you can't be trusted. The day we find any gold going into your pockets is going to be a real unhappy day for you."

No one had anything to say on that matter.

Zac was seeing Phoebe in a new light. He knew she didn't learn what she knew about wages and business during her slave days. It must have been the years of leading by Mrs. Watson that had opened her mind and taught her to think. It had probably started with the grocery shopping, but Zac knew he would never ask.

But now there were some things he had to think through. It was time for a walk. Alone. He couldn't think with others chattering around him.

CHAPTER THIRTY-FIVE

Early the next morning Zac and Phoebe were headed down the hill, on their way to Denver. The carpet bag of papers was stowed under the seat, ready for the lawyer. Zac had removed the bundle of cash, hiding it in the big tent.

When they arrived in Idaho Springs, Zac drove directly to Big Mike's locked-up house. He loaded a mattress from one of the beds into the back of the wagon. On top of that went a bundle of blankets and a few pillows. Bringing the kids up the hill at wagon speed would be a long day, plus a part of a night. If the kids were to be comfortable, they would need the bedding.

Of course, there was no guarantee the marshal would release the kids to them. But Phoebe was pretty determined. Zac would leave the whole thing between the two of them.

From Mike's house they drove to the general store. Phoebe picked out enough food items to cover the needs of the two-day wagon trip, plus some treats for the kids.

On the way out of town, Zac stopped at the lawyer's office. With a grin, he dropped the carpet bag full of papers on the man's desk and waited for a reaction. The lawyer looked into the bag and groaned.

"This might not be such a good idea after all. How am I going to sort out this mess?"

Zac chuckled and walked to the wall behind the desk. He glanced at the diplomas, held his fingers on some small print and said, "Well, looky here. It says, 'with honors'. Imagine that."

Gomer Radcliff laid his forehead back on the palm of his hand. "Get out of here!"

As Zac was chuckling and heading towards the door the lawyer held out a piece of paper to him.

"Your appointment as trustee. Signed by the judge, all fit and proper."

Zac stuffed it into a shirt pocket without looking at it.

After a long trip down the hill and a night in the hotel, Zac was ready to face the marshal.

The quiet hours on the wagon seat and the lonely night at the hotel had brought unwelcome and uncontrollable thoughts roiling through his mind. The only partial solution he had found to his horrible depressions was activity and then more activity, as if the use of his muscles and mind would drive the darkness away. Or at least hold it at bay.

Confronting the marshal would be a welcome relief from the stillness.

When he arrived at Rebecca's the next morning, where Phoebe had spent the night, Rebecca insisted that he sit down to breakfast with the others.

With a large breakfast tucked behind his belt

Zac pushed his chair back. Sipping his second cup of coffee, he started to understand why Phoebe was drawn to this pleasant house. It was a welcoming place to all who came in peace.

It was true that all of Rebecca's borders were black but that didn't prevent Zac from feeling the welcome.

The town was coming alive when they pulled up in front of the marshal's office. Zac swung down from the wagon seat and pushed the office door open.

"Shut the door, I'm purely not attracted to an early morning chill. Reminds me that winter's just around the corner."

"Seems there's not much you're attracted to or happy with. But I'm thinking I can change that this morning, chilly or no."

The marshal leaned back in his wooden swivel chair and took a long look at his visitor.

"The last time you was here, you caused me no end of work and trouble. Ain't done with it all yet. Got Gus and Esther held as prisoners in the town lock-up, taking up my time.

"Now you come with more promises. OK, I saw your lips moving and I hear some noise, but I don't hear anything yet that helps my day."

"Well, how about this? I've come to relieve you of the burden of those two kids."

The marshal leaned forward, as if the chair was his mode of expressing his thoughts.

"And just how are you going to do that?"

Zac answered, "Big Mike's business was all up in Idaho Springs. I've been appointed trustee of his estate."

He dropped the unopened trustee appointment document on the marshal's desk.

"We have reason to believe those kids belong to a couple of mine owners Mike was blackmailing, just like he was forcing Gertie to toe the line by holding her son captive.

"I can't imagine how he ever figured he could get away with such as that but there she lays.

"Anyway, we managed to pair Gertie up with her baby. I suspect we'll find the other parents up the hill, as well. Why don't you just take me to the kids? We'll load them up and you'll be shut of the matter."

Zac could see the thoughts churning in the marshal's mind. He waited, figuring he had already said all that needed saying. After a lengthy pause the marshal stood to his feet.

"Wait till I get my horse saddled. I'll meet you out front."

It took the most of a half hour, winding through several back streets of Denver before the marshal pulled up in front of a large, white-painted house. He tied his animal and walked through the gate. Zac tied off the team, then he and Phoebe followed.

On the veranda, Marshal Haubner turned the crank on the brass bell, creating an annoying, ringing sound inside the house. He repeated that action two more times before a pretty, black girl dressed as a maid, opened the door.

Rocky Haubner didn't wait for the girl to ask their business.

"Miz Grinder in? Tell her Marshal Haubner's need'n to see her."

A stately looking woman, wrapped tightly in a flowing dress that probably fit her sometime in the past, gently eased the maid aside.

"Thank you, Tillie. I'll talk with the marshal."

Tillie stepped back and disappeared, as if that was her practiced response to her employer.

Asking no questions, but simply tilting her head back grandly, as if she was condescendingly receiving a lesser mortal, Hermoine Grinder waited for the marshal to state his reasons for being on her porch.

Having met people like her in his past, and finally seeing through their hollowness years before, Zac came near to laughing out loud.

The marshal whipped off his hat, as was the custom of the day.

"Miz Grinder, these folks have come for the children."

Mrs. Grinder turned her haughty look first at Zac and then, tilting her head back even further, at Phoebe.

"And why would I release the children into their unknown hands?"

Rocky Haubner had his limits of deference to this pompous woman. It hadn't taken long to reach that limit.

At the first arrival of Mrs. Grinder he had pulled his hat off and held it in his hands. Now, he put it back on his head, adjusting it carefully. He smiled just a bit, like a coyote might smile at a rabbit.

"Why, Miz Grinder, simply because I say so. That's all there is to it, really. Nothing else to the matter. Now, please bring the children here. They have a long day ahead of them and they need to get on the road."

"And where do you think you get the authority

to demand anything of me? The committee and I have found a perfectly suitable orphanage to place the children in, although they were reluctant to accept the black child."

She glanced again at Phoebe.

"You should be grateful that you had our assistance. The folks from the Cheyenne Children's Hostel telegraphed that they will be here tomorrow to transport them."

"Well, I'm sure we're all grateful for that, Miz Grinder but my order still stands. I want the children brought here now."

The door swung open a bit more widely. The black maid stood there with a child clutching her left hand while a little black girl held firmly to her neck as Tillie embraced her in her right arm. Without asking permission from her employer, and saying nothing, she passed the girl to Phoebe and held the boy's hand out to Zac.

Mrs. Grinder sucked in a big breath and turned to her maid.

"Tillie, I'll not have this insubordination. Go pick up your things and leave my home."

Tillie didn't look surprised nor disappointed. She simply nodded her head and disappeared again. Perhaps working for Mrs. Grinder hadn't been all the young lady had hoped it would be.

The marshal turned to go, but some inner thought held Zac back.

Phoebe noticed and stood quietly herself, waiting. Without seeming to question, the little girl had transferred her affection to Phoebe. The little arms circling her neck brought back long held memories from decades before.

Zac was sometimes unpredictable. Phoebe would try to run interference if such was required.

The marshal noticed that the other two were not following. He stopped and waited, studying Zac and Phoebe.

Mrs. Grinder waved her hand as if dismissing lesser beings.

"You have what you came for, Mister Haubner. I doubt you have any idea what you're doing but take them and go. And God help those children, with these two…"

She stopped talking but held her fierce look on Zac and Phoebe.

Zac had endured about all he could take.

"Woman, you need to understand that Phoebe, here, is every inch a lady. Her husband and I are partners in a mining venture. They are honourable in every respect. I doubt as how the same could be said for you."

Mrs. Grinder looked as if she was ready to explode but Zac turned his back on her and started down the stairs, still holding the boy's hand.

Before the departing group reached the bottom of the stairs Tillie was back. She was dressed in her street clothes and her arms were loaded with her few items of spare clothing, along with the children's clothing, and a couple of small toys.

She eased past her ex-employer and stepped onto the porch. After a brief eye contact with Phoebe, who was looking back up at her, the young girl smiled, crossed the veranda, and skipped lightly down the stairs, as if experiencing new freedom. Phoebe suspected it was loyalty to the children that had held her in this cold house.

At the wagon, Phoebe placed the baby gently on the mattress. She then took the unwrapped bundle of clothing from Tillie's arms and laid it in the back of the wagon.

Zac lifted the little boy onto the mattress, where he experimented with jumping on the soft surface before moving to the side, sticking his thumb into his mouth, and taking a hold on the wooden sides of the wagon box. He had a questioning look on his face, as if he'd never seen a mattress before.

Tillie said, "These poor little people have been tossed about so much they don't know who they are anymore. I'm truly hoping you can find the proper homes for them. I'm sure the parents are frantic with worry."

Phoebe touched Tillie's hand, holding it for just a moment.

"Do you have somewhere to go?"

"Nowhere I wish to be Miss. But away from this awful place would be a good start."

Zac turned around from the high seat.

"Climb up here, the two of you. We can figure it out along the way."

The marshal had simply tipped his hat to Zac, grinned, and ridden away. Zac was surprised at the casual way the children's welfare was handled. He pictured his own little Minnie in similar circumstances and shuddered a bit at the thought.

Tillie stepped onto the wheel hub and then rolled herself into the back of the wagon, clutching her flowing skirt the whole time. She gathered up the little girl, whose age Phoebe guessed was around two years, and held her on her lap while she leaned against the side boards.

The four-year-old boy was entertaining himself, bouncing on the mattress again.

Phoebe had to raise her voice a bit to be heard over the rumbling of the steel rimmed wheels on the dirt and gravel roadway, when she turned to talk to Tillie.

"You speak very well, Tillie. It took me years, along with a lot of teaching from a good friend, to lose my slave talk, but I still don't come up to your standard. How does that come to be?"

Tillie set the baby down on the mattress and stood. She stepped up to the seat and held onto the backrest, to make talking easier.

"I was never a slave. As an adult anyway. I was born in the south, but my brother and I were very young when we were bought by the man who raised us. He was on a business trip down south and happened to witness a slave sale.

"He says it broke his heart when they started offering children. He bought all he could afford, which was just the two of us. He often said he wished he could have afforded the other three children being offered.

"He and his wife gave us a good home and lots of love."

The intensity of Phoebe's gaze startled Tillie. It was a moment before she continued with her story.

"My parents weren't rich, but we weren't poor either. I've been to good schools. So, it all came more or less naturally."

Phoebe let all that soak in for a moment before asking, "How do you happen to be alone in Denver and working for the likes of that woman back there?"

Phoebe thought she might have heard a quick intake of breath. Perhaps it was the start of a sob, she couldn't be sure.

Tillie answered, "My folks and a couple of my uncles and aunts joined a wagon train coming west before the war. The uncles turned for home, half-way along. They got discouraged with the distance and the dry plains we were crossing. They chose to return to their known surroundings.

"It was a long, long trip but my parents and I arrived safely. Father was an excellent tailor and clothing retailer. He set up a very nice shop in town. 'Harper's tailoring and fine men's wear', he called it. The business was doing fine, but a year or so ago Father took sick.

"I still don't know what disease gripped him, but whatever it was, it proved to be contagious.

"My brother was away at the time. Mother sent me to stay with friends to keep me safe while she nursed Father. The outcome was, of course, totally predictable. Mother was taken with the illness and I lost them both.

"They left me a bit to live on, but not much. I still have most of what I inherited when I sold the store. I only work so I don't have to dig into the little bit I've got set by."

Phoebe said, "I think you should come with us for now. You can always come back here if you wish. We'll need help with the children until we get it all sorted out. They already know and trust you, so you'll be a comfort to them.

"There's money in the estate we're working to settle. I'm sure we can at least match the wage you were earning in that big house.

"And we'll tell you the whole story when we don't have to shout to do it."

CHAPTER THIRTY-SIX

It was drawing on to midnight when Zac pulled the wagon with its weary passengers up to the door of Big Mike's house. The women carried the children in while Zac toted the mattress back to the bed it came from. They were quickly settled down, with Phoebe taking one bed, along with the little boy and Tillie in the second bed with the baby.

Zac lit a lantern and led the tired mules to the small stable, after watering them. A manger full of hay would hold them till morning.

Zac would make do on a corner of the floor, rolled in a blanket right inside the door. No one was going to open that door without moving him. With that measure of security, and his Henry and Colt close by, the group put the long hill trail behind them and slept.

The challenge of where to start faced the group in the morning. Phoebe was anxious to get back to the mine, but the welfare of the children had to come first. Breakfast at the hole in the wall café they had come to think of as a comforting place, where everyone was made welcome and the food was good, got the day started in the right direction.

The next stop was at the lawyer's office. Gomer Radcliff looked as if he hadn't been to bed since Zac was last in his office, two days before.

Zac stood inside the door, trying not to laugh. The two men studied each other while Gomer absently shuffled papers on his desk. Zac was the first to speak.

"You look like you could benefit from breakfast and about a dozen cups of coffee."

Gomer stood and reached for his coat. Without a word he stepped forward. Zac opened the door, indicated the wagon, and said, "Hop on."

The lawyer was a moment sorting it all out. Finally, he said, "You found the children."

Zac ignored the obvious answer and instead introduced the ladies. Tillie offered to swing into the back of the wagon to make room for the lawyer on the seat, but Gomer waved her off.

"Thank you, Miss. I'll be just fine back here."

Without trying to talk over the noise of the steel wheels on the rocky road, they sat in silence while Zac drove back to the café.

With several chairs bunched around the small table, they shared the stories of the past two days. Zac went first because the tale was short, and the evidence of their success was sitting right there at the same table.

He noticed Gomer's eyes flicking frequently in Tillie's direction. The young black girl was, indeed, very attractive, with a figure that would turn heads. It certainly turned the lawyer's head, tired as he was.

For her part, Tillie pretended not to notice while she fussed with the baby.

They let the hungry and tired man finish his breakfast before telling what he had found.

Zac and Phoebe seemed to have unlimited tolerance for coffee, while Tillie asked for a cup of tea. The waitress brought the children a small glass of milk each.

Finally, Gomer pushed his plate away and looked around the group.

"Thank you. That hit the spot."

Zac chuckled a bit before saying, "I won't ask how many hours you've been at that pile of papers. Maybe just tell us what you've found so far."

Gomer looked around the room. He was cautious about being overheard with others sitting so close.

"How about we go back to the office. In fact, I'll walk back. I need to stretch my legs a bit."

Zac joined the lawyer on the walk while Phoebe drove the team. With just the two chairs in the small office, Zac was left standing. The ladies took the chairs while the children played on the floor.

Gomer indicated a small stack of papers on one side of the desk.

"These are deeds and claims for mines Mike Mullins owned outright or professed to own."

He laid his hand on another small stack.

"These are mines and claims he was receiving royalties from, as part owner."

He touched a third pile.

"There are other strange claims here, claims that are not quite so clear. Also, a couple of town properties he seems to have title to. All in all, it's a substantial amount, if the mines are worth what Mike was valuing them at. Of course, his saloon property no longer has much value."

Zac chose to ignore the dig about the burned down saloon.

Tillie asked the first question. "Are any of those owners black?"

Gomer smiled a bit as he looked at her.

"Well, there are no tintypes included here, and I can't tell from the names, so I don't have a ready answer for you. I'd guess though, from the fact that that little girl sitting at your feet is black, the chances are pretty good."

Zac asked the next question.

"Have you had time to examine the records at the claims office?"

"No, that will be my work for today."

Phoebe spoke for the first time.

"That's assuming you can stay awake."

Gomer smiled at her.

"Yes, making that assumption."

They were all silent for a bit before Gomer asked, "What about all of you? Where can I find you when I need you?"

Zac answered for the group.

"Phoebe and I should really return to the Freedom. I can come back down whenever I'm needed. Tillie has no real responsibility in this, but she'd like to stay with it until it's all sorted out and the children are cared for properly.

"We offered her a decent wage from the estate funds to care for the little ones. She thinks she'd like to keep the children at Mike's old house. That's where we stayed last night. But it's a ways out of town and pretty isolated. I don't like the thought of her being alone there with two little ones. Can you think of a better location for them?"

Gomer rose to his feet.

"Let's go see my landlady. There are two or three empty rooms I know she'd like to be gaining rent from. Missus Templeton is a widow. Depends on the rents to hold it all together. I'm thinking she'll welcome Tillie and the kids. It's close enough to walk too, so Tillie wouldn't be stuck out in the country where she can't get to town.

"Of course, if this all goes well, the children will soon be back with their parents."

The group left the wagon where the team could rest in the shade. The boarding house was less than a fifteen-minute walk.

Gomer gave the landlady a quick explanation of the issue the group was trying to sort out.

Mrs. Templeton nodded her understanding. With a simple, "Follow me," the landlady showed Tillie to a room.

"Will this do if we bring in a cot for the little boy?"

Tillie confirmed the arrangement and the deal was set.

Zac counted out one week's rent.

Within one half hour Tillie and the children were settled into the nice, sunny room. A cot was pulled in and placed close to the big bed so the little boy would have his own sleeping place but would still be close to Tillie, who he was treating almost as he would his mother.

With everything settled, Gomer walked Zac and Phoebe to the door.

"I'm going to catch a couple hours of rest, then I'll walk back up to the office. I'll get to the claims' office this afternoon. When I find something out, I'll get a horse from the livery and ride up to the Freedom to let you know."

CHAPTER THIRTY-SEVEN

Two days later, Gomer Radcliff staggered into the yard at the boarding house and flopped into an oversized wicker chair on the veranda. He was weary beyond description after a day of riding from mine to mine looking for owners, or information on past owners.

Mrs. Templeton was sitting in her favorite rocking chair with a sleepy little boy on her broad lap. Tillie, as usual, was holding the girl.

Whispering, so as not to wake the boy, Mrs. Templeton said, "Lemonade on the counter in the kitchen. You'll have to help yourself. All the time assuming you can walk that far."

Gomer removed his hat, setting it on the floor beside the chair.

"I'll own up to being a bit weary, that's a fact. I haven't ridden that many miles in years. But lemonade sounds good. I'll just rest a moment before I tempt my tired legs any further."

Tillie eased the child from her lap into her arms and stood. With a mischievous grin she placed the girl on Gomer's knees.

"Here, you hold Cierra. I'll bring you a glass."

The lawyer, full of smarts and with honors spelled out on his law degree had no idea at all what to do with a baby. Both women chuckled as they watched the helpless expression form on his face.

With the cool lemonade securely in Gomer's hand and the baby safely back with Tillie, Gomer took a sip, paused, and laid his head against the high back of the chair. He was asleep almost instantly.

Mrs. Templeton managed to lift the lemonade glass from the lawyer's hand and set it on the floor.

"Let him sleep", she whispered, "I expect he's earned a rest."

***

Early the next morning, Gomer was back in the saddle, headed up the hill to the Freedom. It was his first visit to the mine. To say he was impressed at the amount of work done by the small group would be nothing but the truth. The men were all working deep inside the mine. The lawyer could hear the clanking of hammer on steel but could see no one.

Phoebe, cleaning up breakfast dishes, watched the lawyer approach. He sat the saddle well enough. He just looked a bit out of practice, and perhaps a bit stiff and saddle sore. She walked out and opened the gate on the small corral.

"Get down. Rest yourself. There's coffee left from breakfast. You help yourself. I'll get Zac."

Sitting around the table, Zac and Phoebe listened carefully to the lawyer's report.

"I found the owners of those mines Mike was claiming shares in. One of them is black. Not really a young man. Almost seems too old to have a baby girl. But you never know, perhaps he had him a younger wife.

"I didn't talk with him directly. I saved myself a long ride with information gained from another miner.

"I said nothing to anyone about why I was asking the questions. It got a bit awkward a time or two, what with the miners being suspicious and wondering, and me say'n near to nothing.

"Everyone knows about Big Mike, of course. So, while they're wondering how that's all going to work out, a lawyer shows up asking questions. I'd wonder too if I were in their boots.

"So now I need your advice. Should I look for the old owners that Mike said he bought out completely or deal more closely with this first group and then move on to the others? We have to consider that some of the old owners may have moved out of the country."

Zac interjected, "Or they could be dead."

Gomer received that suggestion with a grim look.

"Yes, indeed, they could be dead."

Phoebe offered her opinion.

"It seems to me that finding the parents of those two babies has become more important than the financial matters."

Zac and Gomer barely glanced at each other before they both nodded.

"There's no question," said Zac. "No question at all. How would it be if I were to ride back down with you? We'll talk to each of those owners again and try to settle a big chunk of the matter today."

With the plan agreed upon, Phoebe refilled Gomer's cup while Zac went to speak to the men in the mine. A quick change into cleaner pants and a just-washed shirt, and Zac was ready to ride.

There were four mines that Mike had claimed partial ownership in. Zac and Gomer chose to visit the black owner last, knowing that if the child was his, there would be work to do, both legally and personally.

The first two owners the men visited offered almost duplicate stories. They had proven up on small, but prosperous mines. The mineral finds were not substantial enough to interest the big mining companies, but they were certainly profitable enough to capture the full attention of a single working owner, with a couple of hired workers. And in the case of these two mines, capture the interest of Big Mike.

Zac asked one of the men how it all came about.

"What attracted Mike to your operation? The hills are swarming with miners, so why you?"

"I wondered about that. I had to be careful who I talked to because Mike threatened serious violence, not just to me but to my wife and family, too. With the men that were hanging around him, I was pretty sure he meant every word of it. And then, just to reinforce the point, he would have a couple of his goons ride past our home every few days. They'd sit out front grinning for a few minutes and then ride away.

"But, still, I know a few people in town. I asked around. On the quiet, you know. Turns out Mike has a paid stooge at the assay office.

"Actually, I shouldn't say has. It's really had. He's no longer there. A couple of the boys rode him out of town a day or two ago, after the news of Mike's demise was noised around. Don't know where they rode him to, but my understanding is that he's not coming back. The boys brought the horse back with an empty saddle and no one's talking, except to say the fella didn't need the animal anymore."

Not wishing to dig further into the matter of the missing assayer, Gomer took over the conversation with the legal issues.

"Sir, Mister Trimbell here is the executor of Mister Mullins' estate. I'm appointed by the court to settle claims and make sure that all the financial and legal paperwork is wrapped up. I think we can say that your mine, in full, will be returned to you. You'll have to appear before the judge to make it all final. That will happen in the next couple of days. I'll let you know. In the meantime, if you could make a calculation on how much you paid over to Mike, there's a chance that some cash will be available to compensate for that. Partially, at least."

Gomer hesitated before continuing. The question was going to be awkward, but it had to be asked.

"Now, my last question to you is very important. I need you to answer honestly. Did Mike take anything else from you, or was he holding anything else over you? You mentioned the threats of violence. Is there anything else?"

The miner looked troubled at the question, as if 'what could be more serious than the threat of violence'. But he soon answered in the negative.

"No. Just the violence. That was enough. The wife and I considered leaving to start again somewhere else. That's how scared we were."

The second miner was almost a duplicate of the first. After a half hour with him, Zac and Gomer moved on to the third owner. This required an hour's ride into the hills south of town.

The sign at the entrance to the mine said, Willow Tree Gold Company, Kerby Mills, prop.

Kerby Mills was reluctant to talk at all. The fear was visible on his face. He evaded everything but the most mundane questions, glancing in all directions as he spoke. The man was beginning to frustrate Zac.

"You do understand, don't you, Mister Mills, that Big Mike is dead. He can no longer hurt you or yours. All we are hoping to do is settle the estate and get you back the title to your property. But we need your cooperation."

"Well, I'd like to help. But believe me, all of Big Mike's goons haven't left the country. The word is that a couple of them are planning to take over the operation."

Zac thought a moment and then said. "You have my, and the court's guarantee Mister Mills, that our operation will not stop until the whole nest of vipers is wiped out."

Gomer gave Zac a questioning look, as if to ask how he expected to accomplish that.

There was a long delay before Kerby spoke again, this time in a barely audible whisper. Without shame, or perhaps without even realizing it was happening, the big, hard muscled miner allowed tears to forge narrow pathways through the rock dust on his face.

"You're only seeing the mine, seeing the money."

His whisper was so quiet both Zac and Gomer leaned closer to hear him.

Zac had never before heard the lawyer speak in the manner he spoke then. Quietly and with compassion, he said, "Tell us, Mister Mills. We're on your side, as is the court."

Zac had never seen a man so broken up as this man was. In only a matter of seconds he seemed to come apart. Even with three years of combat experience and all the heartaches of loss seen and mourned over in battle, this was a new experience. Zac decided to take a chance.

"Mister Mills, listen carefully to me. I suspect Big Mike has done something dreadful to you and your family. We had some help with our work, our investigations, that enabled us to find out some things. We found three children being held in a house down in Denver. One child is now back with his mother, travelling somewhere, out of the country.

"We have the other two children, a little boy and a young girl safely in our possession. We're trying to identify their parents. Is that little boy yours, Mister Mills?"

Kerby Mills collapsed onto the ground, his head in his hands and with his shoulders heaving, while he sucked in great gulps of air.

"Oh God, Oh God, You can't imagine. My poor wife hasn't stopped crying for months. Have you really got our little boy?"

Gomer took over the conversation.

"We have a young boy, perhaps four years old,

safely hidden away, with good care. Why don't we go for a ride right now and see if he's your son?"

Kirby Mills, sitting bareback on a mule, never said a word for the entire hour's ride down the mountain and through town. His facial features swung between hopefulness and abject misery. Neither Zac nor Gomer broke the silence.

Pulling up before Mrs. Templeton's boarding house, the three riders saw the women again sitting on the veranda with the children.

'The fact is,' thought Zac, 'those two women seem to be enjoying themselves with the children.'

The boy was playing on the floor with some doodad he'd found somewhere. Mrs. Templeton was looking protective and grandmotherly.

Kerby Mills leaped from his mule and nearly tore the gate from its hinges, trying to get into the yard. He finally got the gate opened and a half dozen running steps took him to the veranda. There was no doubt from that moment on.

Kerby fell to his knees in front of the boy, first just looking and then reaching for him. The boy looked up into the eyes of his father.

"Daddy. Daddy."

He reached his arms out and was soon scooped into the embrace of the tough, hard rock miner.

The two women moved into the house to give the father and child their privacy. Zac and Gomer walked out to the fence, where they stood talking. In just a few moments a plan was formulated. They walked back up to the veranda and spoke to Kerby.

"Mister Mills," said Gomer, "I can't let you take the child just yet, but it won't be long. I need you to stay right here and wait for me to come back.

I'm going to see if the judge has time to see to the matter right away. I'll also go after Missus Kirby if you'll tell me where I might find her."

With the directions to the Mills' home and a visit to the judge's office, there was soon another grand reunion, this time between mother and son.

The judge led a quick discussion with the parents. Both Kirby and his wife signed a document for the judge and the matter was closed.

Zac spoke up at that point.

"Folks. Until we're sure all of Mike's goons have given up on this thing, I'm thinking it would be wise if you could keep out of sight. Is there anywhere you could go for a few days, perhaps down in Denver?"

Now that the Mills' family was complete again, Kerby Mills was able to assert his true nature.

"I'll put the wife and child on the stage tomorrow morning. They can stay with friends in Denver. For me, I'll be at the Willow Tree with my rifle primed and ready. Nothing I'd like better than to get one or two of those goons in my sights.

"You men come to where you need some help, you give me a call. With my little boy safe, I'll not be running anywhere but where I might shoot me a Big Mike goon."

The day was already well spent. It wasn't long before dinner time. Zac and Gomer decided to hold off on visiting the last miner.

CHAPTER THIRTY-EIGHT

Riding up to the Hollow Hole Mine the next morning, Zac said. "Tell me this man's name again. Seems like I've let my mind wander to where I can't remember some things."

"Jedediah Miller. I expect he goes by Jed, but I can't be sure. Black man. Whether he was freed or escaped or was never a slave I have no idea. I don't plan to pursue that either. None of my business.

"Works this Hollow Hole diggings with two black workers hired for the task. Folks tell me he's a gentle giant with a streak of reckless anger bouncing around the edges. We'll just have to see what's true when we meet him."

"That's far enough. Halt and state yo business."

The shout came from inside the dark mine entrance.

Zac removed his hat, hooking it on the saddle horn. He wanted the mine man to see his face clearly. He held his hands out sideways, at arm's length, to show there was no threat. Gomer followed Zac's example.

"Looking for Mister Miller. Jedediah Miller."

"Zac Trimbell here, and Gomer Radcliff, lawyer. Working for the court. We need to talk to Mister Miller. It's important. We'll step down here and wait. We offer no threat."

The two riders stepped their horses a few feet to the right before dismounting and tying them to some high-mountain brush growing from a crack in the rock. Zac made a show of laying his gun belt over the saddle before stepping away from the horses. They stood, bareheaded and empty handed, waiting.

A shout back into the mine brought the two labourers to the entrance. As a hurried discussion was held, the two new arrivals studied Zac and Gomer. They then reached into a long, narrow, wooden box and lifted out two rifles. As the miners held their weapons at the ready, the third man slowly walked across the tailing pile and gradually made his way to where Zac and Gomer were standing. He too, held his rifle at the ready, but not directly aimed at his visitors.

"Yo talk'n. What yo wants?"

Zac responded, "We're needing to talk with Jedediah Miller. I assume that's you."

"Dat me. I's ask'n agin. What yo wants?"

The sun was hot on their heads with the slanted morning brightness causing them to squint.

"Well, first, Mister Miller. We'd like to put our hats back on. This low-lying fall sun strikes hard on our eyes."

Without asking for permission Zac stepped towards the horses.

"Careful yo don't go 'n' try fo' no pistol. I's goin'

shoot yo ears off, yo do dat."

Zac settled his hat in place before lifting his hands to show they were empty. He then passed Gomer his hat. With their eyes shaded to where they could see the big man before them, Zac introduced themselves again.

"Now Mister Miller, you've been told that we work for the court. We're charged with wrapping up the affairs of Mike Mullins' estate. I'm sure you know by now that Mister Mullins is no longer with us. But he claimed part ownership of the Hollow Hole diggings. We need to talk to you about that. That and some other things as well. Please listen to Mister Radcliff as he explains the situation to you."

Gomer looked at a ledge of flat rock, a few feet away.

"Let's sit down, Mister Miller. We have a lot to talk about."

Jedediah Miller sat a bit apart from the other two, where the rock formed an angle that allowed him to face his visitors. He relaxed a bit but still held the rifle.

The explanation was short, as it had been at the other mines, but it took considerable time to break through Jedediah's suspicions.

Finally, the black miner said, "Yo tell'n me dat I's gitt'n de papers fo' da mine back? Dat no thugs be a'visit'n here no mo'? Dat I don't gotta pay no mo'? Zat what yo say'n?"

Gomer smiled, seeing that his message had been understood, even if there was still some doubt or unbelief in Jedediah Miller's mind.

"That's exactly what we're saying. But we have

more to talk about. Something much more important. I'd feel better Mister Miller, if you would tell
us what that might be. What else Big Mike might
have done to you or your family."

The response from this big, black man was totally different from Kerby Mills. Both were big,
strong men but Jedediah Miller had that added
edge of barely suppressed anger. Zac figured that
anger could easily turn into violence if the man
was provoked enough.

"Wot dey done to me 'n' my Ruthy ain't no human bee'n could'a did. Dat man not human. He be
evil. He be dev'l from hell. An' dose what be wit
him be jes' as evil."

Gomer was careful, recognizing the potential
of finding himself on the wrong side of Jedediah's
anger.

"You need to tell me the details, sir."

Jedediah laid his rifle down on the rock beside
him. Then he turned to the two miners who were
still standing guard. A simple wave of his oversized
hand was enough to have them place the rifles back
in the wooden box and close the lid, before turning
back to work. He glared hard at Gomer and then
at Zac.

"I tell yo. But yo be ly'n to me 'bout who yo am, I
crush yo head like a melon."

He demonstrated the movement with his big
hands. Zac and Gomer couldn't stop themselves
from leaning back a bit, away from the show of
anger.

"Big Mike, he send da goon. Tell me I's guin'
have ta pay. I lay da goon's body on da hoss, 'n' ride
down da hill ta de sal-oon. Drop goon on ta da flor.

"Da next day dat dev'l, he go to house 'n' beat my Ruthy. Took'd da baby. My litt'l girl baby.

"My Ruthy, she die from da beat'n.

"Da sheriff, he do nott'n. Say I got's no proof. I'd a give da man dis here mine if id'a know they's goin beat my Ruthy, 'n' take da baby.

"Da goons, dey come back to da mine. Say I pay or not see da baby agi'n. What I'm goi'n do? My baby. My little girl. I dig. I pay. I wait. Someday I kill dis Big Mike."

Zac and Gomer were silent. The extent of Big Mike's crimes grew with each victim's story. Again, Gomer slipped into that gentle voice Zac had heard when they were dealing with Kerby Mills.

"Mister Miller. We are very sorry that all this happened to you. It isn't right and I think you are correct to call the whole affair evil. But Mister Miller, we found your little girl. She's safe and well. She's with friends here in Idaho Springs. Get your horse and we'll take you to her."

The intensity of Jedediah Miller's stare was frightening.

"Yo be tell'n me da trut? Yo not be ly'n?"

Gomer stood and put his hand on Jedediah's shoulder, squeezing just a bit. He returned the black man's intense stare with his own sincere look.

"Come see."

Swinging down from the horses in front of Mrs. Templeton's boarding house, Jedediah gave a suspicious look at his two escorts. Gomer opened the gate and walked to the veranda.

Mrs. Templeton heard him coming and met him at the door. One quick glance at the black man following behind Gomer caused her to turn and call into the house.

"Tillie. We have important company."

In just a moment, Tillie stepped into the doorway. With a gasp, she turned back into the house. She was back almost immediately, holding the little girl's hand. The baby, all decked out in a pretty blue dress with white frilly edges, walked out the door and into the sunlight seeping under the veranda roof. She spotted the big black man immediately.

Struggling with her youthful memory, she reached with her other hand, firmly gripping Tillie's fingers with both of her little hands. Tillie had become the sole source of security to the little girl.

Jedediah stood as if thunderstruck. His five second stare seemed like full minutes, one tacked onto the end of the last one.

Gomer quietly said, "Is this your baby, Jedediah?"

The big man, awkward now, didn't seem to know what to do.

Tillie held the baby's hand out to him. Slowly, cautiously, he knelt down on the veranda floor and took her hands in his. His gentleness with the child was in strange contradiction to the strength and anger expressed against Big Mike.

The baby stared as if she was trying to figure it all out. Perhaps trying to remember.

With a glance behind him to make sure the chair was where he thought it was, Jedediah sat down. He picked the little girl up in his arms and held her close to his chest. Carefully, very gently, he stroked her hair. With tightly closed eyes he held the child, his head tipped back, as if looking to the heavens, his lips moving. No words were heard by the onlookers.

The women stepped from the doorway, onto the veranda and took their chairs, Tillie in the white wicker and Mrs. Templeton in her rocker. Gomer and Zac sat on the steps. Everyone was studying the baby and this giant of a man.

Jedediah held his stoic reserve for awhile but finally his bottom lip began to tremble. Fighting tears, he opened his eyes and cast a look at the gathering around him.

Tillie was the closest and had the best look at his struggle for dignity. Hoping to relieve some pressure from Jedediah, she quietly asked, "So what name did you give the baby?"

The question brought him back to the present and gave him something to talk and think about. He looked at Tillie with a questioning glance, as if he couldn't remember the answer to her question.

Finally, he said, "Why, me 'n' Ruthy, we was both gett'n to where we was too old fer ta have chil'n. Dis hear lil girl chil', she be lac a mirac'l. Lac in de Bible, whar ol Abrah'm, he and Sarah, dey have da boy chil' when des old. Named him Isaac, he did.

"Isaac no name fer a lil' girl baby. Closes't we come was ta call dis here lil' chil' Issie. So dat who she is. Dis my lil' Issie."

Tillie smiled at the humble man.

"That's a beautiful name. We didn't know her name. We've been calling her Cierra. I hope you don't mind?"

Gomer explained the matter of needing the judge to finalize the return of the child. He then went on to talk of the possibility of some repayment of the blackmail paid out to Big Mike.

"Tillie will take good care of your daughter while I ride and fetch the judge."

Jedediah nodded his understanding. He passed the baby back to Tillie while he left to make arrangements of his own.

"I's gots ta find someone ta kir fer da baby. Da baby an da house. I be back jest as quick as I kin."

Zac and Gomer talked quietly at the end of the sidewalk, as they watched Jedediah Miller ride away.

***

Two days later Jedediah arrived back at the boarding house with a middle-aged lady, riding in a rented livery buggy. He swung down in front of the gate and made his way to the veranda stairs. Mrs. Templeton saw him coming from the kitchen window.

With a shave and haircut and wearing his 'go-to-meet'n' clothes the big miner looked like a different man.

"Good morning, Mister Miller. Have you come for the baby?"

"Yas'm. Missus Fernandez, she goin' come take kir a da baby. Da baby an me, both."

It was the first time anyone had seen the big man smile in many months.

Tillie stepped out with the baby in one arm and a bundle of clothing in the other. With all the legal matters already handled by Gomer and the judge, there was nothing else to do, except wish Jedediah well.

Tillie carried the baby out to the buggy and lifted her into Mrs. Fernandez' welcoming arms. Jedediah stumbled through an awkward introduction, expressed his profound thanks to Tillie, and the buggy was soon disappearing around the corner.

***

The two women took their seats on the veranda and talked about all that had happened in the past week.

"What will you be doing now, Tillie? Will you stay on for a while or will you want to be getting back to Denver and your friends?"

"I really don't have any close friends, and no family near by. There's nothing drawing me back. I'd stay on here for a while if you'd let me keep the room. Perhaps I could find office work in one of the big mines. Or maybe I could clerk in a store. I know my race is a drawback to some employers, but the folks of Idaho Springs have been welcoming so far."

CHAPTER THIRTY-NINE

Zac and Gomer had another short meeting with the judge to tie down the details of the work done up to that time.

At the end of the meeting, the judge fixed his stern eyes on the two men.

"You ride carefully my friends. I've picked up a rumor. Just a whisper, mind you. But it's worth listening to. This may not be over yet. One of Big Mike's henchmen apparently has the idea to step into Mike's place and keep the scam going. Fella named Blackie Caldwell."

Gomer looked at Zac, with concern in his eyes.

"I've never heard of Blackie Caldwell before. Know nothing at all about him. But if the rumor is true, Zac, you'll be the main target."

Zac thought on this before saying, "You'll be a target too."

The three men sat silently for a bit, lost in their own thoughts, examining the possibilities.

Getting back to the purpose of the meeting, Zac said, "I'm going to leave the search for the missing mine owners to you, Gomer. To you and the sheriff."

With the children back home and safe, Zac's interest in the whole matter was beginning to fade just a bit. Sorting out the issue of the kidnapped children, and returning those children to their families, had clearly been the most important part of the estate settlement. He was also anxious to get back to the Freedom.

Zac could see that both the judge and Gomer were working up responses. Before they could speak, he raised his hand to stop them.

"Look, men, dealing with the first group of miners was relatively easy. They were still operating their mines. They still lived in town. They weren't hard to find.

"Now, with that successfully behind us, the unsolved issues come down to money. To sort that out, the missing mine owners must be found. Or at least as many as can be located. There may be some who will never be found.

"There are no children's lives at stake. It's time to bring in the law. And maybe the local newspaper. Maybe publish the names and ask the public for information.

"And when you find the miners, all it really comes down to now is money. Money, and returning full title to their own holdings."

Looking at the two men sitting around the table he said, "Judge, Gomer, you two are far more able to deal with land titles and money than I am. And I have partners filling in for me while I'm away from the Freedom. I need to get back to work."

The meeting broke up with a nervous Gomer agreeing to take the lead on the search for the other mine owners.

***

The season was growing late. The partnership still had not decided what to do over the cold months. The only thing they were sure of was that the tent would not see them through. They could build a cabin but there were drawbacks to that, too. If the snow got deep on the hillside and stayed for any length of time, they would be isolated, possibly for weeks. If the snow kept the workers isolated it would also prevent the ore wagons from making their hauls.

One thing they decided on, both for the weather and for security, was to have a strong door built into the mine entrance. Zac set one of the hired men to chiseling a notch up both sides and across the roof of the tunnel. They would set the heavy timbers well into the rock.

On his next trip to town, Zac located a carpenter who seemed to understand what they wanted. He was hired with the promise that the work would be done well, and quickly.

After hours of discussion it was decided that the Freedom Mine would purchase Big Mike's small house from the court. Lem and Phoebe would make their home there. Zac and Dominik would take up residence with Gomer and Tillie, at Mrs. Templeton's boarding house.

Phoebe would send Lem off each morning with a lunch. There was no need of her suffering through a long high-country winter at the mine.

Mrs. Templeton would do the same for Zac and Dominik.

CHAPTER FORTY

The light snow cover on the rocky trail muffled the sounds of approaching horses. The carpenter was busy cutting three-inch-thick, sawn planks into the lengths required for the mine entrance door. At the sound of a rifle shot and a bullet whining off the rock above his head, he dropped his tools and dove for cover. The bullet ricocheted off a couple of rock walls inside the mine before imbedding itself in the clean-up pile littering the floor.

Phoebe, working at the back of the tent, packing things for the move down the hill, dropped to the floor. She then wiggled on her knees and elbows, scrambling for her reticule, and the pistol that still made its home there.

Even down the length of the rock shaft, with the hammers striking steel, Zac and the crew heard the gun shot.

Zac dropped his hammer.

"Take cover. Stay here. Blow out those lamps."

Hidden in the interior darkness, Zac made his way cautiously towards the tunnel mouth. He could see the three mounted men, but he was sure they couldn't see him through the gloom. He edged along the wall to where his Henry carbine hung on the pegs. As he was lifting it down, he heard footsteps behind him. Turning, he saw Lem and Dominik sneaking forward. They were each carrying a rifle that they had hidden in the shaft, much as Zac had hidden his, months before.

"Keep back, you two."

They ignored his advice.

Dominik edged carefully along the wall opposite to Zac. Lem was close behind him.

Dominik was no longer the shy, apologetic Polish immigrant. He had captured a good lot of the English language. He had also seized a big portion of determination to hold onto what was his.

The mine was his. He had studied to know rocks. He had travelled an ocean and thousands of miles of strange lands. He had looked for, and found, the mineral. He had broken the first rock and dug the first hole.

No gunman was about to take it from him without a fight.

He foolishly stepped away from the wall, exposing himself just a bit while he shouted at the riders.

"What you want? Why you shoot at mine?"

He was answered with another whining ricochet that barely missed him. Instead of cowering for cover as he might have done months earlier, he lifted his rifle and shot the rider holding the smoking gun. The man dropped his weapon, grabbed his chest and rolled from the saddle.

The look on Dominik's face almost made Zac laugh out loud. Surely everyone remembers the first man he kills. Dominik had just crossed that line.

Lem's rifle spoke almost as quickly as Dominik's, downing a horse. That rider was dumped unceremoniously into the snow, with his leg trapped under the dead animal.

In the split second that followed this action, Zac heard a pistol shot from the tent. He couldn't see the tent from where he stood, but the shot could have come from no one but Phoebe.

The third rider was busy trying to control his horse. The frightened, stamping animal's movements caused Phoebe to miss the rider. Instead, her shot laid a groove across the animal's rump, causing it to buck and jump even more.

The rider, a miner, not a cowboy, and clearly not up to the challenge, dropped the reins and dove off the uncontrollable animal.

With all three riders down, Zac charged from the mine entrance, across the tailings pile and skidded to a snowy stop where the dead rider lay.

He looked at the other two men and said, "Looks like your friend is dead. Either of you wish to join him, I'd be happy to oblige."

The man trapped under the horse dropped the Colt he had pulled and lifted his hands above his head.

"Now that's wise."

Looking at the man who took the desperate dive from the saddle of the terrified bronc, he asked, "And what about you?"

"I'm done. Didn't come to get into no shoot'n match. Came to talk. That fool Milo, him that took those shots and now's bled-out into the snow, he's got no more brains than's necessary. Don't guess it matters much to him now."

Dominik and Lem had arrived, each still pointing a rifle. A moment later, Phoebe stepped to the front of the tent. She was content to stay there. She carried her reticule on her left wrist but there was no sign of the pistol.

Zac stepped aboard the now settled-down horse, loosened the rope from the horn and tossed the end to Lem.

"Slip that over the horn on that saddle."

With that done he eased the animal away. When the rider's leg came free, Lem took him by the collar and pulled him clear. He didn't appear to have anything more than a slightly twisted ankle.

The two raiders stood to their feet and studied the miners and this black woman who didn't seem to hold any fear of them.

Zac hollered at the carpenter. The cowering man had wiggled almost out of sight behind some tailings.

"You can get back to it. This here's all over."

Turning to the men, he asked, "So what's this all about? And before you answer you'd better think on this; right now I'm trying to decide if I should take you down to the sheriff or shoot you both and drag you over that hill yonder and leave you for the coyotes."

The two men looked at one another for just a moment before the one who had been trapped under his horse said, "We come with a message. Wasn't to be no shoot'n."

Zac was getting impatient. He was pretty sure the message would be from Blackie Caldwell and would be a repeat of the earlier one from Big Mike.

"So, what's the message?"

"Blackie Caldwell, he's taken over from Big Mike. He wants the title to this mine, and he wants all of you gone. Gone clear out of the country. Else you'll wake up dead and won't even know it's happened. You've caused more than enough trouble. You'd be safer somewhere else. Like, maybe Montana. You get yourselves gone, else Blackie, he'll come see you his own self, and that won't be no good day fer y'all."

Zac thought immediately about Big Mike and his treatment of women and kids.

"This Blackie. Has he sent other goons like yourselves to harm the women and kids again?"

"No. noth'n like that. Blackie said to leave the women strictly alone. That was Big Mike's downfall. Ain't going to happen again."

Zac turned to Lem.

"I'd appreciate if you'd throw some harness on those mules and drag this dead horse over the hill somewhere. Far enough so's the stink won't reach to camp. Then stand guard here."

Turning to Dominik he said, "You hold your rifle on these two while I saddle my horse."

Pointing at the raiders, he said, "You tie your partner over the saddle of that horse. You can ride double down the hill after we rope you up just a little bit. We'll just go have us a visit with this Blackie Caldwell person."

CHAPTER FORTY-ONE

At the same time the three men were dispatched to the Freedom Mine, Blackie sent another to the Hollow Hole and two more to visit the Lawyer who was causing so much trouble.

Jedediah Miller never would talk about what happened at the Hollow Hole. All anyone knew was that the man sent there by Blackie Caldwell was never seen again.

But what happened with the lawyer was news all over town within an hour.

Gomer had closed his office early and gone home to the boarding house. When two riders pulled up at the gate in front of Mrs. Templeton's boarding-house, one of them hollered for Gomer to come out. Several close neighbors heard the holler and came into their yards to see what the fuss was about. The shout was heard inside the house, as well, and soon the lawyer was strolling down the walkway towards the two men.

A quick, sharp exchange of words caused Micky Danube to swing to the ground. He pushed the gate open with an oath and said, "You sawed off runt, when I talk to you, I don't expect to hear no back talk. You shoulda' listened. Now I got to teach you by hand."

With balled-up fists and great confidence, he approached Gomer. The lawyer never moved. Micky swung a fist, planning to lay the smaller man low with a single blow. Without hardly moving, only shifting his upper body aside a half foot, Gomer grabbed the man's wrist, drove his other hand brutally under the extended elbow and heard the ugly snap of breaking bones.

Micky's scream of pain could be heard all around the area.

With his hand held flat, his thumb and fingers forming a 'V', in a hand and arm that were deceptively strong, Gomer aimed a merciless thrust, this time at the man's Adam's apple. Micky gagged horribly and flopped to the ground, out of the game completely.

He lay on the sparse grass coughing and retching and gasping for breath, holding his injured throat with his unbroken arm. Gomer looked at him with no mercy before he turned his attention to the other rider.

LeRoy Carnes was a big man. Heavy in chest and shoulder, and proud of his strength. He had spent his own years pounding steel in the mines and had the power in the arms that attested to it. Looking to the slight, almost sickly-looking lawyer, and wondering what trickery had been played on his partner, he stepped off his horse and approached carefully.

With no words spoken, he entered the yard,

his hands and arms held at waist height as if to grapple with the smaller man. But as he stepped within grappling range, Gomer swept his own leg sideways, out and back, with everything his thigh and hip muscles could put into it. He connected a pitiless blow to the bigger man's knee. The joint bent inward, as no knee is intended to do, and the fight was over.

With a screech of pain, LeRoy joined his friend on the yard grass of the boarding house yard.

Tillie and Mrs. Templeton rushed down the walkway to stand beside Gomer.

Mrs. Templeton hollered at a neighbor boy who was watching from two doors away.

"William. Run and get the sheriff and the doctor. Hurry."

Tillie placed her hand on Gomer's arm.

"Are you all right, Gomer? That was awful what those men wanted to do. They didn't hurt you, did they?"

Mrs. Templeton said, "Girly, take a look at the mess cluttering up my front yard. Don't hardly look like they done any harm to Gomer. Might have misjudged him just a bit, is all."

Gomer, still fixing his eyes on the men of the ground, had nothing to add.

Micky was lying still, his hand no longer gripping his throat. Mrs. Templeton bent and placed her fingers on his neck, feeling for a pulse. She lifted his eye lid and then pushed it closed again before feeling for a pulse a second time.

She looked up at Gomer.

"I do believe this man is dead."

Gomer's face took on a more serious expression,

but he said nothing. Tillie simply sucked in a big breath and stood silently.

It took almost a half hour for the sheriff to arrive and another ten minutes for the doctor to whip his buggy horse down the street and draw it to a halt in front of the boarding house.

Young William ran all the way to the sheriff's office and then to get the doctor. After running all the way back, he stood, bent over in the yard with his hands on his knees, while he puffed out his exhaustion.

The sheriff took a look at the small space behind the doctor's buggy seat and decided they would need a larger conveyance.

"William, run and get Slade. Tell him to lock up his barber shop, put on his undertaker hat, and get himself down here with his meat wagon."

The boy, not running nearly as fast as before, disappeared around the corner.

LeRoy Carnes, still in abject misery with his broken knee, looked up at the sheriff.

"Could be you should just shoot me and load me on the meat wagon along with ol' Micky there. Never going to have much life with just the one leg."

"Don't tempt me."

The doctor tried to comfort the badly-injured man.

"I'll do my best to put you back together."

LeRoy simply looked at him, not at all comforted by the man's reputed surgical skills.

While they were waiting for the undertaker, the sheriff took a seat on the veranda with Gomer. He asked the women to leave.

"Cain't hardly question the suspect with y'all

hang'n about. Might need ya to testify at the court if'n I decide to charge the lawyer with murder or some such."

Mrs. Templeton didn't move.

"We saw everything that happened, Beamer Wallis. And I'll not have you browbeating one of my tenants whether you're on my front porch or in a court of law. You go ahead and ask your questions, sheriff. And try to remember back to when you were plain ol' Beamer Wallis. Remember too that you got that job by just fourteen votes. I'll vote fifteen times myself to lose you your job if I don't like your talk."

Sheriff Wallis heaved a sigh of resignation and asked Gomer what happened.

It took all the willpower either Mrs. Templeton or Tillie could gather up, but they managed to stay silent while the lawyer told his story.

The sheriff heard all he wanted to hear before interrupting Gomer.

"Are you telling me that the Big Mike thing ain't done with?"

"That's what I'm telling you, sheriff. I don't know who's behind it all but there's more work to be done cleaning the whole nest of vipers out."

"I know who's behind it." The voice came from the stairs. Neither Gomer nor the sheriff had heard Zac walking up. The women, seated where they could see the yard, had watched his approach in silence.

Sheriff Wallis turned sharply around. After studying Zac for only a moment he stood and turned towards the front road. The doctor and the undertaker had the dead Micky and the injured Le-

Roy loaded into the back of the meat wagon, as the sheriff had called it. But beside them were several horses, one of them clearly carrying a dead man.

As they watched, the undertaker untied the man from the saddle he was draped over. With the help of the doctor, he wrestled the heavy man into the wagon. LeRoy screamed out as the dead man's arm flopped onto the broken knee. In another minute, the doctor turned his buggy to leave, followed closely by the undertaker.

The horse with the two well-secured riders stood idly by the fence it was tied to.

Zac was grim as he looked at the sheriff. Just as he began speaking, the sheriff cut him off.

"I'm interviewing a murder suspect here. I'd appreciate if you'd step back to your horse. I'll get to you by and by."

"You'll get to me right now. You're questioning of Gomer is finished. You have more important things to do. We have to go and arrest a man. Or maybe shoot him. What happens will be up to him. Now let's get a move on."

Beamer Wallis didn't move. He was about to argue but Zac got the first word in.

"Sheriff, you were useless in dealing with Big Mike's crime spree. Now someone named Blackie Caldwell's trying to take up where Mike left off. You can arrest him, or I'll shoot him. Have it whatever way you want."

Gomer spoke for the first time since Zac's arrival.

"All these men are a part of the old Big Mike gang, sheriff. I'd saddle up and go with Zac if I was you. Could save you a bunch of trouble later."

When Gomer and the women were alone again on the veranda, Tillie asked, "How did you do that to those men? I've not had much experience with men fighting but I'm pretty sure that's not a typical barroom battle."

Gomer hesitated before he answered, his mind still fixated on the fact that he had killed a man. Finally, he looked at the women, first at Mrs. Templeton and then at Tillie.

"My father is just a bit bigger than me, but he's still considered a small man on the San Francisco docks where he's put in a lifetime of hard work. He had to learn to defend himself or get bullied out of a job. He learned some things from a couple of the China Boys, as they're called on the docks. That's Orientals; men from many nations, who arrive on the ships.

"When I was coming of age, Father sent me to see a man named Chinh. Turned out he wasn't Chinese, but from a country named Vietnam. I'd never heard of it before. The fellow spoke no English, so we talked with smiles and nods and actions.

"Toughest man I ever met. Perhaps not the strongest. But surely the toughest. He showed me some self defence moves. It's come in handy a time or two."

CHAPTER FORTY-TWO

The sheriff and Zac, leading the mine raiders' horses, with the raiders still riding double, pulled up in front of a house the captives directed them to. Leaving the two men still tied to the saddle, the sheriff approached the front door. The single window on that side of the house was covered with a cloth curtain of some type.

A city block before reaching the house, Zac peeled away from the sheriff and the tied-up raiders. He circled around through the overgrown grass, rusted cans and old outhouses, until he was at the back of the building Blackie Caldwell was using for his operation. He tied his riding animal and cautiously approached the rear of the small house on foot. He moved onto a covered porch, leading to an unlocked door. He peeked through the small window built into the door, before turning the handle.

Stepping inside, Zac heard voices from another room. He crossed the floor carefully, stopping at the doorway.

He was just in time to hear a gruff, self-assured voice say, "Sheriff, I have no idea what you're talking about. I'm a businessman. I own parts of a few mines and a couple of them outright. These men with me are my foremen, doing their daily tasks. That's all there is to that.

"I don't know any Micky or LeRoy, or what they might have done up at the Freedom Mine. How about you take your troubles somewhere else and let us get on with our business."

The gravel-voiced man was putting on a good bluff. But what the sheriff couldn't see was that Blackie Caldwell was holding a Colt on his knees behind the desk. Zac saw the weapon and immediately took action.

Taking two quick steps into the room, intending to lay the Henry's barrel across Blackie's wrists to immobilize him, his boots made a scrunching noise on the dirty floor.

One of Blackie's men heard the noise and hollered a warning when he saw Zac holding the Henry.

Lifting his Colt as he shouted, he snapped off a shot towards where the sheriff had been standing a moment before. The sheriff, moving more quickly than Zac thought possible, given the bulk and girth of the man, had dived to the floor, rolling over once. When he was again lying on his left side, with his right hand holding his own Colt, he lifted the weapon and drove answering shots at the shouting man.

With a cry of anguish, the shooter dropped his weapon and grabbed his stomach. His knees slowly folded and he dropped to the floor.

Blackie, seeing Zac for the first time, whipped his weapon up, already spouting flame and lead. The speed of Blackie's actions took Zac by surprise, leaving him no time to move. Blackie's first shot took him in the left hip, staggering him. The stagger saved him from the second shot, which went wide by inches.

His Henry sagged down, to point at the floor.

Ignoring the pain as much as humanly possible, as he had been forced to do a few times in battle, Zac lifted his Henry onto his target again and pumped off four shots as fast as he could drop and lift the lever. Blackie went over backwards, his swivel chair crashing under him. With barely ten feet between them, Zac knew where he had put the shots. There was no need to worry about the man shooting again.

Zac reached for a chair with the intention of sitting down. He missed and fell to the floor, blood soaking through his canvas pants and spreading onto the pine flooring.

The entire episode had taken mere seconds, but in that time the sheriff had gotten a bead on the second of Blackie's helpers. The man threw his weapon into the corner and raised his hands, shouting out, "Don't shoot. I quit.".

Sheriff Wallis tried to steady his Colt as he slowly regained his feet. He took a quick glance at the blood leaking from Zac and made a decision.

Looking at the man who had surrendered he said, "This here's a one time offer fella. You mess up, I'll find you and I'll shoot you deader than those two lying over yonder, even if it takes me a year. You grab you a horse and scoot as fast as you can for the doctor. Get him here as quickly as ever is possible.

"You do that, you can point your animal downhill and don't ever come back. That's the best deal you're likely to get, in this lifetime or the next."

Chapter Forty-Three

The little house was crowded, threatening to outdo the doctor's tolerance level. His attempts at patience, beyond, his normal endurance, was about to create an explosion. Mrs. Templeton came to his rescue.

"Clarence. Come sit out back with me for a bit. I saw some lemonade in your kitchen. I'll bring a glass for each of us."

The doctor heaved a great sigh of resignation and left the house.

The news of Zac's hip wound had brought the folks who knew him, together all at the same time. The buzz of conversation was loud and annoying to the injured man. When he realized that everyone was wrapped up in conversation with another visitor and that no one was talking to him, he closed his eyes and tried to put it all out of his mind.

But how do you put the thought that you may never walk normally again, out of your mind?

***

When he was first hauled to the doctor's small clinic, he had experienced a couple of tough days, first being shot and then suffering through the doctor's not so gentle ministrations.

As if that wasn't enough for Zac to wade through, when he had finally awakened from the surgery his stomach had been in terrible knots, his mind was a blur and his eyes wouldn't focus.

The worst was that he had no hope of controlling his nausea. His bouts of vomiting were horrible to live through and to remember.

It was the ether sleep imposed on him by the crudely trained doctor that led to uncontrollable vomiting, and other side effects.

He tried to apologise to the young lady the doctor hired as an assistant, but he couldn't find the words.

A bit later, when his ether befuddled mind finally found and sorted out the words, his tongue was so thick and his throat so sore he couldn't get the words out of his mouth.

Whatever the doctor was paying the girl, it wasn't enough. He promised himself that he would put a little something into an envelope for her when he got the chance.

To add to his misery, Dr. Goodfellow had pulled a chair up beside his bed just that morning and cheerfully laid out some facts for him.

"I've done what medical science is able to do for you, young fella. You can figure on a few weeks lay'n a-bed whilst that damaged bone heals itself. If it's any consolation to you, your future looks brighter, so far as walking goes, than that feller in the other room.

"That would be the one your lawyer friend laid down. Never saw so many chips and fractures in one small gathering of bones. If he ever walks again it will be with a crutch and a badly warped knee.

"Nothing I, nor you, can do to speed up the healing process. Time is what it takes. Time and rest. If all goes well, by spring you'll be up and rar'n to go. Or you might find you need a cane or even a crutch.

"While you're waiting for that hip to heal, you might want to consider all that happened, and give thanks to whatever god you worship, that you didn't bleed out, lying on that cabin floor. Another few minutes and you would've avoided all this pain and misery, with ol' Slade, him that does the undertaking work here abouts, doing for ya.

"Now what I'm tellin' you is how it'll be, all the time assuming that no infection sets in. What I'm try'n to say is that you might just as well lay back and gain some rest. You've got serious healin' to do."

***

The injury, following another hated gun battle where he had killed a man, was in the process of driving him into a deep depression. He was constantly aware that he lived close to the edge of some unknown mental precipice, forever fearful of falling over, or of sinking into some quicksand of the mind.

Time after time he had attempted to protect

himself from this invisible enemy. Nothing seemed to work for very long. He had found some release since the end of the war, with travel, hard work and good friends. But what can a man do to keep his mind and body busy when he's flat on his back, confined, for how many months he had no idea?

He didn't mention his depressions to the doctor for fear the man would jam another ether-soaked wad of cotton over his nose and mouth. He somehow felt the medical man would say something like, "This here will help you rest," when Zac himself knew it would do no such thing.

The conflict between the injured man and the healer went unmentioned but it was real just the same.

The doctor was concerned only about the healing of bones and muscles.

Zac was concerned about that too, but mostly he was concerned about holding on to his sanity. He had taken the tightest grip he was able to put together, but there were times he wasn't sure it was enough. That old feeling; the fear of falling into a dark hole, crowded itself upon him when he least expected it and was the least prepared.

***

At least he still had his friends and the Freedom Mine. As thankful as he was for that, he wished his visitors would leave and allow him to sleep.

Phoebe walked to the bedside. "Zac, I'm going

to push these people out of here so you can rest. Is there anything you need?"

"Just a new hip and leg. Shouldn't be too much to ask."

Phoebe patted him on the hand and pulled the bed covers up, tucking them under his chin and pressing a few wrinkles out.

She turned to the group and raised her voice just a bit.

"That's enough, people. Zac needs to rest."

CHAPTER FORTY-FOUR

Two weeks after the gun battle that put a final end to the mine grabbers, a few of Zac's friends arrived together, at the doctor's office.

Gomer, in an annoyingly cheerful voice, shook his shoulder and said, "Wake up there, my friend. Time to say goodbye to this grim space."

Zac shook himself into semi-wakefulness and looked up as the bunch entered the room, crowding around the bed. Again, Phoebe took control.

Zac studied the small crowd and then looked at Phoebe.

"What's happening?"

"We're taking you home. It's a nuisance having to come all the way out here to visit, so you're going back to the boarding house."

Zac saw through the ruse immediately. The rescue had nothing at all to do with travel time or the location of the doctor's office. His friends were thinking solely of him, and his comfort.

Doctor Goodfellow pushed a couple of men aside as he entered the room.

"All right, you've told me what you intend to do. I'll not argue with you any more than I have already. You take him and go. Carry him gently and hold that hip firmly in place. If you drop him, I'll have to think carefully about whether or not I'll want the bother of fixing him up again."

Phoebe smiled and said, "Doctor, I'm sure we are all impressed with your attempted gruffness, but I don't believe a word of it."

Dr. Clarence Goodfellow, a frontier doctor with only medium skills, and almost no bedside manners at all, waved his arms as if in surrender and left the room. The group heard him talking to LeRoy in the next room.

"And I suppose your friends will be coming to take you somewhere too. I'll warn you again, that knee can't stand any movement for a long while yet. I've already told you that it should be taken off. Might have to do it yet."

The patient's quiet answer took on a dejected tone.

"I've got no friends, Doc. Hasn't been nary a soul darken that door since I come here."

There was a short pause before LeRoy said, "Mostly dead anyway, I'm guessing. Shot down."

Neither the doctor nor anyone in Zac's room had anything to say that might encourage the injured man.

***

Besides Mrs. Templeton's own room, there was one small bedroom on the main floor that Tillie had been using. The only two women in the boarding house agreed that for decency's sake, having a stairway between them and the men upstairs might stop some of the wagging tongues among the housewives of Idaho Springs.

Showing no concern at all about her safety or her reputation, Tillie had changed rooms. She carefully moved Zac's clothing, weapons and whatever else he had accumulated, down the stairs to her room and then carried her few possessions to Zac's now vacated space. She gave both rooms a thorough cleaning and even though the late-fall day had a distinct chill in the air, she opened the windows wide, allowing the wind free reign for an hour.

The two strongest men in the Freedom Mine and lawyer combination were Lem and Jedediah Miller. Phoebe assigned each of them to take the primary load during the transfer of the patient, with Gomer and Dominik taking one side each, to hold Zac steady. Zac had no idea where they managed to find an unused door, but it served adequately as a stretcher.

Settled into his new room at the boarding house, Zac quickly fell into an exhausted sleep. Although the men had been as careful as possible during the move, his hip was still sore from the bouncing and jostling in the wagon. Somehow the injury seemed to drain every ounce of his stamina. He slept for hours and still wanted more rest.

***

When Zac awoke, Tillie came into his room, fussing around, tugging the blankets this way and then that way, making sure he was comfortable and asking all kinds of foolish questions that the patient had no answers for.

But it was Mrs. Templeton who came to his rescue with a cup of much needed coffee.

With the men going back to work, and Tillie spending the days at her new job in the office of the Big Star Mine up on the east hill, the boarding house soon fell into a comfortable rhythm.

Mrs. Templeton found a few books for Zac to read, or at least pretend he was reading. She brought him coffee at regular intervals but otherwise, went about her day as if he wasn't present.

Using extraordinary care, and a pair of crutches Gomer had discovered hidden away behind some shovels and such in an empty wooden barrel at the general store, Zac was able to slowly make his one-legged way to the outhouse. He counted the accomplishment as being one of his greater achievements, freeing him from the dread and embarrassment of the chamber pot.

CHAPTER FORTY-FIVE

Two weeks before Christmas, Dominik stomped the snow from his boots as he stepped into the enclosed back porch of the boarding house, closing the door quickly to keep out the still falling snow. After hanging his winter coat on one of the many wall pegs, and tugging off his boots, he chaffed his hands and pulled off his winter hat, the one with the fur lined ear laps. His hair stuck up in all directions and crackled with static, in its dryness.

His first stop was at the big kitchen range that was never allowed to cool off at this time of year. Mrs. Templeton had her cooking pots loaded with fragrant offerings for the evening meal, taking up most of the cast-iron surface.

As Dominik held his cold, chapped hands over the hot cast-iron stove top, relishing the heat, Tillie poured him a cup of coffee, placing it on the table, ready for him. He took a seat, commenting to no one in particular, 'Cold'.

Zac had also heard him stomping around on the porch. The reluctantly house-bound patient was getting around quite well with the use of the crutches. He made his way from the bedroom to the kitchen, sitting across from Dominik, and motioned for Tillie to join them.

As if a bell had rung on the streets of Idaho Springs, announcing the end of the workday, Gomer too, stepped into the back hallway, repeating the actions that Dominik had so recently worked his way through. He even announced his own arrival with, 'Cold'.

Zac, ever eager to know how it was at the Freedom Mine, put the question to Dominik.

"Much snow. I am think, maybe too much snow. He held his hand at the level of the tabletop to demonstrate his point. Lem, he agree. We lock door. Go back after snow gone."

Zac took a while to think that through but finally said, "That's probably a good decision. It's too hard on the riding animals to get y'all up there each morning and then they have to stand around in the cold and snow all day. Too hard on you men too. The gold will still be there come spring."

The final decision would be made when they were together with Lem and Phoebe but, for now, the mine would stay locked.

Gomer had news of the estate settlement.

"We've found the two men who sold their claims to Big Mike, accepting ten cents on the dollar rather than six feet behind the church. They've been digging again, working together this time.

"Staked a claim up some draw, way off to the north of town. They've shut down for the winter.

"It was that notice we put in the newspaper that brought them out. The notice appeared some time ago, but their fear of Big Mike and his goons was such that they were reluctant to step forward. Then they read the news about Blackie Caldwell and the others. But still they waited.

"In town for the winter, with nothing to keep them busy, they decided to come to my office. I cross-checked their information with the original claim data and confirmed that they were telling the truth.

"Now I need them to meet with you, as the executor, Zac, and the judge. There's no reason we can't get their mines back for them. I'll arrange a meeting tomorrow, if possible."

"What about the third guy? He seems to have disappeared."

Gomer looked troubled as he paused before speaking.

"The word I get, from his wife and everyone who knew him, is that he hasn't been seen for months. I expect he's dead, but I don't know of any way to prove it.

"What I have in mind now, is having you and the judge declare that the estate rightfully belongs to his wife. That way, if he ever shows up again, he only has to deal with her. We won't be involved. In the meantime, perhaps she can either sell the mine or hire a crew to work it for her.

"If we can clear that up, our jobs will be finished except for distributing the funds left in Big Mike's bank accounts."

As that conversation came to a close, Mrs. Templeton picked up an envelope from the kitchen windowsill. She held it out to Dominik.

"What is? I don't know this word."

He showed Zac the envelope with his finger held below the troubling word.

"That says 'telegram'. That means there's a message in there for you. Open it. Maybe they're inviting you to come home and be the king of Poland."

"Poland no have king."

"Well, open it anyway."

As if he feared what might pop out at him, Dominik slowly opened his first ever telegram. He placed the torn envelope on the table and unfolded the flimsy paper the message was scribbled on. Between Dominik's poor command of the written English language and the decidedly scratchy penmanship of the telegrapher, he was unable to make any sense of it. Finally, he gave up and passed the message to Zac.

Zac took it and flattened the crinkled paper on the tabletop. He took a few seconds to scan the message before his eyes returned to the top. He read it out loud.

"In New York. Stop. Bianka. Stop. Antoni. Stop. Roman. Stop. Coming to Idaho Springs soonest. stop. You wait. Stop."

When Zac was finished reading, every eye turned to their Polish friend. Dominik was clearly dumbfounded by the message. He picked up the paper, but the words still didn't jump off the page at him. He laid it back down.

"What this mean? All this stop?"

Zac explained, "It's just used as a way to separate the words. It keeps the message clear."

Tillie asked, "Who are these people?"

She picked the paper up and read, "Bianka. Antoni. Roman."

Again, every eye turned to Dominik.

"Roman my brother. Bianka is girl from farm close to my place. Antoni, Bianka's brother."

Tillie smiled at her friend.

"So. A neighbor girl is travelling halfway around the world to see you. Were you two sweethearts?"

Dominik looked from one face to another around the table. He didn't know what to say. Finally, he pulled the paper to himself again and held the flat of his hand on it. His neck and face were flushing just a bit. It might have been the heat in the room.

"Bianka," he said quietly. "Maybe come this place."

Into the stillness that followed that short statement, Gomer, ever the practical lawyer said, "You told us how your father had to sell a cow and then you had to work on the docks and on the boat to get here. Now your brother and two neighbors are coming. They're already in New York. How many cows did your father have to sell for them, I wonder?"

Dominik came out of his wondering stupor. His intention was to send money to help his family, but he hadn't done it yet. He shook his head as if he was casting off one thought and then another.

"Not have so many cows. My family very poor. After university no money left. This my family do for me."

He left the thought there, and the question unanswered.

***

After a night of tossing and turning, thinking one thing and then another, Dominik talked to Gomer at the breakfast table.

"You know this telegram thing? You know how works?"

"I know a bit, but not much. What do you want to know?"

"How I send money to Roman in New York?"

Gomer leaned back in his chair and studied his friend.

"That's a good question. The bank can wire funds anywhere there's a telegraph, but how would they find Roman and the others?"

They all ate in silence for another couple of minutes. Finally, Gomer laid down his knife and fork and pushed his chair back.

"Tell you what, my friend. Let's you and I walk down to the telegraph office right after dinner. We'll find out how to do what you want. You bring the telegram with you."

The telegrapher took a quick look at the page he had written out the day before and said, "If you've got two dollars you can answer this. Ask whoever's on the other end for an address. Best we can do."

Dominik laid out the money while Gomer wrote down the message. Idly he wondered if one of the three travelers had learned English or how the messages were translated.

The wire was sent with a promise to have any answer forwarded to the boarding house.

Dominik and Gomer then walked to the bank to enquire about wiring funds. With that all straightened out, Dominik walked home while Gomer went to his office.

CHAPTER FORTY-SIX

Within a week the legal and estate matters were settled, the funds distributed as fairly as the group could calculate and the matter was closed. Zac heaved a sigh of relief when he was out from under the executor obligations, having completed all that was legally required. He was entitled to a portion of the estate as payment for his services, but he turned it down.

"Along with everything else going on, I don't need to be accused of conflict of interest."

During the final meeting with the judge, Zac had laid out the bundle of cash he kept hidden at the mine. Added to the stake impounded from the banks, it was a considerable sum.

The impressive stack of printed bills and the sack of gold coins would be deposited to a trust account controlled by Gomer's law practice.

The judge, acting just a bit officiously, now that Zac and Gomer had done all the work, looked at the bundle of cash Zac laid on the table.

"And, exactly why, sir, did you not bring this

matter forward before now?"

Zac smiled at the judge, keeping his deeper thoughts private.

"Because I had no idea how this was all going to play out, judge. We didn't know for sure that the banks would truly release the account proceeds. If there was trouble on that end, we would at least have the other amount to distribute. It wouldn't be enough to change anyone's life, but it seems the best we could do."

As the judge glared at Zac, Gomer was grinning at his mining friend.

CHAPTER FORTY-SEVEN

Christmas Eve fell on Sunday. The small church, just a short walk from the boarding house, was having an evening hymn sing service. Everyone from the boarding house had agreed to attend, even though it would be a new experience for Dominik. Gomer had never mentioned spiritual beliefs, so he remained a mystery.

Lem and Phoebe joined the group for the dinner and the evening. They had sold the little house on the south side of Idaho Springs, feeling it was too far from everything. They purchased a small, but satisfactory, home close to the boarding house.

With Tillie's help, Mrs. Templeton put out the evening meal, took her place at the head of the big oak table and said, "Zac, will you return thanks for us this evening?"

She had long been in the habit of asking her tenants to give thanks, sometimes surprising a short-term guest who was not aware of this practice. It produced its awkward moments, but it also opened interesting conversations.

Zac's faith had been severely tested during the war years as he watched and participated in the butchery of his fellow human beings.

Arriving home to find his family murdered, drew him close to the breaking point, emotionally and spiritually. But as time passed, and as he shared stories with Lem and Phoebe about their slave days and their lost children, with Lem reminding Zac that there are no guarantees of an easy life found anywhere in the Scriptures, he slowly began his spiritual recovery.

The whole process was driven largely by the challenge of Rev. Moody's question; "Is it still well with your soul?"

Zac's truthful answer would have to be 'no', but he shared that thought with no one. He admitted to himself that any recovery was slow in coming, and setbacks were frequent.

He was still reluctant to fully trust. But at least he had quit fighting the process.

Even in the few times Zac addressed his Maker privately, his prayers were shallow and perfunctory. But when Mrs. Templeton asked, he managed to stumble through a short prayer, giving thanks for the meal.

***

By the time January rolled around, Dominik had received a telegram from New York confirming that his money had found its way into his brother's hands. The funds would ease the next steps in their travels.

It would take considerably more time to hear if

the funds he sent to his father in Krakow had been received.

Sending money out of the country was a complicated and slow process, with a lot of trust involved.

Trusting the bank to honestly and accurately calculate the value of Polish funds was perhaps the biggest test for Dominik.

And then, remembering the slow, arduous Atlantic crossing, with its never-ending risk of storms and other hazards, cost Dominik some hours of sleep.

Once the ship arrived in Hamburg, there would be the complications of sending a wire through Germany and Poland, ending in Krakow, at a bank that could handle the procedure. And somehow the bank would have to locate the Kowalski family; a perhaps difficult task.

Dominik doubted that his father had ever had a bank account or that anyone in Krakow would know the family.

It all added up to an almost formidable challenge to the young geologist.

The returning confirmation telegram would take just as long.

A newspaper left at the boarding house mentioned some talk about a financial adventurer attempting to connect North America to Europe with an underwater telegraph cable. But so far that was only talk.

Some underwater cables had been successfully laid but these were for much shorter distances. The North Atlantic presented a significant challenge.

Dominik's father spoke no English. He could read and write, but only poorly. And of course, he would have no concept of telegrams from halfway around the world.

What funds the small farm produced were spent almost as fast as they were earned. The bit of excess was kept in a tin stuffed into the back of the kitchen pantry.

There had never been any family connection to a bank, that Dominik could recall.

Trusting that, somehow, the system would work, he had sent a considerable sum, an amount that would change the lives of his parents and of the farm. Now he could only hope and wait.

Of course, he had sent a letter with more details, but when would that arrive?

***

The winter weeks crawled past with Dominik pacing the floor and making plans for opening a new work, where he had marked the quartz seam on the back side of the rocky claim. He would have to dig out samples and have assay work done before any of that could happen.

He purchased paper and pencils and made drawing after drawing of possible extensions to the Freedom claim.

He was determined to drive a shaft to daylight from the farthest point of the tunnel.

With the poisonous gasses released in the blasting process, the air was often questionable. And the light was always poor at the working face, even with the use of kerosene lanterns.

They would have to do something for light and ventilation if they were to go deeper.

Zac paced the house as much as Dominik did. Where Dominik was fussing about the mine, Zac's goal was the strengthening of his shattered hip.

It was coming along well, according to the doctor, but Phoebe wasn't so sure. She did everything but tie Zac to a chair to keep him from overdoing things.

With a break in the weather in mid February, Zac convinced Lem to bring his gelding from the livery. Again, Phoebe objected.

The first ride went well enough, although Zac kept it to a scant half hour. The worst part had been gaining the saddle.

He had finally talked gently to the horse before mounting from the offside.

As it did in battle, the animal stood like a statue while the struggling rider sorted it all out.

Firmly grasping the crutch alongside his left leg allowed Zac to keep the weight off his still-healing hip. Lifting his right foot into the stirrup he gently swung the wounded leg over the saddle. There was some pain from the unfamiliar movements but nothing he couldn't handle.

After that, he rode whenever the weather allowed. By full spring he should be ready to do his share of the riding and the work.

CHAPTER FORTY-EIGHT

Dominik couldn't stay away from the mine. It was all he thought about. Well, that and the promise that Bianka would somehow find her way across the continent come springtime.

At the least break in the weather, the novice geologist was out of the house and riding up the hill. He found that with a better saddle he was able to make the trip on the rattle-brained, flighty animal Gertie bought and left with Zac.

He was no judge of riding animals, but he thought the one he rode might not make the grade if it were to be judged alongside a good cow horse.

He knew he would never be a rider by western standards, but he was a miner, not a cowboy, so it didn't matter.

Dominik had no intention of working the Freedom by himself. That wasn't why he returned when the weather allowed. His goal was to take a closer look at the other promising locations he had seen, further up the hill and off to the right of the Freedom vein.

Even after doing that he would have explored only a small portion of the entire claimed area.

He carried just enough rock tools with him to expose the outcrop so he could examine it more closely and take some samples. If the vein looked promising after a further examination that morning, he would cut out a larger portion for an assay.

As he neared the Freedom, he saw human foot tracks in the snow. A few were older, with sloped sides and a bit of crystallized snow around the edges, indicating they were made before the last small melt. Other tracks were fresh, but off to the side, seemingly bypassing the entrance to the Freedom adit.

He unsaddled the horse and left it in the corral. There was no feed for the animal, but he hadn't intended to be long away from the boarding house stable.

With his rock tools slung over his shoulder in a burlap sack, and his rifle in his right hand, he went to examine the tracks. The disturbed snow made a wide circuit, away from the face of the Freedom.

Glancing up as he passed the tunnel face, he could see hammer, and perhaps axe marks on the big wooden door, as if someone had been attempting to enter the workings. By all appearances, the door had held firm.

He moved around the bulging rock that marked the edge of the claim. The strange tracks continued up the hillside. Stepping cautiously, he followed. A half hour later he could see that the tracks had skirted around the outer claim posts and headed off into the bush, well beyond the area Dominik held interest in. Satisfied that another prospector was simply exploring, he turned back.

Deep snow and the steep, uneven rocks present-ed a challenge, but Dominik finally made his way to the site of one of the promising quartz showings. As he dug out his tools he wondered if he would be lucky enough to find visible gold; a mix of min-erals, or would his effort be rewarded with barren bull quartz?

He took a careful look around the area before he leaned his rifle against a shrub and bent to his work.

He was nervous, and still wondering about those tracks in the snow. As he worked, he took regular glances behind himself and then all around the mixed pine and aspen forests bordering the uphill side of the Freedom claim.

When he first arrived in these hills, he had few tools and less knowledge of the country rock form-ing the hillside. But with the assistance of his new partners, he had an abundance of tools available to him.

As he worked the Freedom, he had been gaining more know-how, along with the knowledge re-quired to prospect more effectively. As the Freedom tunnel was extended into the hillside, he carefully studied the mineral-bearing rock. He believed he was gaining a good working knowledge and un-derstanding of the vein system in the mountain.

Months before, on his first efforts on the hill-side, he had attacked the quartz directly, chipping out small pieces, hoping for a showing of mineral.

Although there were long odds against that kind of exploration, his efforts had been proven successful. The Freedom was the result of this slow and tedious struggle. But he acknowledged that he couldn't plan on beating the odds again.

During his wanderings over the claim in the summer months he had scraped moss and chopped brush as he clambered over the rocks, studying anything that might hold a promise.

That earlier work had exposed a three-foot long section of quartz veining, but with the limitation of the tools he carried with him, the smooth rock face resisted sampling. Now, with the heavier chisel and hammer he planned to cut a channel across the section to expose fresh rock and get a good sample for assay. The quartz and rock proved to be tough, and progress was slow and difficult.

Working with cold, wet and tired hands added a bit of misery to the task. He dropped the chisel into the snow several times. He hit his thumb twice.

But he was a geologist and a prospector. 'This is what I do', he kept telling himself. 'For this I studied in the university'.

Although there were a number of quartz vein exposures across the mountainside, prospecting had shown that not all carried mineral. From working the Freedom vein, he had come to recognize the particular type of quartz that held potential.

The showing he was chiseling on looked promising, so he continued cutting out rock, even though his thumb was swelling and throbbing in pain.

If the values that he hoped for came back after the assay, he could open a fresh adit, in the spring and drive forward on what looked to be a strong vein system.

To get the sample he needed for assay he would start by cutting a notch several inches on each side of the quartz. His plan was to chisel deep enough into the native rock to form an undercut, in order to remove the rock and quartz together.

Nearly broke, and desperate when he first explored this knobby hillside, he had satisfied himself with chipping out a few small pieces of quartz here and there. The tiny bit of gold exposed in the white rock where the Freedom now stood was enough to drive him forward. And it had been the catalyst in his search for development partners.

Now, with some funds behind the mining venture he would carry the rock dug from this morning's work down to the assayer. Two or three samples from the quartz riddled hillside should determine the potential value of the claim.

Digging out a single piece would be enough work for this one cold day.

He had to get it out in a chunk. The assayer insisted on seeing the rock as a whole. He wouldn't provide an assured assay if he didn't break the rock himself.

Dominik focused his efforts on some surrounding rock that already had a few small fissures running through it. Perhaps chipping into the tiny cracks would make his task a bit simpler.

Muscles that had grown slack over the weeks of winter cried out for mercy, but he remained determined. Two hours of steady work had the job nearly done. He balanced his hammer in the notch he had created and stood erect. With his hands on his hips he stretched his upper body as far back as he could, attempting to ease his back and shoulder muscles into something approaching normal. As he tipped his head back, he saw a flicker of movement in the bush off to the left.

Dominik immediately dropped to his knees in the snow and grabbed for his rifle. Glancing around, he convinced himself that there was only the one man. He saw no immediate threat from the approaching walker.

Heavily bearded, wearing a bulky, buffalo hide coat, with his head swathed in scarves, the strange looking intruder trudged steadily down the slope. He was reversing the tracks Dominik had followed uphill earlier, never turning his head towards Dominik or seemingly acknowledging his presence. The man showed no signs of carrying a rifle or other weapon, but Dominik watched his every move anyway.

Not a word was spoken. There was no motion of greeting. The man never slowed down, his steady steps pushing the deep snow aside as he walked.

Within a minute the strange visitor rounded the knoll of rock and disappeared onto the trail to town. Dominik scanned the area carefully again before standing to his feet. The questions he would have liked to ask the fellow would forever go unanswered.

On his travels from Poland to New York to Chicago to Denver, Dominik had heard stories of gold-struck prospectors; men who had spent their entire lives in mountain and desert, searching for the elusive yellow treasure, some losing half their minds in the process. Was this traveler one of those? He would never know, but it looked likely.

By the time he had the rock loosened and ready to lift out, his stomach was reminding him that he should have brought a lunch. Well, he had been hungry before. He remembered cooking the raccoon and hoped to never again be that hungry.

Dominik gathered up his tools, placing them in the burlap sack. He slung his rifle over his shoulder and bent to lift the loosened rock from its natural cradle. His cold and work weary hands grasped the sides of the rock sample. He lifted it, finding it much heavier than he had guessed. He kept it from falling into the snow by jamming one knee against the rock face and resting the cut portion of the rock on his thigh. In the process he dropped the tool sack, and then the rock sample slid into the snow.

Frustrated, and knowing the snow-slippery sample would be even more difficult to carry, he stood erect and wondered what to do. Finally, he cleared the snow from around the rock and eased the burlap bag over the top of it. With some careful wiggling and by lifting a bit at a time, he managed to roll the jagged rock into the sack, nestled on top of the tools.

He twisted the sack top until it resembled a large rope. With strong, but wet and half frozen fingers he took a grip and slung the burden over his shoulder.

He carefully reached for his rifle, slipped his hand, and then his arm, through the sling and soon had it draped over his other shoulder. He then took a two-hand grip on the heavy sack, steadied himself, and started down the hill.

Not being a horseman, he was unprepared for the problems he would face getting aboard the skittish horse.

He saddled the animal with no problem and slid the rifle into its scabbard. He lifted the heavy sack, balancing it on the pommel. With a few wiggles he tried to fashion the loose tools around the saddle horn. The result was shaky at best. The animal was uneasy with the amateur handling, but Dominik didn't notice.

He had become chilled and wet after working in the snow all morning. The horse was stiff and cold from standing in the corral for several hours. It was a poor combination for the inexperienced rider.

To make matters worse, the stirrup was designed for a riding boot. Dominik was wearing miner's thick-soled lace-up boots.

With great determination but little skill, Dominik turned the animal to face downhill, gathering the reins in his left hand. He grasped and balanced the sack as best he could with the extended fingers of that same hand, his thumb throbbing in pain. He took a grip on the cantle with his right hand and lifted his foot.

Fighting cold, fatigue and heavy, clumsy clothing, he missed the stirrup, kicking the horse in the process. The startled animal skittered away, ripping the reins from Dominik's hand and dumping the sack into the snow.

With his head held high and to one side, to avoid the dragging reins, the animal headed down-hill, kicking snow in all directions.

Dominik stood in mute despair as he watched the horse round a corner and disappear from sight.

With, at the most, three hours of daylight left, Dominik faced the fact that he would be walking to town. He had done it before but didn't relish the thought of repeating the walk, with the snow cover hiding the many slippery rocks and hidden traps for his cold feet, and with the heavy sack over his shoulder. He considered locking the sack in the Freedom tunnel, but his stubbornness got the best of his thoughts. He twisted the sack top into a rope again and hoisted the burden to his shoulder.

Bent under the weight of the rock sample and the tools, he hadn't gone fifty feet before he slipped on a snow-covered rock and fell to the ground. It was a portent of what was to come on the long, snowy trail.

***

The early, winter evening was nearly upon the land when Zac rounded the corner onto the trail to the Freedom. He saw the struggling Dominik a quarter mile away.

Leading the escaped horse that had shown up rider-less at the boarding house corral, Zac rode his faithful cavalry animal to where Dominik stood waiting. The heavy sack was resting in the snow at the miner's feet.

Zac instinctively understood that this was the time to keep his thoughts to himself and simply get his partner home, to warmth and food.

Riding a bit past Dominik before turning the animals back towards town, Zac dismounted and passed the reins of his own trustworthy animal to the weary man.

Taking a firm grip on the reins of the skittish run-away, Zac mounted. He then held his hand out for the heavy sack. Dominik understood the wordless gesture and hoisted the burden one more time. Zac lifted it onto his lap while Dominik mounted the more stable animal.

Still wordless, they made their slow way to the boarding house. A noisy reception gained no response from the half-frozen man. He simply hung up his coat, removed his cap, which left his hair standing up in several directions, and dropped into a kitchen chair.

Tillie and Mrs. Templeton commented and fussed around, but Dominik had nothing to say. Tillie finally placed a cup of steaming coffee before him while the landlady was ladling out a bowl of freshly made cream of potato soup. Several slices of homemade bread and freshly churned butter sat in the center of the kitchen table.

Dominik sat in wondering silence, his stiff hands wrapped around the hot mug, as he waited for his fingers to warm up enough to hold the coffee cup, and the spoon.

With a shaky voice he looked at Zac, who had just come in from working over the horses. "Tank you."

He then turned his eyes to the women. "Tank you. Tank you."

Zac was fighting a serious limp. It seemed no one noticed the pain in his eyes. He sat for just a minute and then made his excuses and limped his way to his own room.

It had been a long, cold ride. Longer and colder than his injured hip should have been subjected to.

***

When Dominik came down for a late breakfast the next morning, Zac was just riding into the yard. He was leading a sturdy looking gray. The hammerhead was no longer in the corral.

CHAPTER FORTY-NINE

The long winter was grinding into a slowly arriving spring. Zac was restless. He had been restless for weeks as he waited for his body to heal completely. He was able to walk and to ride, but for only short distances.

Although he was anxious to get back to work at the Freedom, during the snowed-in lull his idle mind was travelling trails far from the hills of Idaho Springs.

Among the trails Zac's mind travelled was the one that led to a burning house and a suffering wife and her little girl, and a group of killers who had escaped into anonymity.

Zac had never thought of himself as one that would seek revenge. Of course, the situation had never before developed to test his reaction. Arriving home from the war he'd entered into a whole new experience.

When he had stepped away from the graves of his family, he was apt to accept the situation as just one more tragedy of war. An unnecessary and evil tragedy, to be sure, but one he could think of no answer to.

In the three years leading up to that time, he had seen so much that was inhumane and ungodly that it almost seemed a part of his soul had become numb.

No one in the district around Carob, Texas had any idea who the raiders were. Their actions had been so swift, so violent, so heartless and so final that anyone who was close enough to witness their deprivations was dead, and anyone who saw the smoke from burning buildings was too far away to intervene.

Lem and Phoebe had hidden themselves so thoroughly in the bush that they saw no individual riders. And by the time Lem ran the half mile to Zac's little farm the raiders were nowhere in sight.

Zac had talked this all over with himself many times. His conclusions were always the same: 'let it go. I don't even have a starting point'.

In times past, the old Zac would have said something like 'leave it with the Lord'. 'He has promised to avenge'.

The new Zac still had those thoughts, but he was more apt to push them aside than listen to them.

Still, if his midnight mind kept seeing burning buildings, and his dead wife and daughter shattered and broken, he might have to try...

Well, he didn't know exactly what he would try. The one thing he was sure of was that his fragile mind didn't respond well to the repeated stress of remembering.

Adding to his stress was the confinement of winter. Having seen only periodic snows and never sleeping outside during long cold nights until the war, he hadn't considered how folks from the northern stretches of the land lived. Now, he had seen about all he wanted to see of high-elevation snow and cold.

He understood well enough that it was activity and constant movement, continuous challenges, that had kept his mind close to balance. He feared losing that balance.

Work. That's what he needed. Productive work. To work himself into a mind absorbing pattern that would block out the dark thoughts. And of course, those efforts he longed for would be directed towards the development of the Freedom.

Strangely, his stress levels seemed to drop when he turned his mind away from himself. When he was helping others, as he did with Lem and Phoebe and with Gertie and with Dominik, with Tillie and the children, with the frightened miners who fell under Big Mike's sway. Under those circumstances he was almost, but not quite, the old Zac. It was as if putting his mind towards those others had the added benefit of hiding or covering his own troubles.

He found it all too confusing to sort out.

***

When the assay from Dominik's ill-considered solo venture to the new quartz showing came in, the results were beyond expectations. But more samples would be needed before funds could be risked on drilling and blasting.

The geologist was not happy at the thought of waiting till spring, but there was no way to get the wagon up the snow-covered trail. Zac needed to get out of the house anyway, so he agreed to accompany Dominik on the prospecting venture.

His healing hip was coming along nicely. He was sure he could handle the ride. Swinging the big hammer might be an altogether different challenge but he was going to give it a try.

Chuckling a bit, Zac suggested to Dominik that the heavy rock samples could be balanced on their saddle horns.

Failing to see the humor in the suggestion, Dominik frowned and shook his head.

After some discussion it was agreed that Dominik, Lem and Zac would all ride. Lem would ride a bareback mule, which he had done many times. He would lead the second mule; with a pack-saddle he dealt the livery owner out of. They would pick up more tools from the Freedom. Working together would shorten the day and lighten the workload. The rock samples would be brought down the hill tied securely on the pack saddle.

***

Another telegram arrived from Roman, advising that the wandering trio of Polish immigrants were in St. Louis. The men were contracted as horse handlers with a westward bound, railway exploration and survey group slated to work west of Cheyenne. They had determined to travel by horseback, tempting the late spring weather and shunning the much slower wagon travel. Bianka was hired as a cook.

With the typical brevity of telegrams, there were many unanswered questions. Those questions would have to wait the much-anticipated arrival of the Polish trio.

CHAPTER FIFTY

The dreary winter was coming to an end. Bare rock welcomed the runoff from the melting snow in the higher-up hills. The tent was pitched again at the mouth of the Freedom tunnel. It would only be used for lunches now. Work was in full motion, with the hired men back on the crew. All over the valley, drilling and blasting could be heard as the mines moved back into full production.

The assays from the rock brought down the hill on the mule confirmed the positive prospects of the two veins that were sampled. Dominik insisted on opening both.

"We look. We see. Maybe both goot. Maybe both no goot. We don't open we don't never know for sure."

Zac and Lem took turns working with Dominik, drilling and preparing the two new quartz exposures for blasting. Black Wiley made a point of riding by to examine the progress and give advice.

It seemed to Zac like no time at all went by before the partnership hired more men to muck out the rock from the two new openings. The assay reports continued to be too good to ignore. So now they had three tunnels under expansion.

As with the Freedom, Dominik spent most of his time on his knees, tapping, breaking and examining each piece of rock before it was shoveled onto the newly forming tailings pile. His excitement knew no bounds as he exclaimed over and over at the signs of mineral in the two new tunnels.

With three openings producing tons of rock, Dominik was kept busier than ever trying to keep ahead of the drilling and blasting crews.

As soon as full-sized adits were opened at the two new sites, the carpenter was brought up the hill again to install strong doors. The partners and the crew would all be staying in town, riding back up the hill each morning for work.

With no close-by security, the doors were necessary to keep prowlers from scooping up any of the high-grade ore.

CHAPTER FIFTY-ONE

The white coated waiter carefully laid the platters of sizzling steaks before Gomer and Tillie. This was the second Saturday evening that they had taken dinner at the hotel dining room. There were fewer whispers this evening than there had been the first time they visited. Tillie was uneasy and a bit embarrassed at the unwanted attention they were drawing. Gomer brushed it all aside.

"Who we have dinner with and where we have it, is no one else's business."

Over the cold months of winter, the duo had started to spend a considerable amount of time together. At first it was evenings sitting by the brass-trimmed pot-bellied wood stove in the sitting room of the boarding house, where much quiet talk and companionable laughter could be heard. They covered their togetherness by playing simple card games with a deck Gomer purchased for the purpose.

That togetherness developed into long walks in the moonlit snow. When Tillie came near to slipping on a snow-covered walkway, it was a natural instinct for Gomer to grab her hand, holding her upright.

To assure them both that she wouldn't risk such a hazard as that again, Gomer continued to hold her hand. He found the matter much to his liking. Tillie didn't pull away, so the lawyer assumed his taking of this small liberty was welcomed.

From there the young couple found the hotel dining room was a pleasant place to share a meal, talk and get to know more about one another.

Things have a habit of moving quickly in new and growing frontier towns. The hand holding moved into giving the beautiful young lady a hug as Gomer helped her with her coat, upon leaving the dining room. The hug became an arm around her waist as they strolled towards the boarding house. Inevitably the hug become a pause in the darkened doorway of a locked-up general store. The kiss that followed seemed natural, almost inevitable. And well worth repeating.

***

Mrs. Templeton picked up some unkind gossip and rumors as she did her normal shopping.

The community was more or less accommodating of blacks who lived and worked among them. The gold frenzy was such that little mind was paid to anything other than gaining riches. And there was always the need for strong backs and willing hands to muck out the tons upon tons of rock that was moved each day.

But a white man courting a black woman might

be taking their accommodation a step too far.

As incensed as Mrs. Templeton was at a couple of overheard comments, she kept her peace and left the store.

She was washing dishes after the evening meal, with Tillie drying and putting them away. Everyone else had gone off to deal with their own matters.

Taking a deep breath and hoping she was doing the right thing, the landlady said, "Tillie, you're a fine young lady and so far as I know, Gomer is a gentleman, with all that title implies. Still, may I ask if you have carefully thought through your courtship and what the future may present you with?"

Tillie was a long time answering. Mrs. Templeton waited silently, giving as much time as the subject required.

Finally, Tillie put down the cloth and turned to her friend.

"I'm not sure it's really a courtship. I've tried to be honest with myself. Of course, in saying that, I must acknowledge that I don't really know where our friendship is heading. Nothing has been said or implied beyond enjoying some time together.

"You will remember that I was raised in the North. While it is not at all common there for mixed races to marry, it is not totally unheard of either.

"Now, there, I just said 'marry'. But I need to assure you that nothing of that nature has been mentioned by either of us, at least until now."

Mrs. Templeton smiled knowingly.

"Young lady, you are either being coy, or you are hiding the truth from yourself. If that young lawyer isn't head over heels, I miss my guess. And you've been a bit dreamy yourself these past weeks.

"You owe me no explanation and I don't ask for one. I only urge you to be sure you use that bright mind the Lord gave you."

Tillie said no more. She simply picked up a dry dishtowel and turned back to the task before her.

***

It was a matter of only three weeks later that the boarding house table was laden with all the delicacies a frontier town could offer for the Easter Sunday celebration. Lem and Phoebe had been invited to round-out the dinner party.

The dinner was lavish by any standard. Mrs. Templeton was pleased and humbled by the praise heaped upon her. She was quick to remind everyone that Tillie had been a big part of the effort, and that Phoebe had baked the dried apple pies.

The men all extended their praises to those two ladies, while Zac went to the big kitchen range and carried in the fresh pot of coffee. With everyone's cup re-filled and the dinner plates removed, the guests slid their chairs back just a bit and settled in for coffee and a visit.

Before any other topic could demand the attention of the gathering, Gomer spoke up.

"I know there has been a lot of talk and sidewise glances for the past while. I need to put that talk to rest, and I can't think of a better time than now, with all our friends gathered around this big, welcoming table.

"Well, the fact is, I have asked Miss Tillie Harper

to be my wife. I have no idea at all what she could possibly see in a half sized struggling lawyer, but somehow, only because of a moment of weakness, I am sure, she said 'yes'."

The dinner table exploded with comments and congratulations. Gomer good naturedly accepted the handshakes and back slaps from the men.

Tillie blushed, and smiled nervously.

When the talk died down Gomer again claimed the floor. Looking directly across the table, he said, "Lem. Phoebe. You have taken so much interest in Tillie's welfare and have helped her in so many ways, I'm sure she has almost come to see you as guiding lights, if not as her adoptive parents. I considered speaking to you, hoping for your approval before we made our announcement, but we finally decided to simply seek your blessing."

Phoebe glanced sideways at her husband. Lem smiled and nodded.

"You two have no obligation to ask Lem or I anything at all on the matter, but we are honored that you did. Yes. My goodness, yes. Of course, you have our approval, and our blessing.

"You will face difficulties in a mixed marriage, but you are young and strong, and the West is mostly a forgiving place, peopled with fine folks. Lem and I wish you every happiness. And we will always be here to help or do whatever needs doing to see you along your way."

The table was quiet for only a moment before Dominik, in all innocence, said what the others had been thinking for weeks. He smiled as he looked at Phoebe.

"You beautiful woman, Miss Phoebe. Tillie beautiful woman too. You look like could be mother and daughter. Goot you meet here in gold mountains. You look much goot together."

The table was silent. It was as if everyone was holding their breath. No one who ever saw the two ladies together could possibly not notice how much they were alike.

Both were beautiful, as Dominik had made clear. Both were tall and slender, with head turning figures. Both were gentle, but firm of voice. Both were graceful in their movements.

The silence and the tension seemed to build until Phoebe put her face in her hands. The brief statement from the Polish geologist struck a bit too close to home. She tried to hide the sob. Lem looked grim and stoic. When she spoke, Phoebe's voice cracked just a bit.

"We had a little girl. Had a little boy too."

Mrs. Templeton laid her hand over Phoebe's and gave a tight squeeze.

Dominik didn't know the story of the sold-off and lost slave children. He looked befuddled and was sure he had done something wrong, but he chose to say no more.

Zac felt the need to say something, hoping it would ease the situation and perhaps bring more happy memories to Lem and Phoebe. Perhaps remind them of the brief joy the children had bought into their lives.

"Lots of heartache in this old world. Sometimes there's no accounting. I lost my beautiful little girl during the war. Name was Minnie. Remember a lot of good, loving times with her though.

"Never going to forget how I lost her, but the hurt seems to get a bit buried under new happenings."

Mrs. Templeton, who never spoke of her life or background said, "Had a daughter. Named her August, for that's when she was born. Love of my life. Would have been near thirty by now if'n the river hadn't taken the wagon, team, my husband, daughter, and all we owned. Swept us all downstream. I woke up, tangled in some brush on the riverbank, hours later.

Never saw hide nor hair of the outfit or my family again. I've never forgotten, but I learned to live once more, and cherish the short memory. No choice, really."

Zac looked across the table at Lem and Phoebe.

"You've told me about the children and the plantation you were slaves on, but I don't think you ever told me the children's names."

Lem, wishing to relieve his wife of more talking and perhaps bring the conversation to an end said, "The boy was oldest. His name Grafton. Little girl we name Cecilia."

Tillie gasped. Everyone turned to look at her. She sat there with her hands holding the edge of the table and with a look of startled amazement on her face. She was casting her eyes between Lem and Phoebe, her gaze intent.

Mrs. Templeton, sitting directly across from her, was closest to Tillie.

"What is it, dear?"

Tillie started to weep, to the point where she could hardly speak.

"Grafton. That's my brother's name. He told Mister Harper his name when we were first together, on the way back north.

"And Grafton has always called me Cecee. He never would call me Tillie."

There was total, shocked silence around the table until Lem asked, with a gravely voice, "Where is your brother now?"

Tillie came out of her trance and studied Lem, as if she hadn't understood the question. She finally said, in a voice so quiet they all had difficulty hearing her, "Why, why, Grafton joined the army. He was hoping to be discharged at the end of the war. He said he would meet up with me in Denver. That's why I left word that I was coming to Idaho Springs."

Lem wasn't finished with his questions.

"Tell me about your Grafton. What does he look like? How big a man is he?"

"Well, I hope I'm not just being foolish, but I'd have to say that he favors you in looks and build. Taller, but not by much."

It was as if everyone around the table was holding their breath.

Lem cast an almost fierce look at Tillie.

"Are there any marks on him? A birthmark or some such?"

Tillie pointed to her chin.

"He has no birthmarks that I know of, just a small half-circle scar, here on his chin."

Sure of his beliefs now, Lem said, "He was running in the grass. Fell on a old piece of metal lyin' there. Cut hisself. Bled som'thin awful."

CHAPTER FIFTY-TWO

There was no possibility of keeping the two new finds on the Freedom claims secret. The fact that a crew was working on an improved wagon road to the mine site would alert even the most unaware resident to the fact that something noteworthy was happening on the hillside.

There had long been prospectors tramping through the woods and climbing across the rocks that made up the mountainside surrounding the Freedom. There was little acreage left anywhere in the area that had not been examined. A few holes had been chipped out and small finds had been made. Claims were posted and worked until the posters gave up in discouragement.

None of that was to suggest that all the prospectors were qualified geologists or that their work was in depth. Many were gadflies, chipping a rock here and there, hoping a fist sized nugget would fall out. But with the news spread abroad about the Freedom, qualified men were climbing the hills, their tool bags over their shoulders, taking another, more careful look.

Work was progressing on all three openings at

the Freedom. The crew was enlarged. The wagon road was nearing completion. The ore was coming in such quantity that there was a steady trail of wagons between the three adits and the mill.

The mill was backed-up, and some other mine owners were screaming about the delay in getting their own ore crushed and processed.

***

Zac was starting to buckle under the pressure.

Mining for gold was all very exciting and profitable. But as an owner of the Freedom, Zac felt great responsibility. Perhaps more responsibility than his often-troubled mind could cope with.

It was unfortunate that, even though Lem and Phoebe had been reasonably well received in Idaho Springs, most folks were having difficulty accepting southern blacks as a part of the business world.

And then, with Dominik's growing but still limited command of the language, it was left to Zac to carry the weight of the Freedom's management with the bank, the mill and the suppliers.

Adding to this pressure was the guilt of watching Dominik rush from one shaft to the next, knowing he could do little to aid the geologist.

As hard as the other owners were working, Dominik was working even harder. Zac was concerned for the man's health but didn't know what to do about it. Even after all the hours of Dominik's teaching, Zac knew the needs of the mine were well beyond his knowledge of minerals.

***

For more than a year, Zac had kept his mind and emotions under check by keeping busy, by concentrating on the tasks and the friends that surrounded him. But even that remedy had its limits. The buzz of activity that he enjoyed was becoming a roar of demanding pressure, increasing, it seemed, every day. He feared his mind was nearing its tipping point.

For relief, as he had done so many times, Zac laid the Henry across his folded elbow and went for a walk. He wasn't going anywhere. He simply needed to be alone, to breath quiet air, to slow his thoughts and his memory down. At Dominik's insistence he carried a hatchet and a chipping hammer. He might see an outcropping that bore examination.

With so many men clambering over the hills, Zac's walking space was limited. He had no desire to talk with anyone. He simply needed to be alone for awhile. To assure his aloneness he decided to stay on the claim. It was, after all, a large area. And not even Dominik had been over all of it.

It was hours later that he walked back onto the original site, heading for the tent. The crew had gone home and the last wagon for the day was disappearing down the trail. Lem and Dominik were seated in the shade of the canvas shelter, drinking coffee, waiting for his return.

"One cup left," Lem hollered as he saw Zac approaching.

Zac silently laid the Henry across the table, poured the last cup from the pot, and took his seat.

"We'll drink this and then I need to show y'all something."

Half an hour later, after climbing over a steep, but short hillside and sliding down the sloping rock on the other side, the three men were in a brush filled hollow at the far reaches of the Freedom claim. They could see some chopped-off scrub lying in a heap at the side of the hollow, where Zac had hacked his way in.

Zac leaned a ten-foot aspen tree away from the sloping rock and indicated that Dominik should take a look behind it.

Eager, as always, the geologist shouldered his way past the tree, pushed some small brush out of the way and stood silently. After a minute had past by, he called Lem.

"Lem. You come. You see. Is goot, I'm tinking."

Zac chuckled to himself.

"I guess you could say it's good. Gold flecks showing right through the quartz. Like an invitation. You might say that's good."

CHAPTER FIFTY-THREE

There was no further word. No telegram. No letter. No announcement of any kind. There was just the rattle of a light buckboard wagon clattering over the rocks at the base of the tailings pile at Freedom One. There were two men and one woman sitting on the high, spring seat.

That noise was followed by shouted instruction to the team, calling them to a stop. "konie zatrzymują się". The shout was in Polish, words that no one in the busy lunch tent understood. Words the horses would have never heard before.

In any language, or no spoken language at all, the team would have responded to the slight back-pull on the reins. The 'whoa' wasn't really necessary, in Polish or in English.

As the curious crew looked on, Roman stepped down from the rig and approached the tent. Again, only a single word was spoken.

"Dominik?"

One of the crew pointed over his shoulder with a turned back thumb.

"In the tunnel."

The mystified look on the enquirer's face caused the crewman to repeat his words, only louder, as if the issue at hand was deafness.

"In the tunnel."

This time the enquirer turned a bit to follow the path the pointing thumb was aimed at. He lifted his own hand, pointing at the tunnel, with a questioning look on his face.

"That's what I said, 'in the tunnel'."

The Polish visitor turned, climbing the crude rock stepping-stones onto the tailings pile. With hesitant steps he approached the dark opening on the hillside.

As he walked across the waste rock, one of the crew at the lunch table laughed and said, "Square-heads. Dutchmen. The lands gett'n run over with 'em."

Another man at the table answered that comment.

"You'd best keep that talk to yourself. We've a good thing going here. Good wages. Place to take our lunch in the shade. Close to town. And all because a Dutchman, as you call them, found a major gold showing. I, for one, ain't got a problem with square-heads or Dutchmen."

Roman approached the big wooden door with trepidation. He had never been in a mine tunnel. He wasn't sure he wanted to go into this one now. He glanced cautiously around and then looked up the slope above the shaft opening. There was a lot of rock up there. He wouldn't like to be in the mine if that rock decided to collapse.

In an excess of caution, he chose to lean into

the dim space, his two hands firmly gripping the door frame on either side, as if seeking this pillar of security. He shouted out 'Dominik?' into the darkened space before him.

He waited perhaps thirty seconds before shouting again.

"Jeste tam brat" (Are you in there, brother?)" he shouted in Polish.

There was an immediate, excited answer, also in Polish and the sounds of running feet on the uneven rock floor. Dominik emerged from the dimness of the tunnel and nearly bowled his brother over in his enthusiastic greeting.

The two men hugged and slapped each other on the back while they danced in a slow circle, both talking at once. Finally, Dominik held his brother off at arm's length to take a close look at him. He then pulled him into a rib straining hug again.

Speaking Polish, Roman said, "Hold up there, brother, you have the arms of a blacksmith. I didn't come all this way just to have you crush the life out of me."

Dominik laughed in joy and turned to the wagon, where Bianka and Antoni sat, watching the happy reunion. He barely glanced at Antoni, but he took a long, approving look at Bianka.

Having assured himself that the two on the wagon seat were truly the neighbor girl that graced his dreams, and her brother, he let loose of Roman and walked to where the wagon sat.

Antoni stepped to the ground and smiled at the approaching geologist. The two men settled for a firm handshake and a greeting before Dominik turned to the girl.

"Bianka, is that really you? I was afraid we may never see each other again, but here you are, halfway around the word. You must have had many adventures getting here and I want to hear every one of them, but not right now.

"Welcome, dear Bianka. How often I have dreamed of seeing you again. You are more beautiful than ever. Oh, my. I don't even know what to say. Welcome. But I guess I already said that didn't I?"

Bianka spoke for the first time.

"Yes, I believe you might be repeating yourself. Perhaps you have been in this lonely frontier for too long."

She said it all with a radiant smile.

"Help me down so I can give you a hug."

Dominik knew this farm girl needed no help getting off a wagon, but it was a gesture he appreciated anyway. The hug was gentle but long enough to lend meaning to the restraining circumstances, with her brother and a tent full of men looking on.

While the visitors were being greeted, Zac and Lem wandered down the trail from Freedom Two. They sized up the situation immediately. Without hesitation they approached the gathering and held their hands out to the men.

Along with the handshakes Zac said, "Zapraszamy", (welcome).

At Roman's raised eyebrows Zac laughed and said, "Dominik has been teaching me a few Polish words."

Dominik translated for the others. The three newcomers nodded in unison and said, "Tank you."

Antoni showed a slight hesitation at shaking

hands with a black man but Roman returned a firm shake. Bianka held out both of her strong hands but Lem very gently took only her fingers and quietly said, "Zapraszamy."

***

Leaving the mining operation in Lem's capable hands, Zac and Dominik saddled their horses and accompanied the wagon back down the trail. They went directly to the little lunch café that the group had originally met in. The harried waitress pointed at a large table in the corner and hollered, "Beef and fried spuds or sausage and kraut?"

Dominik translated and confirmed that they would all have the beef.

After the leisurely lunch the group made its way to the boarding house. It had been decided that Dominik would give up his room so Bianka could stay there, with the other women. The men would go to one of the other boarding houses in the area.

A more permanent solution would be needed but that could await another day.

CHAPTER FIFTY-FOUR

Knowing they already had more on their plate than one beginner geologist and a couple of helpers could cope with properly, the group was reluctant to spread their efforts any thinner. Still, curiosity, if nothing else, demanded that they do an assay on the quartz outcrop Zac had uncovered.

Wishing to keep the find as secreted as possible, they were careful not to damage the trees around the site while a good sample was hacked out of the rock. They settled for just one sample, feeling they already had a pretty good idea what would show in an assay.

With the rock removed, they carefully pushed the surrounding trees and brush back into place.

A week later the assay report lay on the table before them. It made their heads buzz with possibilities.

***

What their next steps should be, and how to proceed, was always the major topic of conversation when the partnership was together. Phoebe drove a good portion of the talk with her insistence that a plan be developed. A plan that was affordable and workable.

Their original plan, such as it was, was simple. Find some gold. There was no more to it than that. But with good fortune they had far exceeded that modest yearning. Now they were starting to feel that they were attempting to hold back an avalanche.

"You men are working yourselves into your graves, but for all the world, I can't piece it together. We already have more money in the bank than we ever dreamed possible. I'd like to see us all enjoying some rewards before you work yourselves to death."

The talk got around to forming an official corporation and hiring the expertise to develop the mine the way it deserved to be developed.

Zac pictured the big mine up on the hillside across town, with all its buildings, its workings, its humming, puffing steam engine and pounding mill, its crew working shifts, its management team holding it all together.

Inwardly he cried, 'no', knowing he couldn't cope with all that busyness and pressure. But for the time being he held his peace.

***

Black Wiley brought it all to a head while he and the partners were drinking coffee in the tent, after blowing another set in Freedom One.

Taking a sip of the hot liquid between each

thought, he slowly said, "Met a man. Couple a days ago. Was in the mining supply store. Look'n fer work. Mine engineer. Fresh down from Virginia City. Tunnel man."

The partners sat silently, studying their friend.

Finally, Black Wiley settled himself into a more comfortable position, set his coffee mug on the table, and proceeded with his thoughts.

"Men. You got yourselves a whoopdinger of a find here. I'm think'n you're goin' to learn that these veins run together, by n' by. And that means a big find. Even bigger than what ya got goin' now. Maybe one of the biggest in the area.

"Thing is though, ya get any deeper ya got some thinking to do and some money to spend. You need ventilation. A lot of ventilation. Else you and your crew are going to find yourselves sicker than you want to be. Lots of chemicals in this powder. That, along with the dust, is a poor combination. Kill ya, ya give 'er time enough.

"You'll notice I don't go back inta the shaft after we blow 'er. Needs time fer the air to purify itself after we let 'er off. Lots of time and fresh air.

"Ya need tracks laid and cars ta carry the ore. Yer gett'n too far in fer wheelbarrows, and its only goin' ta get to be a bigger problem, each foot ya blow.

"And then there's sure to be more side veins show up as you dig 'er deeper. Yer already follow'n the one. Track'n them side veins is going ta force you ta think of the roof. Yer alright with just the one narrow passage but ye open 'er up and yer faced with some bigger matters.

"There's other things to think about. That's why I mentioned the mine engineer. If he knows his stuff, he could earn his pay easy enough. But he's going to tell you just what I already told ye."

With a grin he said, "Only thing is, he'll want ta git paid fer the tell'n. I just did 'er all fer free.

"Now then, is there any more liquid in that there coffee pot, or did you hard rock men drink 'er all down?"

Zac shook the pot. Judging by weight and the sloshing sound, there wasn't much left.

"I'll put on another pot."

***

Lem had listened carefully to the powder man and had the question that was on all their minds.

"Fergett'n all the details fer now, what's yer suggestion?"

Wiley took a slow look around the gathering, judging their feelings.

"Can't tell you what to do. But if she were mine, I'd be talk'n ta one of the big companies. Someone with the knowledge and the dollars ta make 'er all come together. I'm think'n you'd get a buyout that'd put a smile onta yer faces. Might even stay on as partners. Collect a steady wage and make yerselves a handful a extra cash come dividend time.

"Now, it's true you might could open 'er up as a company, issue shares and all that. You might even make more money that way. But ye need ta notice that I said 'might'. Might also all blow up in yer faces."

The partners had many questions but nothing more was said at the time.

CHAPTER FIFTY-FIVE

Two matters were obvious right from the start, with the arrival of the Polish immigrants.

The first was that Dominik's mind was never very far from the peasant farm outside Krakow where a cow-milking neighbor girl lived. She had never been far from his mind, when it came right down to the rights of it.

He had seldom talked about her during the time he had been working with the group. Perhaps his lack of English held him back.

He had also been unable to find a solution to his one-sided, long distance dream.

Then there was the fear that she could already be married to someone else. Could be raising a family by now.

The second matter. One that delighted the geologist, was that the arrival of the neighbor girl was a sure sign that she had been thinking of him too.

The courtship of these two Polish wanderers was short and decisive. To Dominik's critical question

Bianka answered, somewhat in amusement, "So, Mister mining man, why do you think I travelled so far? You think I just wanted to see the world, maybe? You foolish man. I came here to marry you. Does that answer your question?"

Dominik could find nothing at all worth saying.

The majority of Polish people were of the Catholic faith but there was a smaller portion following the Eastern Orthodox path. Dominik and Bianka's families, Orthodox to the core, both held strong feelings about the Catholics.

After discussions with Zac and Phoebe, with Dominik repeating everything into Polish, the young couple decided they could consider themselves to be adequately married with the services of the Baptist Pastor.

It was either that or the Catholic meeting place and that wasn't to be considered.

To their surprise and delight, Tillie and Gomer invited them to join their service and have one large, double wedding.

***

The matter was settled and over with so quickly that Dominik was still in a bit of a haze, wondering if it was all real.

With the simplicity of a small, frontier town, the fancy fixings that might have made the occasion more festive or colorful were simply not available. The brides agreed that none of that was necessary to make the day special.

Zac, looking on from his position as best man

for Gomer, decided that more effort had been put into fixing up the ladies' hair than all the rest of the ceremony put together.

Tillie was somewhat limited by the curly nature of her black hair, but somehow it was still special, with a bright red ribbon skillfully wound through it.

Bianka's long, blonde tresses, were unwound from the large braid she usually twisted them into. In place of the braid was wave after wave of curls and pleats.

The result for both women was outstanding.

Along with the simple, but still elegant dresses purchased for the occasion, the desired effect was accomplished.

Bianka, built a bit sturdier than the tall and slim, but well-formed Tillie, were both pictures of grace and expectancy.

The two grooms, stiff in newly purchased suits, along with shirts, high collars and string ties, watched their brides walking down the center aisle of the little church with wonder at their good fortune.

To ease the situation for Bianka, the pastor paused long enough for Dominik to translate.

When it came time to ask who was giving these ladies to be married, Antoni spoke on behalf of his father, knowing their far away parents would approve of the marriage.

When the same enquiry was made about Tillie, Lem nearly burst out of his shirt with pride as he answered, "Her mother and I do."

There had been much discussion before making that public declaration, since there was still some doubt about the accuracy of the statement. But it was finally decided that it was correct in spirit and intent even if not in true heritage.

***

The pastor kept the service short but still found time to emphasize the rough nature of the new West and especially of their gold mining high-country town.

"Love each other unconditionally and keep The Lord as the center of your lives. That's the formula for a long and happy marriage, here or anywhere else."

Walking back down the aisle after the service, Gomer looked as if he just might crack his face in half if he smiled any more brightly.

Dominik had all the appearance of a man who had just witnessed a miracle.

***

Mrs. Templeton and Phoebe had worked closely with the hotel to arrange for a dinner following the service. The hotel couldn't close the entire dining room on a busy Saturday evening, but they marked off a space along the back wall exclusively for the wedding party.

Housing was not plentiful in Idaho Springs,

with its growing population, but Gomer managed to find two cottages that would do for the newly-weds until better arrangements were made.

Dominik showed up at work two days after the wedding. Even a new bride couldn't keep him away from his beloved Freedom Mine.

CHAPTER FIFTY-SIX

After a tour of the workings, both Roman and Antoni were more convinced than ever that they had
no interest in becoming miners.

"We are farmers," Roman said to Dominik. "I
don't think I would enjoy living like a mole."

Although they had both picked up a smattering
of English on their trip west, their conversations
with Dominik were held in Polish.

"We travelled through some fine farmland north
of Denver. Maybe we will go down there. Perhaps
there will be jobs available."

Dominik understood their dislike for the mine
and their attraction to the green lands to the north,
in the shadow of the Front Range. He, too, saw this
land on his way west. While he saw the land for
what it was, he was determined to become a miner,
leaving the farming and ranching to others.

"You go and look. But you don't look for jobs.
You look for land. When you find what you want
you come back here.

"I will ask Gomer to go with you to negotiate.

We will purchase the land and you will do with it whatever is best. Maybe you grow grain. Maybe you raise cattle. Maybe you have fruit trees. And maybe our parents will also come here to farm."

With a short farewell lunch, the two men mounted their wagon and headed down the trail to Denver.

CHAPTER FIFTY-SEVEN

The partnership was trusting Gomer more and more as they thought of the good work he had done in settling the Big Mike Mullins matter.

Zac knew that none of them in the partnership were truly businessmen. They had gotten to where they were through hard work on a solid mineral find. But to expand the mine was beyond their full understanding.

And they knew Black Wiley was correct; the whole thing could blow up in their faces if they were to a make a critical mistake.

They would need knowledgeable help in whatever they did.

Following instructions from the group, Gomer made contact with a large mining company in Denver.

"We've certainly heard of the Freedom find," Col. Miles Bellows, the puffy, somewhat overfed manager of the Upcountry Mineral Company, said.

"It's all talk, of course. Little more than barroom chatter at this point. We haven't seen any actual reports or numbers. Exactly what is your interest Mister Radcliff?"

"I've been tasked by the partnership to shop the mine to a knowledgeable and honorable mining company. And believe me, Colonel, the Freedom is not mere barroom chatter.

"The purpose behind our enquiry is to either sell the holding in its entirety, or to bring in a working partner with the financial strength and expertise to take the project forward on a profitable basis.

"If you were to express interest in the proposal, we could proceed to a detailed examination of possibilities. If, on the other hand, you tell me that you have no interest, I would simply thank you for your time and move on."

Miles Bellows, who liked to be called, Colonel, tilted back in his big swivel chair and tapped his teeth with the end of his pencil. He studied his guest with intense eyes. The fact that this man had picked up on the name preference bode well for his intelligence.

Gomer, a pretty good negotiator himself, sat silently, returning the steady stare. The leather satchel with the mine assay and production reports was left untouched at his feet.

After a full two minutes of silent deliberation, Col. Bellows came back to an erect position in his chair and then stood to his feet. With four steps across the board room floor he reached a side door and turned the knob. Pulling the door open, he leaned only his head and shoulders around the door frame.

"Erasmus, I need you."

Gomer watched as a ruddy faced man came

through the doorway. Erasmus was a big man in his shoulders, chest and arms, with all the rough appearances gained from years in the outdoors. By looks he would fit in where ranchers or prospectors gathered.

The introduction was casual.

"Erasmus, this is Mister Radcliff. Lawyer from up in the Springs. Wants to sell us the Freedom."

He turned to Gomer. "Erasmus is our main engineer. Knows more about rocks and holes in the ground than anyone I know."

Gomer stood and the two men shook.

"Not much on the Mister, Erasmus. Just call me Gomer."

The engineer showed a small smile and took a seat.

Wishing to show he was in charge, the Col. said, "So tell us what you've got, Mister Radcliff."

Gomer reached for the leather satchel.

"I'll simply let the reports do the talking."

He pulled out a sheaf of papers and laid them on the desk in front of the Col. The company manager merely slid them sideways, stopping them in front of the engineer.

Except for the shuffling of paper and the occasional 'hmmm', from Erasmus, the office was silent for a full ten minutes.

Gomer needed all his willpower to sit silently, waiting.

The Col. restrained himself for a few minutes and then shuffled his feet before standing and walking to the window. He stood there, looking to the hills above Denver, his hands locked behind him, until Erasmus pulled the papers together, tapped them on the tabletop, side to side and then top to bottom, creating a neat bundle.

The Col. Didn't bother turning around. He simply said, "Well?"

Erasmus was clearly a man of simple thoughts and words. "Best I've ever seen, Colonel. Even better than the Blue Girl, up to Cripple Creek."

Another full minute of silence went past. Finally, the Col. said, "What brought you to my office Mister Radcliff? Was it just chance? Or have you been going from company to company hoping to find an interested party?"

Gomer chuckled and said, "No Colonel. It's not at all like that. I've been researching and fact finding for the past month. With the magic of the telegraph it's actually fairly easy to do.

"I have contacts in the banking world in San Francisco. I also have law associates in several towns across the west, men I studied law with. A couple of them are in towns where you own mines. The Pinks are also easily contacted.

"I gathered information from each of those contacts.

"I needed to know two things: Is your company stable financially and are you, and the people working under you, morally trustworthy?

"I know you have had some problems with your silver deposit up on the Comstock, but even there you seem to be trying to make it right. I'm told that if you get the tunnel stabilized, you'll be back into a profit position.

"All in all, Colonel, I know quite a lot about you and your company. And the fact we're sitting together in your board room should indicate that I found little to trouble me or my clients."

The eyes that studied Gomer were the fieriest he had ever seen. He could think of no one who could hold up under that scrutiny without flinching.

Finally, with a glance at his engineer, the Col. said, "I commend you, Mister Radcliff. That's something I might have done, but few others would bother with it. This is a fast moving, big money industry with a lot of fly-by-night investors either getting rich or going broke. There seems to be no happy medium with that gang."

Gomer nodded in understanding.

"Believe me when I tell you, Colonel, that my clients are not fly-by-night types. Nor are they in this for the fast dollar. They have worked incredibly hard to get where they are. They're not about to quit or give it away."

Erasmus asked, "Why exactly are they searching the market?"

"Because they are intelligent enough to realize that they either have to do that or hire the expertise and find the capital to pull it all together."

The Col. showed the first sign of a small smile.

"In other words, they're in over their heads."

"Not yet, they're not. But that could happen, and they wish to prevent it."

The Col. turned to his engineer.

"What are you working on, Erasmus? Could you let it go for a few days while you take a look at this show?"

The engineer glanced at Gomer.

"How are you traveling, Gomer? Did you ride down or come in a wagon or buggy?"

Gomer laughed as he got to his feet.

"I'm afraid I ride like a lawyer, Erasmus. No ranch would hire me, but I somehow get where I'm going. But I'm no fan of wooden wagon seats either. So, I'm riding."

The engineer smiled and said, "Well, I ride like an engineer. I'll meet you in front of this office at sunrise tomorrow. We'll go for breakfast and then take to the hills."

CHAPTER FIFTY-EIGHT

Dominik, Zac and Lem escorted the engineer through the workings and then showed him the quartz seam hidden behind the alder bush. After a slow walk across the remainder of the rocky claim, he stopped at the highest point of rocks. Erasmus had seemingly missed nothing. He asked few questions but appeared to notice every detail. He frequently jotted a few words in his pocket notebook.

"Men, I'll stay the night at the hotel and ride down in the morning. We can meet for dinner this evening if you wish, but there'll be no discussion about the mine until I have instructions from the Colonel. My report will be on the Colonel's desk tomorrow afternoon. He's known for taking his time with the research but also for making quick decisions once he has the research in his hands.

"Now, we still need to discuss what you're offering. Do you want a full buy-out or do you wish to stay on as working partners or simply as investors? That information needs to become a part of my report.

"I don't need values from you. If he makes an offer at all, the Colonel will place his own value on the Freedom, depending on my analysis."

Zac explained how the partnership shares were distributed. The engineer was surprised to hear that Phoebe was a full partner in Lem's share but he had no objection.

Zac took a seat on a protruding rock. The others followed suit.

Erasmus lifted the notebook from his shirt pocket and prepared to take notes.

Zac continued his explanation.

"We've talked this over pretty thoroughly, Erasmus. We all have a lot of blood and effort in the development of the Freedom. And, of course, it's Dominik's discovery. The partners preference would be to continue on as owners but to bring in your group as managers and financiers.

"How each person's skills are put to use could be negotiated. I think you'll agree that Dominik has proven to be an above average geologist and prospector.

"Lem is very good with the men and could probably be put in charge of all the labor force.

"Phoebe has a good command of the language and of numbers. She might be found to be of assistance in recordkeeping or bookkeeping."

Erasmus waited for Zac to point out his own strengths and preferences. When nothing was said he looked at Zac.

"And you?"

Zac sounded like he didn't really want to answer, as if the truth were somehow hurtful, but necessary. He had come to fully recognize his limitations.

It was true that with the trauma of the war and the murder of his family, he had needed the busyness and the hard work and the trusted friends. He believed those things together had kept him from a full mental breakdown. In some ways he was hiding from himself and from the facts. But he made no apologies for that.

But now he needed peace. And some space of his own. A large and thriving mine was clearly not going to provide either of those. In any case, the others didn't need him anymore. They were all well established financially and had developed a solid foundation from which to grow into the future. He was free to stay or to go, as he felt best.

"I'll be pulling out, Erasmus. There're several reasons for that, all of them totally personal. No one could ask for a better group of people to work and live with and no one could ask for a more profitable life than working the Freedom. But it's time for me to do what's best for me."

Dominik and Lem looked startled at the news but left the questions for a later time.

Zac continued.

"I'll leave my share as an investment. It there's dividends at the end of the year they can be deposited in my account. I'll catch up to that news sooner or later."

When Erasmus finished writing all that down, he said, "One more thing. The Colonel will need to have a majority position before he moves ahead. He won't bite on a fifty percent position."

It took a moment for the group to let that soak.

Zac finally said. "He can buy out half of my shares. That would give him his full half plus another eight and leave me with an eighth."

***

Within a week the deal was done. Zac had his share purchase money safely tucked away in his bank account, and the share structure of a new company was formalized.

Gomer was hired to be the local comptroller, looking over all the mill reports, as well as the wages and the purchases for the mine.

Erasmus moved his wife to Idaho Springs and the development of the Freedom was soon fully underway.

Zac watched the beehive of activity around Freedom One, sitting in the shade of a hillside pine grove. The more he saw the more he was content with his decision. He would be riding within a couple of days, as soon as he made his final arrangements.

CHAPTER FIFTY-NINE

Zac gave one final wave as he pointed his cavalry mount out of Idaho Springs. His pack was tied securely on the big gray he had purchased for Dominik to ride after his ill-fated venture in the deep snow.

There were no actual tears at the dinner the evening before, but there had been few smiles and no outward show of good cheer either.

He had tried to explain his reasons for leaving, avoiding the most personal parts of the decision, but he wasn't sure his friends and partners, except Lem and Phoebe really understood.

Those two saw the bigger picture for Zac but chose to say nothing in front of the group.

As he swung up the trail to the south west of Idaho Springs, he began feeling a sense of lightness. A sense of relief or release, almost. Perhaps he hadn't really understood the weight of responsibility he had loaded onto his own shoulders.

He only had to watch that the release didn't collapse into pointlessness. His life had to have meaning, or he would be in danger of giving in to melancholy. He was sure he would be alright by himself for a few weeks, or for however long it took to get to New Mexico. But he would remain vigilant of his emotions in any case.

CHAPTER SIXTY

Zac was in no hurry. He didn't have a schedule to meet. And this was all new country; beautiful and fit to explore. The evenings were getting short, with fall coming on, but that suited him fine. He didn't want to ride long days anyway. The early mornings would be chilly, but again, he didn't mind that. He had purchased a tanned buffalo robe to use as a cover against the cold nights. And he had his sheepskin coat.

***

The trail to Silver City and Fairplay was well marked. It would be tough going for a wagon, but the horses handled it well. He had no way to know for sure, but as he felt the horse struggle, and as he sensed his own need to breathe more deeply than normal, he guessed they were topping ten thousand feet, and perhaps more on some of the hillsides.

Zac had no particular reason to go to either of the mining towns. But perhaps he would sit down to a hot meal or two along the way, if something looked promising.

By riding the back way, avoiding Denver, he was simply side-stepping traffic and people. And seeing some new country. His goal was Santa Fe.

He had never been there and didn't know anyone who had, but the talk around town was that the winters were short and mild. Short and mild sounded just fine to Zac. He had convinced himself that he couldn't survive another high-country winter.

Zac managed to push his short ride into a ten day stretch, wandering and exploring and dawdling about, along the way. Finally, riding into Silver City at mid-day, he was struck by the similarity to Idaho Springs. The hills were different, and Silver City was higher in elevation, but that it was a mining town could not be missed. The thunder of the big stamp mills overshadowed every facet of the town.

The single road into town expanded into several trails that branched into the residential districts and to the outlying businesses. Zac chose to ride through town until he found a livery stable. There he boarded his two animals, storing saddles and pack in the small adjoining room.

Many towns were shying away from carrying weapons on the streets, but he toted the Henry along anyway. His belt gun was sheltered from view by his sheepskin coat.

He took lunch at a small café and then registered at the hotel. With two days rest, he was again saddling his horse.

The ride to Fairplay was short, but pleasant. There were trails everywhere. He chuckled to himself as he pictured hundreds of seekers chopping trails, riding, walking, tapping rocks, building hopes and suffering disappointments. Only the odd few were as fortunate as Dominik.

He turned the one-day ride into two and arrived at Fairplay in time for dinner and a night's sleep. A stroll around town the next morning convinced him that he might just as well ride on. One mining town looked pretty much like another.

The difference with Fairplay was that it was on the edge of a great grassy plain. With mountains to the west and a few broken hills close by, the land opened onto a high mountain valley, broken here and there by rock upthrusts.

Zac, feeling much more at home on the grass than he ever did in the mountains, pushed his animals south by east, following the grassy carpet and avoiding the hills. Again, he explored as he rode.

He saw just a small scattering of cattle close to a rough built shelter. He saw no people.

He knew the country would one day support large herds, but that time was not yet.

Twice he saw herds of buffalo in the distance. He gave them a wide berth, not knowing anything at all about the beasts and not wishing to learn the hard way.

Five days of slow riding took him through a more mountainous area, finally arriving at the banks of the Arkansas River, although he didn't know its name at the time. He turned east, following the watercourse until the land again opened before him.

Zac was thoroughly enjoying his lonely ride. It seemed like forever since he had been alone. In fact, including his time in the army, and with Lem and Phoebe and the mining partners, it had been near enough to five years that he had people around nearly all the time.

Since the war he had taken a cautious path on his desire to be alone, knowing that it was work and good company that was holding him on a somewhat even keel.

Setting out on this trip to Santa Fe he had assured himself that if his mind started slipping into dangerous territory, he would find emotional shelter with other people.

That thought had him thinking about his friend Moody Tomlinson and the little church in Carob, Texas. Would he ever again find a friend like Moody? It was doubtful.

Thinking about Moody, his mind logically went to Moody's question, 'is it still well with your soul'?

Zac held his thoughts still for a minute or two. Then, feeling a bit of something come over him, perhaps nostalgia, perhaps a prompting from the Lord, he looked up to the bright blue sky.

"Are you still there, God? I'm right here on the back of this horse in the middle of a magnificent country. Can you see me?"

CHAPTER SIXTY-ONE

Only once, in the distance, did Zac spot a small band of Indians. He knew this had all been Indian country not long ago, and some of it still was. Seeing the group of riders a half mile to the west, he waved his hat in the air but kept riding.

There was a lengthy pause as he continued to watch the group. Finally, one warrior lifted his bow above his head, waving it just a bit. They each went their way with no more contact.

After another day's ride, he was sitting on the edge of a small rise, leaning against a burnt-out pine tree when he saw dust in the east. He checked his Colt and pulled the Henry within easy reach. As he continued making his meal, he kept a close eye on the horizon.

There was far too much dust for a single rider, or even for a group of riders. It could only be a buffalo herd on the move or a bunch of driven cattle. He could see no reason there would be an army patrol in the area that would be large enough to kick up that much dust.

Zac decided there was nothing to fear and no reason to saddle up. Not yet anyway. If the circumstances changed it would take but a minute or two to be underway.

Within the hour Zac could clearly identify a herd of cattle with several white topped wagons in the lead. Cowboys were holding the herd together and driving them forward. He watched a single horse ahead of the wagons until he could identify it as an Appaloosa. The rider was slouched over carelessly, as if he had found a comfortable position and had no intention of giving it up. He was clearly not an ex-cavalry man.

It took almost another hour for the rider on the Appaloosa to swing south, leading the group to the edge of the same rise Zac was sitting on, about a half mile away.

Riding up to the edge of the rise, the lead rider swung to the ground and waved for the others to walk up. A large group of people stood down from their wagons and horses, edging up to the lip of the rise.

He saw the man who rode the Appaloosa pointing across the land before them, casting his arm from east to west, as if presenting the land for examination.

Zac was too far away to hear any words, but he imagined the leader exclaiming about the sight before them.

What was being pointed out was thousands upon thousands of acres of grass. Miles of grass. Grasslands with just a few rocky upthrusts here and there.

***

Although he'd been sitting at his fire for the past two hours, enjoying the view, Zac couldn't help following the pointing arm.

It was all a sight to see. Beauty that city folks never saw. Grass, mountains, open spaces. What more could any freedom loving man or woman wish for?

Far off to the south could be seen a hazy outline of mountains. Zac, looking at them earlier figured they could be in New Mexico, but he wasn't sure.

Many miles to the west stood more mountains. Someone had told him there were snow capped hills down this way that folks had named the Sangre de Cristo Mountains. This could be them. He would have to ask someone. If he ever saw another person, in this lonely country, that had the time to visit.

***

At a signal from one of the men, the cowboys started moving the cattle forward. They skirted the wagons and slowly pointed the animals south. The beeves were soon slipping and skidding down the short slope, their front feet digging into the grass.

As the herd reached the bottom, they spread themselves along a small creek. Water was always welcome in this semi-desert country.

Suddenly three young men rode their horses down the hill and out over the grass. Standing in their stirrups, their arms held wide and yelling Rebel yells that Zac could faintly hear, the riders galloped over the welcoming sod.

Zac had no way of knowing who these folks were or where they had come from, but he could clearly see that they considered themselves to be at home. To have arrived.

As the men eased the wagons down the slope, the rider on the appaloosa rode over to where Zac was sitting.

Zac could see now that he was an older man, dressed half like an Indian, wearing a much-abused Stetson with a feather sticking up behind.

"Saw you here, just a-sett'n. Figured ye might have a spot of coffee ye could spare."

"Get down and make yourself to home," answered Zac.

Almost as an afterthought he said, "Beautiful horse."

The man turned and looked at his animal. "Ol' App and I been together a while now. Couldn't ask for a better mount. Seen most of the West together, and some of the East, time ta time."

The old man dug into a saddle bag and found a dinted and scratched metal mug. He picked up the pot and poured just a half inch into the cup. After sloshing it around for a few seconds he threw the dregs into the grass.

Zac figured that was as much cleaning as the mug was apt to get.

Finding a piece of grass to his liking, the visitor folded his knees and sat. He stuck out a dirty hand.

"Known as Jimbo. You ask anyone in the know about Jimbo, they'll point me out. Been around these parts since those mountains was just hills."

Zac introduced himself and the two men concentrated on their coffee.

Finally, Zac said, "Quite a herd. Looks like several families."

Jimbo turned and looked affectionately at the people pitching tents and lighting supper fires.

"Salt of the earth folks. Met Mac before the war. Called himself Walker back then. Knew then he was a special sort of feller. Now, here again our paths crossed. Back in Fort Dodge. Only this time he's married and driving cattle. Veteran of that Eastern foolishness.

"This grass has been waiting all eternity for just these settlers, and for no one else. Couldn't have a happier situation."

Zac watched the activity for a minute. Far in the background he could see buffalo grazing.

"Not settling just yet, myself. I've been up to Idaho Springs for the past while. Partner in a gold mine. Good mine. But I've had enough of cold winters and dark tunnels. Heading for Santa Fe. Figured the winters might be a bit more friendly there.

"Anyway, I'm getting a mite tired of bland, Northern food. Longing for something I can taste."

The two men sat in companionable silence as they drained the coffee pot.

Finally, Jimbo rose to his feet.

"Ride down and meet Mac and Margo and the folks if ye wish. You'll like them."

Another few seconds went past.

"Santa Fe, eh? I'm longing to go with you, but I got things holding me here for just a while yet.

"Good town Santa Fe. You'll enjoy it.

"Say holo to the señoritas for me when you get there."

Zac rose and shook Jimbo's hand.

***

When he was alone again, Zac picked up the saddle and walked to his horse. Within five minutes he had the pack in place on the gray, his fire put out and was sitting the saddle himself.

He pointed his animal down the slight grade and out onto the flat.

"Might meet those folks another time. Looks like they got their hands full without me getting in their way. For me, I think I'll get a few hours closer to Santa Fe before the sun goes behind those snowy mountains."

A LOOK AT: MAC'S WAY

Raised in poverty in Missouri, Mac is determined to find a better life for himself and the girl who is still a vague vision in his mind. Work on the Santa Fe Trail, and on a Mississippi River boat give him a start, but the years of Civil War leave him broke and footloose in South Texas. There he discovers more cattle running loose than he ever knew existed. Teaming up with two ex-Federal soldiers, he sets out to gather his wealth, one head at a time.

While gathering and driving Longhorns, Mac and his friends meet an interesting collection of characters, including Margo. Mac and Margo and the crew learn about Longhorns, and life, from hard experience before they eventually head west. Outlaws and harrowing river crossings are just two of the challenges they face along their way.

AVAILABLE NOW ON AMAZON FROM REG QUIST AND CKN CHRISTIAN PUBLISHING

ABOUT THE AUTHOR

Reg Quist's pioneer heritage includes sod shacks, prairie fires, home births, and children's graves under the prairie sod, all working together in the lives of people creating their own space in a new land.

Out of that early generation came farmers, ranchers, business men and women, builders, military graves in faraway lands, Sunday Schools that grew to become churches, plus story tellers, musicians, and much more.

Quist's writing career was late in pushing itself forward, remaining a hobby while family and career took precedence. Only in early retirement, was there time for more serious writing.

Woven through every story is the thought that, even though he was not there himself in that pioneer time, he knew some that were. They are remembered with great respect.

Find more great titles by Reg Quist and Christian Kindle News at http://christiankindlenews.com/our-authors/reg-quist/

Made in the USA
Middletown, DE
08 February 2023

24305583R00224